Dirk's

America

Unifies

Collection

www.BarbarianSpy.com

This book is copyright © Dirk Hessian 2017
Dirk Hessian asserts his right to be known as the author of this work.
Published by BarbarianSpy in 2017
Cover design © S Bush 2017
Cover images: All Manipulated: All from Deposit Photos.com: flag © nazlisart, Sheep © Orientaly, Cowboy © konstantynov, Burning barn © Jasiek
ISBN: 978-1-925190-94-6
All rights reserved

BarbarianSpy
Toronto, NSW
Australia

Dirk's America Unifies Collection

Dirk Hessian

Table of Contents

Introduction

Dirk Hessian specializes in gay male historical action/adventure novellas and novels. His works are set in a wide variety of historical time periods and event settings from the ancient times of the mystical past through medieval and American history up to modern times worldwide, as far afield from his home setting of the United States as France, Scotland, the Black Sea, and China.

His shorter works, previously available only in e-book form, are now being brought together in print collections. This is the third of that series and the second of Dirk's "America" series, and includes works covering the American Civil War and expansion west, *Blue and Gray*, *Confederate Gold*, *Fire Down the Valley*, and *Ridden West*. The first collection in the "America" series, *Dirk's America's Founding Collection*, included works covering the period of the American Revolution *Colonel's Treasure*, *To the Hessian Hills*, and *Soldier, Spy*.

Blue and Gray is a personalized Romance of two men on different sides of a conflict. During the Union retreat from the American Civil War battle of Port Republic, Virginia, two soldiers from opposite sides find themselves alone in the ruins of an old mill. In the tense moments of their meeting, the wounded Union sergeant, Able Jenkins, experienced in warfare and guile but troubled by the thought of men coupling with men, must scheme for his survival, while the vulnerable Rebel private, Josh Hardy, inept at war but known by men, is beset by temptation. Both men survive the encounter, but neither does so unmarked. And what they each think is a shameful end to their forced relationship is destined to become anything but that.

One of the mysteries of the American Civil War is what happened to the Confederacy's treasury in the waning days of the war. In the novella, *Confederate Gold*, paralleling actual events, fictional hunky Confederate cavalry officer and aide to President Jefferson Davis, Charles Singleton, is literally caught with his pants down in a Richmond male brothel when he is informed that Grant's Union forces had breached the city's defenses in Petersburg and would be in the capital by 8:00 that night. Commandeering both the young quadroon slave prostitute who was servicing him, Eaton Matthews, and the brothel's wagon and horses, Singleton oversees the transfer of the Confederate treasury into rail cars to follow the train of Davis and his cabinet to presumed safety in Danville, Virginia. What follows in the adventure in which Charles and Eaton grow progressively closer and more reliant on each other as they dash south with the bullion train going off the rails and the treasury slowly dwindling is a bittersweet lesson in the slavery of love.

Fire Down the Valley is the first of two novellas in this collection on America's expansion west toward the Pacific Ocean. As civilization begins to reach the Colorado of the 1870s in the form of roads and telegraph lines snaking west, young Cal, thrust into the world of the white man without even knowing his birth name, faces wars between worlds he can't fully place himself in. The sole survivor of a wagon train massacre and raised by the Arapaho, when the cavalry arrives to move the Arapaho into reservations, Cal is "rescued," pulled out of the only life he remembers. He subsequently is fostered by a sheep herding family in a Rocky Mountain valley on the verge of a range war between the cattlemen, the sheep men, and the farmers, and is thus thrust between worlds he doesn't completely identify with. Cal also finds himself torn in finding his sexual identity between an Arapaho brave, a half-breed cowboy, and a cruel ranchman. Calamitous events in the unsettling birthing of Colorado and the effects of encroaching eastern civilization claw at Cal to take sides and make momentous decisions of his own—if the men overpowering his life will give him choices.

In *Ridden West*, a story of one young man following the Horace Greeley "Go West, young man" dream, Billy has aged out on a Kansas orphanage farm in the late nineteenth century with enough sexual experience with the farm's owner to prompt the farmer's wife to sell him to two pimps supplying a male brothel in a Colorado mining town. Billy's goal is to reach California, and he willingly goes to Colorado with the thought that California is just over the next mountain from there. After some rough sexual encounters in the mining town, an aging Utah rancher entices him to move to his ranch to nurse the rancher to sexual satisfaction. The rancher's son has other ideas, though, for Billy, who winds up shared out to the ranch hands and a few Indian braves and finds himself headed back to Kansas. Will he ever make it to California alive?

Blue and Gray

Chapter One: Able Starts West in Pennsylvania

Able Jenkins didn't have to go to war. That southerners wanted their own country and wanted to keep darkies as slaves was no skin off his nose. He was exempt from being conscripted as well and had no truck with darkies. He'd rarely even seen one. And yet, as far as Able could remember it, it was a darkie by the name of Jeremiah that led to Able going to war.

Darkies weren't a problem in the Pennsylvania town of Hamburg in the early 1850s; there weren't any there that Able could recollect. And they weren't the reason that Able left Hamburg. It was because of Germans that Able first learned of the petty and mean side of his father. But isn't because of all Germans; only the new ones.

Adam Jenkins owned and ran the small town's general emporium, and he'd always had a reputation as a pleasant and helpful man and, more important perhaps in an area dominated by Amish and Quakers, an upstanding and righteous man. Although it wasn't all that apparent to others, to Adam's family that all started to change because of political strife in the German revolutions of 1848 and the refugees fleeing to the United States. Those of this influx were known as the Forty-Eighters, and they were unlike the German immigrants in years previous in that they didn't diffuse in Pennsylvania when they arrived. They formed unitary communities, communities that sought self-sustainment, communities that created their own schools and networks and, most damning, communities that wanted to have their own stores.

Adam Jenkins's store began losing some of its German-ancestry patrons because even the Amish began to be drawn by their "own kind." Slowly the new German immigrants were buying up the farms around eastern Pennsylvania. Adam Jenkins's business was dwindling and he started talking about moving west. He talked more and more of the Horace Greeley "go west young man" spirit.

There was little likelihood that Adam himself would remove his family to the less-civilized and populated western sector of the state. Whenever he mentioned the possibility, he would end with the observation that it might be something he would have done if he was younger. However, his son, Able, *was* younger. So, in the end, perhaps it was all Adam's fault—that Able ended up going to war when he didn't have to.

The petty streak in Adam showed in his starting to call in the credit he had extended to German families living around Hamburg—even ones who had been rooted there before Adam's family arrived. He did this out of spite as punishment to those who were shunning his store and buying only from German merchants. That this drove customers that he had right to the German folds he was railing against didn't seem to occur to him. The mean streak, however, concentrated on a particular friendship his son, Able, was forming the flew in the face of the losing battle Adam was fighting.

"I don't care if he is teaching you more about boxing than anyone else, son, I don't want to hear you've been with that Wasser man again. You can surely find friends more your age. He is a rotten apple, that one is. And he is too old to be someone you are carousing around with."

"No one my own age can help me like Heinz can, Papa. You yourself encouraged me to take up the boxing. You said it would make a man out of me. And you don't know anything about Heinz—other than he is one of the new Germans. There's nothing rotten about him. He is a fine man."

"You are from the town; he is from the farm. And he can hardly speak English yet. My customers do not like the thought of you mixing with his kind."

"His kind just meaning that he is a new German, Papa. Isn't that true? Isn't that all you have against him?"

"That would be enough. But no, there is talk about him. There is talk of him being too interested in young men like you. It's not something you need know anything about, but I want your contact to end now. You can learn all you need learn about boxing from the fine young men down at Elden's barn on Saturdays after you have done your chores. Do you hear me on this, Able?"

When there was no answer beyond a sullen look, Adam repeated, "Have you heard what I said, Able?"

"Yes, Papa."

Able Jenkins had heard more of what Adam had been saying in recent months than just that there was nothing good about the new Germans. Able had heard his father say that he would go west to make his fortune as others were if he just was still young.

Well, Able was young, barely past his majority, when he answered the "Go west, young man" call himself. He heard the call the night that he woke to pebbles being tossed at his window and he opened it to a vision of Heinz Wasser, with a pack over his back, saying he was leaving that night, riding the rails out of Berk County, west to work in the iron foundries, where a man who wanted to be a boxer of any fame could make himself a man of steel—and get paid a living wage for doing it. He was riding the rails to this new adventure, and he wanted Able to come along.

Able had just had another fight with his father that made Able feel like he would be under his father's increasingly mean thumb for life unless he escaped. To him, his friend, Heinz, was the perfect escape.

Able quickly made up a pack for his own back of necessary clothing and equipment for a long ride on the rails, and he was out of the window and going west with Heinz hours before he was missed.

If he'd stayed until the morning and the spread of the news around the town, he would have learned that Heinz was being sought on a charge of debauching a young man on the neighboring farm, which was a horror not openly talked of in Berks County unless it could be avoided. It was behavior that was not tolerated, and Heinz would have been hunted down and severely dealt with—with the blessing of even the new German community—if Heinz could have been found anywhere.

* * * *

"The night is cold. You are shivering. You must be freezing."

"I should have brought two blankets instead of one—and warmer clothing," Able answered in the dimness of the open-doored box car as the last of the lights of the villages around Harrisburg slid past.

"*Comst du hier*—Come over here, my friend. We will bundle up. It can get very cold in the Alps of Germany too—much colder than here. We learn to share our body heat there. We did whatever we could to survive."

"You haven't said much about Germany and why you and so many others left."

"There was war. Too much war."

"They speak of war here, too, Heinz."

"*Ja*, they do. But Heinz is the clever one. That is why I go to the iron foundry. I know of one in a place called Brady's Bend. Others have told me of this place. I told you that working there would make a man of steel of you. And *das ist*—that is—true. But for a man like me, tired of generations of war in German, fighting for causes that are other's causes, not mine, the iron foundry is an answer. Iron is needed for war. It is needed so badly that workers in the foundry aren't conscripted."

"Aren't what?"

"Aren't conscripted—aren't impressed to become soldiers and go to war. It is coming, Able, I can see it. This struggle between your North—now *meine*, my, North as well and your South is going to end in war. Mark my words. I've seen it in Germany. There will be war. And war needs the bodies of young men to throw into the caldron. If you had not so willingly left Hamburg with me, I would have told you that your choices were dwindling. You are the perfect age and healthiness to sacrifice to war. They would have come for you.

A store keep is not needed for anything better than to stand in the front line and protect the general's horse from bullets. A man who makes iron, though. He is too valuable where he is."

Able sighed. "The world is just too hard for me to understand."

"You should have been born in Germany. You would understand the world quickly—or you would be trampled under the feet of the hooves of all the Napoleonic horses."

"What kind of horses?"

"Never mind, my innocent Able. There is no need of you knowing such things before your time. Come, now. Come over here. We will bundle and share our heat."

Able moved farther into the interior of the box car, where Heinz had settled against a rotting and split bale of hay. They arranged both of their blankets around them and huddled closely together.

The innocence of Able was such that the heat this closeness brought him failed to categorize itself as the same kind of heat it was stoking in Heinz. And the hardness Able felt was not something he realized was an arousal for the closeness of him.

Heinz ached for the innocent young man, and he intended to have him. There had been several young men in Hamburg who also would have been willing to leave with him, young men who no longer needed to be seduced to open their legs to Heinz. But it was the seduction that was the most interesting to Heinz. And he had been cultivating this delicious young man for too long to just walk away from him when one of Heinz's conquests had turned on him and forced him to leave Hamburg on no notice.

"Here. If I put my arms around you and hold you close inside them, we will both benefit tenfold from the shared heat."

"Ummm."

"You asked about the wars in Europe, Able. So much of it is about honor and chivalry and loyalty. And about the close bonds formed between men. The deep affection borne of loyalty and commitment. It is much the same in the circles of boxers, don't you think? Don't you feel the connections there, the feeling of being almost one? Of the intricate dance in the boxing arena, the unity of it. When you are in the ring, do you not feel the connection to your opponent, the two of you moving as one, as one connected unit?"

"Ummm."

"Almost, dare I compare it to, a union of a man and woman—a marriage of sorts and all that goes with that."

"I'm not sure I understand. I—"

"Have I told you of a famous boxing fraternity in Bavaria, where I come from—of supertalented boxers who train and live together and are totally devoted to each other. Who gain strength from each other by melding their passion— their passion for the sport of boxing. And, when they are totally possessed by the sport, their passion of each other? Have I mentioned the Society of the Buried Sword?"

Heinz had been speaking in a sing song voice. He could feel Able relaxing against him. The young man, certainly, was drifting off to sleep, but he was entering the perfect state of approachability for the beginning of what Heinz had in mind. It was this talent of his for seduction that was why he'd been able in times previously to coax a young man to his first masturbatory experience with another man just by lulling him into a state like this so that the young man was already past that first, all-important stage of giving in to him before he even realized it was happening.

"The Society of the Buried Sword?" Able murmured drowsily.

"Yes, it is a very special brotherhood, one that—"

Heinz stopped abruptly. They, quite suddenly and unexpectedly, no longer were alone in the boxcar. The train had come almost to a rolling stop at the Carlisle Barracks army post train stop, and two dark shapes had hoisted themselves into the boxcar and rolled into the shadows not far from where Heinz and Able were huddled. Able grew alert and instinctively pulled away from Heinz—who let him go so that, although the blankets were still wrapped around both of them, they no longer were touching beneath the covering.

"Geez, I told you this one wouldn't be empty, Jim," a voice hissed out from the darkness.

"Any port and all that," came a second voice. "This'er's Jim and I'm someone else," the voice called out in the direction of Heinz and Able. There was a laugh and a cough and then the voice resumed. "Either one of you have a light? Or a stogie to share?"

"If I've told you once, I've told you once again, Chauncey. No lights when the cars are near a station. Don't cher remember nuffing?"

Heinz sighed. No doubt these interlopers would remain with the train even beyond Brady's Bend, which, of course, they did. It didn't matter much, though, he thought. It made the wait all the more sweet. Able was a tasty and easy mark. Most of the others had cottoned to what he was up to by now—and some had even objected and resisted him—but he'd had them all. They would be in Brady's Bend within two days, and there was all the time in the world then.

There certainly was time when Heinz and Able reached the Brady's Bend Iron Company, but there was little opportunity. The foreman had quickly signed on Heinz and was glad to have such a large, strong, well-muscled man—glad enough that he took on Able at Heinz's insistence. It was just that Able seemed so young. The foreman could see that he could develop into a good iron worker too.

Brady's Bend Iron Company was quite an operation. It was such an organized operation that it had its own village and company store and even its own saloon and a church. And it took care of every aspect of its employees' lives so carefully that it had dormitories for its single male workers. Regimentation of these extended to barrack room assignment by surname initial. The cutoff was between H and K. So, Able was sent to one dormitory and Heinz to another.

This was not something Heinz had foreseen, but there was time, and the risk and maneuvering all heightened the pleasure of the eventual seduction and debauching.

* * * *

"Next Sunday, how 'bout you and me do some hiking along the Alleghany. I'm bustin' to get away from this prison."

"Ah, Heinz, it ain't so bad here. We get three squares a day and a bunk with clean sheets and they even wash our clothes for us. And I'll bet the prices are cheaper in the company store than in town."

"Yeah, well, I feel trapped. Same old routine, same twelve hours of work, six days a week. and lights out for eight hours—and you better be in your bunk." He didn't say "alone," but he thought it, even though Able had yet to start filling in those dots.

Heinz and Able were sitting on the wooden steps up into Able's dormitory. It was late on a Sunday afternoon, and Able had just come out from having slept the entire day away. It was their third week here, and this was the first Sunday— their only day of the week off from working in the iron works—that Able had come out of his dormitory room on his day of rest at all, even for meals. Increasingly Able was toughening up for the job he'd been given, shoveling coal from the bins to the furnaces, but it was taking time. And it was taking a whole lot out of him. Heinz was on the casting team. He was one who forged the iron in the furnaces and beat it into the desired shape. He'd come much tougher than Able had, and he was managing the work without any trouble.

"Not today, Heinz. Sorry. I just can't think of anything except sleep on my day off yet. It's getting on toward supper now. Maybe next Sunday we can do something here. Play some cards or something. A walk on the river still sounds too much like work for me."

"There's no privacy here," Heinz complained. He was on edge. Part of that was that he'd waited here all day for Able to wake up so that they could have some time together, so that Heinz could resume his dance of seduction. The need for seduction was the other thing that had him on edge. Heinz was about ready to explode; he had all this jism built up inside him. Something had to give—and soon.

"That's what I mean by prison," Heinz continued. "They got the whole place fenced in, there ain't two trees standing together in the compound to provide a place to rest in the shade in private, and guys are just milling about in here on

Sundays. There ain't no place a guy and his friends can go for privacy."

"The fence is to keep people out, Heinz," Able said with a laugh. "'Cause we have it so much better in here. I've never eaten as good as this. I bet you haven't either. And privacy? We're sittin' here and talkin'. There's nobody listening to us. Nobody's lookin' over our shoulders."

"Everybody walkin' around like this, I don't feel like it's private. Let's walk down to the river tonight. We'd need a pass to get back into the gate, but I can get a couple of those."

"Ah, gee, Heinz. Me and a couple of the other guys have a card game on for tonight. But you could come in on it too. Right here in the dormitory."

"Yeah, OK. *Das ist*—that's OK."

It wasn't anything close to OK, but at least they'd be there together this evening. There could be some smilin' and a bit of touchin'.

But Heinz had this raging need right now. He looked up to see one of the other coal shovelers walking by. It was sort of a surprise to see Jeremiah on this side of the compound. He was a darkie, and they had their own dormitory on the other side of the common buildings. The darkies and the whites were kept separate here—as they were almost everywhere else. That much the North had in common with the South.

Jeremiah was an easy lay. Heinz had heard talk about him already, although he hadn't done much about it. He was a darkie. What Heinz wanted was Able. But Jeremiah was OK. Not a bad face for a darkie, and he had a slim, sinewy build— more pliable and resilient than raw muscle power. He was good with the coal shovel, each time carrying what looked like more than his weight. And he wasn't the talking kind. Heinz had heard that he liked cock but that he wasn't real showy about it. He didn't talk much about what he got.

"Hey there, Jeremiah. It is Jeremiah, *nicht wahr*—ain't it?" Heinz called out.

The darkie turned and looked in the direction of Able and Heinz, both still crouched down on the wooden steps up to the dormitory. Heinz stood up so that Jeremiah could see him. His hand went to his crotch so that Jeremiah could see that too, although Heinz was careful to turn so that Able couldn't see it.

"Yas, that's me. I be Jeremiah."

"I'm hankering for walk down to the river. Interested in going down there with me?"

Jeremiah's eyes narrowed and he took an all-over look at Heinz. He must have liked what he could see, because he smiled and said, "Yas, that were be nice. A nice walk down to the river." Jeremiah knew what an evening stroll to the river meant.

Able didn't catch on to a thing then. Of course he wasn't looking for anything. When he first saw what was in the air wasn't until late in that work week. He and Jeremiah were running coal from the bins to a furnace. It wasn't even the furnace that Heinz was working. It was hot, even without the furnaces going, and every man in the place was stripped to the waist. The sweat was flowing off their coal dust-encrusted chests. No matter what the job, this was hard muscle work, so there wasn't a man on the floor of the factor who wasn't a magnificent specimen in the torso department.

Able and Jeremiah had been working in relay for some time, and Able made two trips before realizing that Jeremiah wasn't there. Just gone to take a piss, Able decided, but when he looked over toward one of the big doors out to the factory grounds, he saw two figures in silhouette that he knew he recognized even before he had time to wonder what they were doing. They were just talking, but it was Jeremiah and Heinz. Heinz usually worked at a furnace at the other end of the big factory building, so Able was surprised to see him there.

He was even more surprised to see the two of them look around—Able instinctively dropped his own gaze so they wouldn't know he'd seen them—and then, first, Jeremiah, and afterward Heinz, walk toward an empty coal bin back in the shadows.

When both had disappeared behind the bin wall, Able put down his shovel and quietly followed after them.

Able never figured out whether Heinz meant him to see them and Heinz probably didn't know himself. Although maybe it was a tactic he was using to clue Able in to the lay of the land before Heinz claimed him.

Whatever it was, it was all out sex—and it had started before Able got to where he could peek into the empty coal bin without being seen. Both men were stripped down and Jeremiah was showing his flexibility by standing but bending over and grabbing his ankles with his fists. His knees were bent just enough to meet the desired level of Heinz's need. Heinz was crouched behind him, his chest hovering over Jeremiah's hips, and he was fucking up into Jeremiah's ass with a hard cock to beat the band.

Able didn't stay around very long—but he stayed around long enough for the dawning of a lot of things in the attention Heinz had been giving him for weeks on end and to catch on to the realization of what was what.

And he stayed long enough to become unsure of himself on just how disgusted he was with what Heinz and Jeremiah were doing. The way they were doing it, sweaty, coal-dusted bodies and all, was more like a dance. And they certainly seemed to be enjoying it. Able could see the lost little smile on both of their faces, and he could hear Heinz's groans and Jeremiah's soft little mewings and moans.

But then he pulled away, and rather than returning to his shovel, he walked slowly back to his dormitory.

There was no walk along the river the next Sunday for Able and Heinz. Heinz was still there, but Able had left the factory and gone into Brady's Bend with his accumulated wages in his pocket and bought a rail ticket back east as far as the Carlisle Barracks, where he signed up with the 110th Pennsylvania Infantry Regiment.

And that is how, despite having found protection from going to war, especially over the enslavement of darkies, Able now was preparing to go to war and all because of a darkie named Jeremiah.

When Able left Brady's Bend, he told himself that is was because he could not countenance what Heinz had revealed himself to be. He told himself this over and over. But no matter how many times he told himself this, he couldn't help being frightened that there was something about what he'd seen Heinz and Jeremiah doing that attracted and aroused him and that this was the reason he ran away from Heinz so quickly. That if he didn't run away from something, he'd be running to it.

Chapter Two: Josh Gives It Up in Virginia

Josh hadn't known there would be this many. Maybe he should have asked for more money, but he was new to this. God, he hadn't ever done it before. It was all because of Tom. Tom was standing there beside him, grinning, and holding the twenty cents they'd agreed to pay. Tom hadn't chipped in any money. He said he'd get his later for setting this up for Josh. Ralph Klingenschmidt was behind Josh's hips. He was grunting and groaning, working his way inside Josh. Josh had already taken Mr. Morris, the blacksmith. They'd all agreed that since he'd come up thickest upon comparison, he'd go first so that once Josh had been opened up, the rest wouldn't be such a chore.

And it had been real rough for Josh to take Mr. Morris. The only one Josh had had before was Tom's—and then just a few times out back of the outhouses at the church while Tom's father was conducting services inside. Tom's had been long, but he hadn't been nearly as thick as Mr. Morris was. Mr. Morris had sat on a felled tree log there behind his barn while the cock fight was going on out in the farmyard, at the other end of the barn. Josh could hear the men shouting as each of the fights was going on. He tried concentrating on the noise from there rather than where he was here. Tom had told him it would be nothing, just a way to pick up some needed money. That once he done it, doing it for more at a time would be nothing. But it wasn't nothing.

When Mr. Morris was sitting on the log, Josh was turned by three other sets of hands to where he was straddling Mr. Morris's thighs, facing away from him. Mr. Morris wrapped his beefy arms around Josh's belly and chest while one of the other men positioned Mr. Morris's cock head at Josh's ass entrance, and then there were hands on Josh's shoulders, pushing his body down on Mr. Morris's hard staff, and men were laughing at the sobbing and groaning Josh was doing as he was settled in Mr. Morris's lap.

Ralph Klingenschmidt jumped up on the log, placed then his feet on either side of Mr. Morris's hips and stifled Josh's cries of anguish by grabbing Josh by his ears and forcing his cock into Josh's mouth. Another set of hands snaked between Josh's legs and grabbed onto his cock and started milking him. Mr. Morris spread his knees wide, forcing Josh's thighs even wider, and Josh bottomed on Mr. Morris's cock. With a grunt, the blacksmith moved his strong, calloused hands to grab Josh's slim waist on either side and begin raising and lowering Josh's torso in a long slide on his thick cock.

The junior constable, Harry Denton, was standing off to the side with Tom, watching it all. When he'd first come around the side the barn, Josh had thought he was going to put a stop to what Tom had gotten him to agree to. But Denton just grinned and handed his own nickel to Tom and was now standing and watching, waiting for his turn.

Ralph was taking seconds, with Josh standing and bent over at the waist, his burnished golden curls cascading down around his face and his hazel eyes watering from the pain and humility. Ralph stood close behind him, one hand palmed on his belly to help his knees from going to rubber and making him fall, and the other fisted between Josh's shoulder blades and holding his chest down so that his mouth was level with Harry Denton's upward-thrusting cock. That third, unnamed man, now was crouched between Ralph and Josh's spread legs, head raised to their crotches, where he was playing with both Ralph and Josh's balls with his tongue and occasionally working Josh's cock with his mouth. He was palming Ralph's bulbous buttocks and helping to propel his thrusts up into Josh's channel.

Josh saw movement at the back of the barn in his peripheral vision and turned his head enough to see that the school teacher, Paul Cushman, had come around, headed for the outhouses. He took one look at what was happening behind the barn, though, and swiveled and made a quick return to the farmyard.

Josh was mortified. Paul had only been in Madison for a little over a year. He wasn't more than a couple of years older than Josh, and they had met and become friends. Paul had been helping Josh with his reading and his numbers. Josh was from a farm between Madison, Virginia, and the base of the Blue Ridge Mountains, to the west of Madison, and, as an only son, his father hadn't given him much time for attending the local school. With his dad dead now, Josh had even less time, but his mother was able to be more outspoken with her lord and master gone, and she encouraged Josh to find the time to improve his education. It had been Josh's mother who had invited the new school teacher out to the farm for a meal often enough that the teacher had felt compelled to stay after the meal and help Josh with his schooling.

It would be mortifying for Josh for the teacher to tell his mother what he'd seen. And worse than that, Josh had a crush on the teacher, who was dark and handsome to the point of being pretty and who had a broody, sensuous-lip face, and beautiful hands with long, slender fingers—and who could quote Shakespeare's sonnets. Josh almost thought that Paul Cushman had been equally taken with him and, just perhaps, was courting Josh just a bit.

Thoughts of this had spun Josh into the arms of the preacher's son. The town twittering had a joke going of both the angels and the devil being wrapped up in the preacher's family. Whereas the preacher and his wife could do no wrong, their willful son was the first one to come to anyone's mind when there had been a prank or a villainy of any sort perpetrated in the county. Tom had certainly slipped in while Josh was mooning over Paul Cushman; had cleverly pulled this hidden, forbidden desire of Josh's from him; and had promptly provided Josh with the cocking Josh had only been dreaming about from Paul.

Playing on Josh's vulnerabilities, Tom had peppered him with declarations of what a sweet lay he was and how much Tom loved being with him—and that now that the deed was done, Josh had nothing to protect and surely would be one of the most popular young men in Madison Country for the favors he could bestow. Why he could even make money from

27

it and become a rich man and not have to live on the edge as a small farmer trying to eke a living out of the rock-laced soil of the Blue Ridge foothills. And it wouldn't be like Josh would be giving up what he hadn't already lost.

Tom had wheedled at Josh enough for Josh to agree to coming to a cock fight that he otherwise wouldn't have attended and to earn a bit of precious money on the side. He had no idea that Tom had set the gang fuck up ahead of time—indeed, had cultivated the vulnerable Josh for it—and that each man was paying fifteen cents for Josh's attentions rather than the nickel Josh was receiving.

The unnamed man milking Josh's cock was satisfied with just that from Josh. What he wanted was a fucking himself from the blacksmith and Ralph, and he was getting that, suspended between them and having his ass played in double time like a calliope as Harry Denton roughly grabbed Josh by the wrist and pulled him into a stand of trees to the west of the barn. He took out handcuffs, snapped one wrist band on one of Josh's wrists, raised Josh's arm to a low-hanging, but strong tree limb, flipped the handcuffs over, and locked in Josh's other wrist, suspending Josh's body from the tree limb. As Josh whimpered and begged, Harry grabbed the legs of the smaller, younger man, hooked Josh's ankles on his shoulders on either side of his head, positioned his cock, pushed inside, and fucked Josh with a strong, pistoning rhythm for longer than all of the others had been inside him altogether.

After he had ejaculated, Harry released Josh from the handcuffs, just let the young man fall into the fern bed at the base of the tree, and strode off toward the barn and the cock fights that were still going on in the farmyard beyond.

Tom found an exhausted Josh there at the base of the tree, bunched up in a fetal position. He gently turned Josh on his back and smoothed his arms and legs flat with long, gentle strokes of his hands. Tom knelt between Josh's thighs, pulling the young man's buttocks on top his own thighs. He leaned his bare torso over Josh's and, with the fingers of one hand, pushed Josh's damp curls out of his face and caressed Josh's check. He leaned down, bringing his face to Josh's, and kissed Josh's tear-stained eyelids. Then he moved his mouth over

Josh's . . . stifling Josh's surprised scream, as Tom's other hand helped his cock head find Josh's opening, and Tom plunged his long, hard cock deep inside Josh's channel. Josh struggled and writhed under Tom's strong control as, with hard, brutal thrusts, Tom took his declared percentage for setting up Josh's group transaction.

* * * *

Josh's mother had been called away the previous day across the mountains to Staunton to help with her sister's birthing. Josh hadn't even thought about his own supper that evening, days after he made it home from the cock fight and there, at the door, was Paul Cushman. It was only then that Josh remembered it was a Wednesday and that Paul always came to supper and a study hour on Wednesday evenings.

Opening the door, Josh stood back, embarrassed and flustered. Both he and Paul covered the embarrassment well, with Josh apologizing that he'd forgotten that Paul would be coming when his mother wasn't there to fix supper. The real reason for Josh's embarrassment was that he had no idea whether or not Paul had recognized him in that pile of entangled naked bodies behind Mr. Morris's barn the previous Saturday. Paul gave no indication that he had, though, much to Josh's relief. Josh stammered that he still could rustle up a meal if Paul didn't mind a cold plate, and Paul said he didn't mind.

Josh continued to be flustered through the supper, but Paul was as smooth as always and kept the discussion rolling along with reports on his students and how different their personalities were.

"It's like some have no appreciation at all what a basic education can do for them and just can't wait for the school day to be over, whereas others want all of the experience they can get and have a passion for living life to the fullest and seeing and experiencing it all."

Josh stammered his agreement, lost more in the sensuous way Paul spoke those suggestive words than in the innocent meanings that no doubt were behind them. He watched Paul chewing at a cold chicken leg, a bit of grease running below his full lips. Paul's tongue flicking out to catch the grease, and Josh had to look away, in embarrassment.

He should clear the table so that they would have a place to study, but he had turned hard at listening to Paul's rich, deep voice and watching him eat lustily—and just imagining all sorts of things and desire-rooted possibilities. It might have been logical that Josh's so recent sexual congress with five men would shock him so badly that he would pull away from any suggestion of sex with a man. But it had had the opposite effect on Josh. Each night since he had dreamed of Paul and had awakened to find himself fisting his cock and streams of semen running down the shaft into his reddish gold, curly pubic hair. It was just as well that his mother had not been here the past two days.

At length Josh had to clear the table, so he stood and awkwardly positioned his hips away from Paul as he maneuvered dishes into the kitchen. When he came back, Paul was standing away from the table, over by a chair where he had dropped his knapsack, and he was rummaging around in the pack and pulling books, a chalk board, and chalk out of the sack.

Josh was seated when he came back, and Paul sat down very close beside him. Josh, trembling, looked at Paul with a question written all over his face.

"We work on cursive this evening. I will have to guide your hand."

Josh was shaking as Paul wrapped an arm around his shoulders and folded a hand over Josh's hand that now held the chalk. Paul's chin rested on Josh's shoulder.

They only made it to L before Josh felt Paul's sensuous lips at the hollow of his neck and Paul's free hand finding that Josh was hard.

"Paul," Josh whispered in a shaky voice.

"Shush," Paul whispered back. His long slender fingers were deftly working the buttons of Josh's fly. "I saw you on Saturday—with those men at the cock fight. And I have so burned for you myself."

"Paul, don't . . . we can't . . ."

"Your body says we can. That it's what you want too."
Paul's fingers had found and were stroking Josh's hard cock.
Josh was moaning for him. "Which door is the one to your
bedroom? The one on the left or the right."

"The right," Josh answered with a groan.

They fucked in the dark, Josh on his belly, after his
knees had given out from being in the dog-fuck position, and
Paul riding his hips in long, sensuous waves.

Tom, waiting out on the porch and peeping in the
appropriate windows, only waited until Paul's cock was first
sheathed in Josh's channel, and then he took the quarter Paul
had given him out of his pocket, flipped it once, put it back in
his pocket, and strode off. He'd told Paul he could only stay a
couple of hours tonight—that after this he could come and go
as he pleased, but only a couple of hours tonight. Tom himself
would be back shortly before dawn to take his commission out
on Josh's ass.

Josh and Paul were lovers throughout that summer.
Increasingly Paul spoke to Josh of the great, sweeping events
that were running through the country. That the North and
South were at each other's throat and that there was nothing to
be done but for the South to secede from the Union, as it had
every right to do, and to strike out on its. own.

"I don't expect the Yankees to let us go without a
fight," Paul murmured in Josh's ear, "but there's no comparing
northerners to our boys when it comes to a fight. It will all be
over in a week. And I don't want to miss it."

They were laying out in the forest on the rise up to the
Blue Ridge from Josh's farm. They were hidden in a little glen
next to a brook. Paul had been reading to Josh from
Shakespeare's poetry when lust had overtaken them. Satiated
now, Josh was stretched out on top of Paul, his back to Paul's
chest, the two of them connected by Paul's still-buried and
softening cock and one of Paul's arms hugging Josh's belly
close to him.

"I don't know, Paul."

"I know you are not in favor of any war. That your
family came here from Europe to escape the never-ending wars
there—and that you fear leaving you mother all alone. But you

31

won't have to go. You are the sole support of a farming family. The war will never come to you. And it will be over so soon that you won't miss me."

"I don't know, Paul."

"I've been thinking, though. No matter how long the fighting lasts, I don't want you to miss me or forget me. I have something for you."

"Something for me?"

Paul stretched his hand out and pulled his knapsack toward him. He put a hand inside and extracted a small silver frame.

"A daguerreotype? It's you, Paul. It's a likeness of you."

"Yes. It cost nearly every penny I have, but I don't want you to forget me. I don't want to take that chance, even if I am only gone for a week."

There were no more words at that moment to be said. Josh was so overwhelmed that he twisted around until he was laying face down on Paul's breast. And they were kissing again, and then Josh was riding Paul's cock.

Two weeks later, they both arranged to be in Madison at the county courthouse, because the recruiters were going through to muster up a Confederate army that almost inevitably would be taking to the field within the month.

There was a gleam of pride and determination and longing in Paul's eyes as they watched the small detachment muster out and parade up and down the main street before the commander of the 10th Virginia Volunteer Infantry Regiment, Colonel E. T. H. Warren, gave his rousing patriotic speech trumpeting the southern clause. Watching his lover's reaction to these ceremonies was overwhelming to Josh—as was the thought of being separated from his lover for even a week.

That evening, Josh went back to his farm only long enough to kiss his sobbing mother good-bye and to pull out his bedroll and change of woolen socks. He already was a private in the 10th Virginia Volunteers.

* * * *

The 10th Regiment only had a few short weeks to drill on the plain of the piedmont north of Richmond before it was on a march north to threaten the capitol city of Washington. The first shot of the war had already been fired at Fort Sumter in Charleston harbor on 12 April 1861. Paul was in his glory, and he took to being a soldier like a natural warrior. Josh just couldn't seem to work up the spirit or master the techniques. However, he was not an unhappy man. He was at Paul's side, mooning over his lover. And Paul was there for Josh, showing him where he had gone wrong in cleaning and priming his rifle, and slapping his buttocks down when they were crawling along the ground, trying not to be a target.

The war had begun, just as Paul had predicted it would. And in the first blush of the 10th Regiment's first action, it looked very much like, as Paul had predicted, the war would last merely a few hours rather than the nearly five years it took to bleed both camps nearly dry and to devastate the South.

Three months after the firing on Fort Sumter, the 10th Regiment was walking seventy miles north from its training ground to Fairfax County, in their commonwealth of Virginia, just south of the Union capitol. Here, along a stream called Bull Run, the arrogance of the South nudged up against the even greater arrogance of the North. So sure were the citizens of Washington, D.C., of the superiority of their army that the wealthy families drove their carriages out into the Virginia countryside, loaded up with their luncheon baskets, to watch their soldiers, under the leadership of General Irvin McDowell, teach the ragtag Rebels a lesson.

In the late afternoon of July 21st, the Confederate forces broke through the Union lines at Henry Hill, and the Union forces turned in panic and raced for the protection of the Potomac River in full rout, running over and scattering the carriages of the wealthy Washingtonians en route. So surprised were the Confederate forces at the suddenness of the break in the battle that they failed to pursue. If they had, they could have occupied the Union capitol in the opening hours of the war.

Although in the thick of the fighting on Henry Hill, neither Paul Cushman nor Josh Hardy were in any way to blame for failing to pursue. Josh had been felled by a bullet to the head at the top of Henry Hill at the height of the fighting and had dropped like a stone. Paul had forged ahead, but sensing that Josh no longer was at his side and feeling the responsibility for being Josh's support and protector, he stopped and turned, only to be gutted by the bayonet of one of his own regimental comrades who was pursuing the enemy and had been unable to stop when Paul did.

Josh's head wound was merely a graze, but his part in what came to be known as the Battle of First Manassas had come to a close. A lesser man would have deserted and returned to his farm in the foothills of the Blue Ridge at that point. Josh had never been lost to war fever, as he lover had, and he didn't take to the life of a soldier.

But as penance—having been able to figure out when he'd found Paul's body on the northern down slope of Henry Hill that Paul had died worrying about where Josh was—Josh remained with the 10th Regiment. The following year, in June, even though Josh had yet to have become a seasoned soldier, when he found himself just on the other side of the Blue Ridge from his own farm, helping to cover the retreat of the iconic Confederate general Stonewall Jackson from being trapped in a pincher movement by two converging Union armies at a strategic Shenandoah River crossing at the village of Port Republic, Josh was still something that Paul, in all of his talent as a soldier wasn't—he was still alive.

Chapter Three: Coming Together at Port Republic

Sergeant Able had been one of the last of the Union soldiers off the North River Bridge over the south fork of the Shenandoah River, where it was formed by the meeting of Broad Run and the South River. The Union troops under Brigadier General Erastus Tyler had made a stab across the middle of Virginia to try to trap the legendary Confederate general Stonewall Jackson and had only managed to back themselves to the in-flood south fork of the Shenandoah. Tyler had counted on being joined by Fremont's army, which never appeared. Now Tyler's forces had to get across the one bridge on the Shenandoah at Port Republic to escape a pincher movement of southern troops coming up from the south and down from the north on the river's western bank.

Once across the river, Tyler's forces had to quickstep back to Harrisonburg to avoid being enveloped by Jackson's army. The pursued had become the pursuer.

Sergeant Able's problem was that he couldn't quickstep. He'd barely made it over the North River Bridge when the Southerners had reached the eastern end of the bridge. They had snipers set up on the eastern bank who were shooting anything that moved. A bullet had gone through another soldier running away from behind him and had grazed Able high on his thigh. The other soldier had been shot through and through, and had landed on top of Able, dead before they hit the ground.

Able heard the Southern troops running across the bridge and deploying themselves along the western bank. Then he heard the bridge blow. There'd be no regrouping by Tyler's troops for another go at Jackson in Port Republic.

Able wasn't dumb. He knew the blowing of the bridge would signal Tyler just not to stop his retreat to Harrisonburg. And Able couldn't walk that far in front of a Confederate advance, even if he dared rise from the scant cover he'd gained when he'd hit the ground. The wound in his leg wasn't fatal, but it would slow him down too much to make a run for it. And it might, indeed, be fatal if he didn't get the bleeding stanched soon.

The first wave of Confederate soldiers fanned out parallel to the river bank and moved toward where Able lay. As they moved across the ground, they prodded Union soldiers who had been felled by snipers and helped along those mortally wounded but not yet gone. Able played dead, his body pretty well covered by that of his dead compatriot, as a battle-worn Reb passed him by.

Able waited for as long as he felt he dared after the Rebs had passed, and then he pulled himself along the ground to the only cover he could see, an old mill house not far to the south of the blown bridge. As he reached relative safety there, he could hear the second wave of the Confederate troops fanning out from the river bank across the fields to the west. Able pulled himself into the dark building and burrowed into some burlap sacking behind a stack of barrels.

His wound was bleeding badly, and he couldn't suppress a moan when the young Confederate private, Josh Hardy, crept into the building in search for exactly what he found—a wounded Union soldier.

A very dangerous moment punctuated the scene when Josh first saw Able. He instinctive lifted his rifle and he could have shot the enemy soldier right there and then and no one would be the wiser. In fact, no one other than Able would care or, probably, ever know the circumstances of his death. It would be less of a hassle all around for the Southern forces. And Josh did raise his rifle, and Able did lift his hands in defense and supplication. But then Josh saw the sergeant's stripes on the arm of Able's blue Union jacket. Josh had been told that they wanted to capture anyone with any rank, if they could, in case they could find out more about Tyler's troop strengths and plans.

Josh lowered the barrel of the rifle, and at that point Able nearly swooned into a faint, both in shock for what had been narrowly avoided, at least for the moment, and from the loss of blood from the wound on his inner thigh.

Now focused on providing a captive for the revered General Jackson, Josh bustled into a preservation rather than a destruction mode. He propped his rifle against a nearby post and grabbed for his canteen and the pack on his back.

Josh stripped Able of his britches and tore strips of cloth from this to use as a tourniquet. He poured water from his canteen on Able's inner thigh wound and then doused it with the whiskey he kept in another small flask in his pack. The wound didn't look so bad now.

Able snorted back to full consciousness when the liquor hit his wound. And he was fully conscious as he watched Josh wind the strips of material around his inner thigh and tie them off snugly. While Josh did so, he couldn't help but brush the backs of his hands across Able's quite able cock, which had been exposed when he'd been stripped of his britches.

Able knew instantaneously from Josh's response what the young soldier's inclinations were and that he'd had some experience. The Union sergeant had been in nearly this same position before. But before the stakes had been quite different from what they were now. He had a very good idea why this private, shaking from fear and the shock of battle himself, hadn't just shot him. The sergeant knew quite a bit about the strength and Shenandoah Valley Campaign plans of Tyler's forces, so he had a good idea what he faced if he was sent back to Jackson's camp. And he knew that there was little or no chance he could get out of this predicament, but that he had to try to do so anyway. It wasn't just self-preservation; he had a duty as a soldier to his regiment.

Josh was young and not that experienced as a soldier, Able could see from how scared and jumpy the other man was, whereas he himself was not so young and was battle tested and resilient. He gauged the distance from where Josh was tending his thigh and where he had propped up the rifle.

Able had never fucked a man before, but that was how this Reb swung and he could be distract by that and, if it required that to get at the rifle, it was something Able would try doing. There wasn't much other choice that he could see of getting out of here. In all likelihood getting to the rifle and killing this Reb would be the easiest part of his attempt to reach the Union lines.

The pursued turning into the pursuer.

The opening was right there beside Able, where it had fallen out of the Reb's pack when Josh had fished around for the flask of liquor.

"He's handsome," Able murmured, pretending now to be weaker than he really was, as he beckoned to the worn daguerreotype of the young man that had fallen out of the Reb's pack.

Josh's head snapped up in embarrassment and surprise. The Union soldier was conscious. Josh wondered, blushing at the thought, whether the Yankee had seen him dreamily eyeing that nice plump cock of his.

"Umm, yes. Ya'all shouldn't try to speak now. I'se afraid I'll have to find something to bind you with. But at least I stopped the bleeding now, so that's to the good."

"Kin of yours, is he?"

"Umm, no."

"Does he have a name?"

"Yes, well, Paul, Paul Cushman."

"And you carry his likeness into battle with you. Is he a special friend then?"

Josh blushed in embarrassment and lowered his eyes, unfortunately focusing on Able's cock, which was harder now, Able having stroked on it while he was getting Josh's attention moved to the daguerreotype.

"Uh, yes, you could say that."

"A lover then?"

Josh melted in shock and confusion and in how easily and openly the Yankee had called him out. He tensed right up.

"Of course not," he declared indignantly, too loud, and without a pinch of conviction as he sat up straight from where he had been hovering over the Yankee's reclining figure.

"You needn't be embarrassed at all," Able countered, lifting an arm and wrapping a hand around the Reb's neck. "I find you quite arousing myself. And I'm ever so grateful that you have bandaged my wound, and ever so ready to show my gratitude. Tell me. Do you make love to him, or he to you?"

Josh lowered his head, not answering.

"He makes love to you, doesn't he? I hope that is the case, because I am aroused by you myself. I would like to make love to you. No one need know. The battle has moved on, I'm sure. And I would guess it's been some time since someone made love to you."

As he talked, Able had moved a hand to Josh's thigh and was squeezing it, knowing that the young man could feel the heat of his touch through the rough worsted-wool trousers.

Able could feel the young Confederate soldier trembling in indecision and disbelief at the forwardness of it all as well as the lack of breathing time and space to work out what was happening. Able brought the young private's mouth down to his and took the soldier's hand in his and placed it on his cock, Josh's hand now wrapping Able's engorging cock and Able held it there with his own until Josh was lost to him and stroking the hard tool on his own.

The Union sergeant's thoughts went back to Brady's Bend and what he'd saw of Heinz Wasser taking Jeremiah Swain behind the coal bin. He would have to maneuver and dominate this young Reb that same way Heinz did Jeremiah if he had a chance of getting out of this predicament. He'd have to convince the young man that he knew what he was doing and would give him what he wanted.

Able reached for the young soldier's face with his hands, cupping his head, and turning it to him. He closed his eyes, wanting to pretend he was anywhere else but here, and he lowered his face to Josh's and pressed his lips to Josh's lips.

When Able knew he'd won the battle with Josh's defenses, when Josh had opened his lips to Able's and was hungrily drinking him in, and when Josh's hand on Able's cock was moving on its own, Able moved his hands to unbuttoning the Reb's shirt and started rubbing the young soldier's nipples with his fingers, just as he had seen Heinz do to Jeremiah to bring him under his full control.

Josh shuddered under the attention, and when Able broke away from the kiss and moved his lips down to Josh's nipples and his hands down to Josh's belt and buttoned fly, Josh, still crouching on his knees, sighed in resignation and need and arched his back toward the floor behind him. As he bent backward, Able's lips followed down the young Reb's sternum and across his belly and down, through his now-revealed bush, and opened up on and then closed over the young man's cock head.

Able had thought this would be disgusting, but he was surprised to find it was not. He was more surprised to find that he felt the beginnings of arousal himself. Just as watching Jeremiah sucking Heinz's cock and then being fucked had surprisingly—and embarrassingly—aroused him, this playing of the Reb was doing the same thing.

Josh was moaning and staring up into the shadows of the eaves of the old mill and moving his pelvis ever so slowly as Able sucked away on his dick, taking more and more of it in with his stroking movement. All the time Able was playing Josh's tool, though, he himself was staring at the pole across the floor that the Reb's rifle was propped against. He was gauging distances, and time, and likelihood. Still too risky, he decided.

Able lifted his lips off Josh's cock, but he continued slowly stroking the base of the hard tool with his fist.

"You didn't answer my question about the man in your daguerreotype. Do you fuck him or does he fuck you?" It was a mere whisper, but the Reb heard him.

A rather long pause. "He did me." Josh spoke of Paul in the past tense, but Able didn't seem to catch on to that.

"Is he the only one who has done you, or were there others? Have you had much experience? Were you willing to lie under others?"

"I have lain under others." I came almost begrudgingly, but with some sense of bottled up release.

"It would not be too disheartening to lie under others?"

"No." Again, acknowledged after a pause.

"It would not be too displeasing to lie under me? I would not be forcing you?"

"No, you would not be forcing me."

40

At least there's that, Able thought to himself with a bit of relief—although he'd been prepared to do whatever it took. Able spit on his free hand and moved it under the Reb's ball sac and started working his moistened fingers around Josh's pulsating rim and into his hole. His lips opened up over the bulbous head of Josh's cock and he ran his tongue into the young man's piss slit before swallowing the cock almost down to the root, closing tightly over the throbbing member, and moving his mouth up and down on the hard shaft.

Josh groaned and moaned. He was panting and breathing heavily and making little mewing sounds. His hips were moving slowly, helping Able with the rhythm of the suck. There was a little lurch and groan each time Able pushed a finger, and then two, and then three, into his ass channel.

Able took his mouth off the young man's cock. He was, he was ashamed to say, enjoying this now. "Does your Paul give you the loving attention I'm giving you?"

The only response was something like a sob.

"Do you want me to stop?"

A moment of silence except for Josh's heavy breathing and a low moan. "No. But . . . but . . ."

"But you want me to stop playing you and put you to the cock?"

"Yes . . . please . . . yes."

Able took his fingers out of Josh's ass and spit on it again a couple of times and moistened up his own cock. Then he lifted the young Reb, who was completely his now, bending readily to any position he moved him to, up to him, chest to chest.

Josh sighed and moaned and gulped as Able brought him into his lap, positioning the head of his cock on Josh's prepared hole and just pulling Josh's channel down the full length of his ramrod-straight cock, mimicking the movement he'd seen Heinz do with Jeremiah when Jeremiah was begging for the fuck.

Josh writhed and rolled against Able's chest in waves of passion, doing much of the work of arousing friction, as Able fucked up into him. Josh had his head buried in Able's shoulder and was whimpering at the deep taking. Able was

41

looking over Josh's shoulder at the rifle propped up against the post across the room. A position change was required.

Able slowly turned his body over on his side, taking Josh with him. Josh looked into his eyes with an unspoken question. Able took the young man by the shoulders and showed that he was to go down on his belly and raise his hips to Able's mastering cock, which he did without objection. It was clear that Josh knew how to do this—to move into positions that gave the cock maximum depth.

Able crouched over Josh's haunches, slowly glided back into him, and stroked him in long, slow, deep thrusts. He reached around Josh's belly and fisted the young Reb's cock and began working it.

Josh threw back his head and howled again and again and again in ecstasy as, himself getting more and more into the arousal of the action, Able picked up the rhythm and fucked with faster and faster and deeper and deeper thrusts.

Able was into it now. He had no idea the sensation of fucking another man could be this pleasurable. For sure he's seen it in Jeremiah's face back there in Pennsylvania at the iron works, behind the coal bins, but he had thought that this was just another man's perverted world. He had no idea that he could be so aroused to greater levels of lust, even, than when he went with women. The Reb's channel was tight; it fit his cock like a glove. The friction was driving Able crazy—he wanted more and more of it. Deeper and deeper. Josh was writing around and babbling about how good it was. How much better than he'd ever had it before.

"Better than your lover back home? The man in the daguerreotype?"

"Yes . . . yes . . . yes." Josh was sobbing, as if some truth had been pulled out of him that he didn't want to admit to, didn't want to give up. But he was in a frenzy, slamming his channel back on Able's cock. All Able would need do now was to stay hard and hold steady. The Reb would do all of the work. But Able was in a state of high rut too, and he slammed his cock home again, and again, and again. He was as much into the fuck as Josh was.

"Of god yes . . ." Josh cried out. "I'm going to . . ."

And then it was over. Josh shot his load on the worn, uneven planks of mill room floor in response to Able's stroking fist and Able came inside the young Reb, totally surprised at how high in the sky the fucking had taken him, how much more satisfying it had been to him than any fuck he'd ever had before.

They collapsed on the floor, Able stretched out on top Josh, his cock still buried deep.

Josh was murmuring and sighing. Able was lost in the moment too.

"Incredible," Able whispered. "I never knew."

"What?" Josh murmured dreamily.

"Nothing. Never mind."

Able rolled off Josh and lay on his back next to the young man. He was breathing heavily, trying to regain his strength and regather his reflexes. Josh was lying there half asleep, well fucked. The more Able recovered his composure, the more he realized he had completely let loose of his predicament and his plan in the heat of the fuck. He had been totally lost to their coupling. He needed to regain his bearings and focus on the task.

Able sat up on his haunches. Josh sighed again, but didn't move.

Able was up on his knees, down near Josh's knees. Pretty much out of the young Reb's line of sight even if he lifted his head, which he didn't.

Slowly, softly, Able was up on the pads of his feet.

Josh felt the hard toeing of the calf of one of his legs, and, still groggy from the fucking, he rolled over on his back and looked up . . . into the barrel of his own rifle.

"What?" was all he could manage.

"Shut the fuck up," Able growled. He had no intention of letting this Reb know how much he had lost his way in the unnatural fuck. He reached over and took up Josh's britches and pulled them on clumsily, needing to keep the rifle trained on the young Reb, now aghast at what had happened and fully returned to reality.

"You just wanted—" The voice sounded wounded, betrayed.

"Shut the fuck up," Able repeated. He was trying to close the britches around his waist, but he was just bigger, more massively muscled there than the young man he'd just fucked. He managed to get a few of the lower buttons of the fly cinched up, though. That would just have to do for now. There might be time to pull an exchange with one of the bodies out in the fields between here and Harrisonburg. His own britches had been cut up for bandages and were of no use now . . . they'd gone for the bandage the young Reb had tied around his bleeding thigh.

Dressed now, Able lifted the rifle and aimed down its barrel at the now-crying Reb, his arms thrust out in defense and supplication.

A long, dangerous moment.

"Fuck it," Able burst out, with a disgust at something or other. He wasn't sure himself. The rifle went to ready rest. It was up to the Reb now whether he wanted to live or die at this moment.

Able leaned down over Josh and lifted his chin and gave him a long, lingering kiss on the mouth.

At the door, he turned, and said, "I'll drop your shirt outside here. I wouldn't suggest raising an alarm or coming after me, or you'll have more trouble than explaining where your britches and rifle ran off to." Then he was gone, leaving the door swinging back and forth on its hinges.

Josh sat there in shock and surprise and gratitude for several minutes before he stirred. He picked up the picture of his lover, took a look at it, and stuffed it back into the pack. Somehow it had lost its luster for him. He sighed as the feeling of double loss swept over him. The regret would always be there now. The Yankee had kissed and fucked better than his lover had done.

Just outside the door, Able stopped and looked carefully around. He was looking for any movement. A few of the wounded soldiers on the ground were stirring a bit, but there was no sign of soldiers on the move. He wasn't sure what direction his unit had taken. He knew at the Stonewall Jackson and one fork of the Shenandoah were to the west of him, though. The mountains were to the east. He thought that was his best bet, to the mountains and toward Richmond. Or he could walk the mountain ridge north toward Washington. There was a river right here to cross first, though, the South River.

Looking around again, Able moved stealthily to the river bank and then waded across in waist-high, gently flowing water. The bridge above his head, on the road to Grottoes from Harrisonburg, was still burning. He got to the other side and was climbing the bank when a shot rang out and he dropped like a stone.

Chapter Four: Make Love, Not War

Able came out of a fever, weak but alive. He was lying on a thin mattress directly on the ground under a tent. There was barely enough room for two mats. A moaning man who was missing at least an arm was stretched out on the other mat. A middle-aged woman in a nurses' uniform and wearing a bedraggled visage knelt between the two mats.

"Good, you are awake. And the fever is going down. We were afraid we were going to lose you."

"Where am I?"

"You're at Belle Isle," She answered. "Both of your wounds are doing well. There was fear for you leg for a while, but the infection has gone away."

"Both of my wounds?"

"Yes. There was the wound in your thigh and another in your back, near the shoulder. That wasn't too deep, though. You must have had something on your back that slowed the bullet."

"Belle Isle?" Able asked. He raised his hand to shoo a fly away from this face only to see that he was shackled to a ring in a short concrete pillar driven into the ground. He saw that another chain led off from the pillar to where the other man lay. The nurse waved her hand at the fly as well and then her hands went back to her lap and she turned her face down and looked at them, in apparent embarrassment.

"What's Belle Isle? And why—"

"Belle Isle is a prisoner of war camp on an island in the James River at Richmond," She replied. "I'm sorry about the tent. They keep saying they will build huts, but they never do."

"Prisoner of war? Richmond?"

"Yes. You were with the Union Army, weren't you? You were wearing a Union uniform when you arrived here."

"Richmond you say? The last I remember I was near Harrisonburg. That's a long way away."

"I understand you were transferred from the field hospital in Gordonsville. That's about half way, but there's still a mountain range to cross. All I know is that they say you were brought in from Gordonsville. I can ask around for more information for you, if you like."

Able didn't answer. He laid back, exhausted and confused, wondering where all the time and distance had gone. The last thing he remembered was fording the South River. And everything around that was hazy anyway and just starting to . . . no, he didn't want to think about that anymore.

"Where are you from?"

"Pennsylvania. Farm country, not far west of Philadelphia."

"Family?"

"Just parents. I'm not married."

"Ah, well . . . but parents worry too. I wish I could say I could write a letter for you . . . letting your parents know you are as well as can be expected. But only trustees . . ."

"How does one become a trustee around here? Will I be staked here forever?" Able lifted his shackled arm in frustration.

"No, that's to keep you confined while you are semiconscious. I'll tell the doctors you are back with us, and they'll send someone to move you to a less-confining tent. Still a tent, I'm afraid. And trustees here help in the mill or the foundry. They produce to help cover the costs of all of the prisoners they have here. I doubt that Belle Isle was set up to accommodate this many prisoners. I'm sorry. The conditions are quite bad. But at least you are alive and out of the war—for now."

"Yes, at least that," Able answered. He wasn't fully attentive, though. She'd said foundry. "I worked in a foundry in Pennsylvania," he said.

"That's good news for you—if you are willing to work here too. It will take time for you to heal enough to do that, but those who can work here fare well enough. The chronically ill and those who have no skills to keep them occupied . . ."

She didn't finish the thought, but Able had quite a good idea of how the conditions were in prisoner-of-war camps in this war. He would gain his strength as fast as he could, and he would work in their foundry.

"Thank you, sister, for being here when I woke—and for many hours before, I reckon. You've been kind."

"It's the least I can do," she answered. "I have no liking for this war—it is bleeding us dry on both sides of it. And I am pleased that you have come out of your fever. I will do report to the doctors. The other man over here should not inconvenience you. We have no idea who he might be. I only hope that he wakes long enough to tell us who he is and where he comes from before. . . . Well, I do try to let the kinfolk know if I'm able. With a name and a town, I have someplace to write with some hope that a letter will go to where it can give some ending of not knowing."

"Yes, sister, if he awakes and you aren't here, I will try to find out his name and home."

"Thank you. It is you who are kind."

No one came again until dark, and Able tried to stay conscious. He wanted to be awake in case the other man became conscious. After a while, though, he drifted off to sleep, still too weak to be fully in touch with the world.

He wasn't fully conscious later, when a hand was laid on his breast and he was being told in a low voice—either in a dream or just beyond his consciousness—that "this food" had been brought for him. He vaguely recalled eating and having a cup of cool water tipped to his face and then a cool, wet cloth bathing his face and his torso and his legs. The sensation intensified into a dream of sex, with someone encasing his cock in a hand while still running the moist cloth over his body. Then he felt the weight of a body on his pelvis and his cock was being enveloped in a warm, moist channel and he was being ridden to an ejaculation.

Afterward the cool cloth was encasing his cock and someone was whispering something in his ear that he couldn't grasp and, although he thought he understood it at the time and that it all made sense, when he woke he couldn't quite grasp what it had meant.

The man on the other pallet had died in the night—not revealing who he was or where he came from. He would be buried with the other unknowns beyond the copse of trees at the eastern tip of the island, on the side away from Richmond across the James River.

Able gained strength through the day, particularly as he was visited by a doctor and pronounced on the mend—and, after he had conveyed that he had experience in foundry work—was shown considerable more attention by the doctor and was promptly brought food and drink that, if only barely tolerable, was of food that would give him strength.

The doctor told him that the next day, when arrangements had been made, he would be freed of his shackles and moved to a better tent and helped to prepare to be able to work in the foundry.

That night Able was less exhausted and delirious when he heard the rustling of the flap of his tent, and a slight figure stole into the tent holding a plate of food, a flagon, and a wet cloth.

"You," Able exclaimed as he sat up on his pallet. Even in the dim light he recognized the Rebel youth who he had escaped from in the old mill room in Port Republic, across the Blue Ridge. Able had no idea how long ago that was. But seeing the young man flooded his memory cells with what had happened in that mill, what he'd had to do to escape. Only to be shot in the back going up the river bank on the other side. Possibly by this man. It was embarrassing and ghastly enough to be suddenly remembering what the two of them had done, but the thought that this was the man who had then shot him in the back . . .

"You're well. Thanks be to god," Josh exclaimed as he knelt down beside Able's pallet and put the plate and flagon down on the ground. He leaned over Able, placing the cool cloth on the Union sergeant's brow and his lips came down to Able's and his other hand slid down Able's chest and belly, searching for Able's cock.

"No!" Able cried out. "What'ur 'yer doing? Be gone!"

Startled, Josh rose back up on his knees and pulled his hands away from Able's body. "Shhh. You'll wake the camp. It's me, Josh. It's just me."

"I know who you are. Leave. Now. I'll have none of you. I'll cry loud enough to have the whole camp in here."

Josh moved back toward the tent entrance on his knees. He gave Able one long, lingering, yearning look full of confusion and astonishment, and then the light in his eyes went out, and he turned away and disappeared from the tent.

The next day, the nurse who had been there when Able first woke was back to tell him that men would be along soon to unshackle him and take him to a better tent.

"I'm glad you came back," Able said. "I looked through the blankets on the other pallet after they took the body away and I found something, there, in the dirt, on the other side of the pallet. Can you see it?"

"Yes, I can. Scratched in the earth with this stick. I think I can make it out. A name, Elmer Hines, and a place, Albany, I think. He must have heard us talking and did what he could to give us the information. Thank you for pointing that out. I will write one of my letters."

"You are an angel," Able said.

"By the way," she said after she'd written the information down on the page of a small Bible she'd pulled out of a pocket, "I did inquire on your coming here. A couple of the guards I asked said you were brought in on the back of a young Rebel soldier. They said he told them, he'd found you beyond the mountains and had taken you to Gordonsville, where you were treated. He stayed with you and when the time came to transfer you here, he'd volunteered to accompany the wagons. The wagon you were on, though, broke down outside Richmond and he'd carried you the rest of the way himself."

"The way I heard it told," she continued, "was that some of the guards wanted to just shoot the patients in the broken wagon and claim either than they all had been too sick to survive the journey or had tried to escape and disabled the wagons themselves. Apparently some of those bringing the wagons were tired of taking the journey for wounded Union soldiers that probably wouldn't survive the prison camp anyway. I didn't hear of any of the other prisoners in the wagon being brought in, but it seems one of the soldiers took you on his back and walked the rest of the way."

Able was mortified. It took him a few moments to gather himself. And then he was so ashamed of himself. He hadn't turned the young soldier away the previous night out of disgust with the young man—or even the act—but in the horror of what he himself had done—and had enjoyed.

"Where . . . where? Could you find the young man for me and bring him? I would like to talk to him and thank him."

"The guards say he left the camp in the night—took one of the supply boats back to the Richmond shore. They say he's gone."

* * * *

It took Josh two weeks, but he finally managed to straggle back to his small farm in the foothills of the Blue Ridge west of Madison. He walked the whole way and mainly at night. A deserter was free target practice for Confederate and Union soldiers equally, and Josh had been a deserter from the moment he'd sloshed across the South River and pulled Able into the stand of trees on the other side and stayed with him until nightfall.

He had been surprised that Able had lived for him to carry over the Blue Ridge and down to the hospital in the railroad hotel at Gordonsville. Josh had thought that he was carrying Able to a Union field hospital and that it would be he, Josh, who became a prisoner of war, but Gordonsville had changed hands again since Josh had been there.

Seeing as how Able was now the prisoner and had two wounds, one of which was festering—the latter one, thankfully having been shallow because of the canteen Able had had strapped on his back when he left the mill—Josh felt obliged to stay with him to ensure he got proper care. And then, having heard Able would be sent to Belle Isle, the reputation of which was quite bad, Josh stuck with him then too.

But Able obviously didn't want Josh to stick with him anymore. Josh had been rejected. It had been true that Able had only done what he did in the mill to gain the upper hand. Josh felt the complete fool. But he wasn't surprised that he'd helped save Able. He was just tired of it all. He just wanted to go home.

So, home he went. His mother was delighted to have him at home, of course, even though there were limits to what he could do. He was still a deserter. And everyone in the Madison area would know that and would resent that he was at home, working on the farm, while their men were off fighting somewhere. His mother kept telling him that there was no one much to know what was happening on the farm or to care— that all of the men he'd known were either dead or at war themselves and the women and children were tied to their own places, trying their best just to grow enough to feed themselves.

But still, Josh went to the fields in the evening or early morning and worked in the woods most of the day, doing whatever he could to scrape up enough to feed two and to keep the woodpile stoked.

He was glad, actually, that most of the men were gone. He had left under the cloud of what he was willing to do for other men. He didn't know if word of that had reached his mother, but he was mortified at how he had scraped together money to buy the rifle he had gone off to war with but had lost in that mill room in Port Republic.

Of course Tom and all of his goading and taking advantage was gone, somewhere down in Georgia his mother thought. Mr. Morris had died at the Battle of First Manassas— just as Paul Cushman had.

Josh instinctively reached into his shirt for the locket he'd put Paul's daguerreotype in while he was waiting out the time in Gordonsville. But it still wasn't there. He'd lost that somewhere and couldn't even remember where. He'd lost it all. He'd lost the memory of Paul and what he thought was an opportunity with Able. And he'd lost his innocence. The only thing he hadn't lost was his urges, his desires. And they had brought him nothing but trouble.

It was a chilly evening in early spring, two years after Josh had come home, along about twilight when Josh left the house and went out into the wood. More firewood was needed, and it looked like rain all day the next day, so Josh needed to lay in some wood that night. He also was feeling particularly morose. Word was that armies were converging on a town south of here called Appomattox and that it wasn't looking good for the South, which had been losing battle after battle throughout the winter months. It had been tough in the folds of the Blue Ridge where Josh's farm was too. Family after family had been receiving the news of a death of a son or husband. Even now more than ever Josh had to be a recluse. It was both depressing and making him feel the prisoner. Every time he talked about going back to the war, though, his mother would start wailing and begging him not to go.

Despite the chill, the wood chopping was such strenuous work that Josh had stripped off his shirt. And so intent was he on chopping while muttering his woes to himself that he didn't hear the sound of the footsteps until they were quite close to him. When he did hear them, knowing them to be too heavy for his mother, who never ventured into the woods anyway, he turned with ax raised. And then his eyes grew wide and he stopped in midair.

"You might best put that ax down before you hurt yourself, Josh."

Josh stood there, frozen, except that his hand holding the ax did slowly lower and he dropped it on the ground next to his leg.

"It is Josh, isn't it? I don't think we ever met formally, but the guards at Belle Isle knew you by name. And, luckily, they also knew where I could find you—close enough that I could ask for your family farm. Don't worry, I told people I met and asked directions of where your farm was, because I had served with you in the army and I wanted to let your mother know that you were alive and would be home soon. I do feel like we served on the same side in the army, you know. Not for political entities but for a section of humanity that has too often been denied and set upon."

"But why?" was all that Josh could say.

"It would be easy to say that I didn't thank you for saving my life—I didn't know you had done it until you were gone. Another reason was because I wanted to return this locket to you, the one with the daguerreotype of your lover in it. He'll be glad that you've recovered that. You left it in my tent the night you left Belle Isle."

Josh lowered his head, thinking back to that night when he had completely misconstrued what Able wanted from him. "Thank you for bringing it. But he won't know. He died. At Manassas. Before you . . . we . . . before Port Republic."

"I see," Able said.

When Josh looked up, he saw an sad expression in Able's eyes. But he saw something else too. Something very much alive.

"You said that was just another reason. Just those two reasons you came here. This is a long way to come just to say thank-you and to return this locket."

"You carried me a much longer distance that that," Able said in a low, husky voice. "But no, that's not the only reason. I came because I want you. If you'll have me. I came because I was struggling with myself—my own desires—when I shouldn't have. I should just have been grateful for what was being offered to."

They stood there silently for a moment. There was a rumble of distant thunder, which was a reminder of the rainy day to come.

"Will they be looking for you?"

"I doubt it. Richmond is in chaos. I became a trustee by working in the foundry. I just took one of the skiffs in all of the confusion on the approaching Union troops and rowed across the James and hid in the warehouse district for two days before setting off west."

"You could have waited for the Union troops to arrive. You were a prisoner of war at Belle Isle. I'm sure they would have believed you. You could have been safe."

"Yes I could have waited for the Union troops to arrive in Richmond. But I didn't. I came here."

"You can come to the house. I'll tell my mother you are a soldier friend who was with me before I left the army— that you've left too and we both are waiting out the end of the war, which should come soon, I've heard. She will be happy to have you here. And if any neighbors come around, that will meet with the story you've already told them. I can just say that I was released from duty and recently returned. But now, I've got to finish chopping this—"

"We can both work on the wood afterward. I see you have another ax there."

"Afterward?"

"After we've lain together."

Josh's knees started to give way from the baldness of the statement—and his realization that he had been aching for it ever since Able had walked into the clearing. But Able, strong as an ox again from the months he'd spent in the Belle Isle foundry, was there to catch him.

Able gently laid Josh down on his side in a bed of ferns and tugged the young man's trousers off his legs. Josh's torso already was bare. Able stretched out behind him and drew the smaller man into his body. He kissed Josh's neck and shoulder and his arm pits and his mouth as he worked the young man's cock and built up his own arousal until he could hold off no more.

Josh, sighed and moaned and cried out and groaned and whimpered and then softly sobbed as Able fully possessed him and marked him as his own.

Confederate Gold

Chapter One: So What to Emancipation

June, 1864, Wellington Place plantation, on the James River, between Richmond and Williamsburg, Virginia

It was no surprise that there would be changes—and probably not for the best—when James Matthew's brother, John, arrived from Mississippi to take up the inheritance of Wellington Place. The biggest change was supposed to be the freeing of the slaves by the Emancipation Proclamation a year and a half earlier. And that may or may not have made all of the difference for Hetty Matthews' man, Obie, or her oldest son, Mathias, both of whom had run off right after the proclamation had become known to them, but neither of whom had written back that they had survived the running off. Not that either one of them could write. It was deemed dangerous to give education to more than a select few slaves needing it for the jobs their owners assigned them.

By the time John Matthews, a fire-and-brimstone preacher by trade, arrived at the plantation, though, Hetty and her daughter, Betty, and younger son, Eaton, were ready for change. It had been four months since James Matthews had died, and they'd been rough months on Hetty and her remaining brood, not the least because of the watchful eyes being held on them because Obie and Mathias had run off.

Hetty, a mulatto slave, daughter from the coupling of a slave woman by the master of the nearby Savery plantation, had been both the housekeeper of the plantation house at Wellington Place and James's bed warmer. James Matthews was the father of her three quadroon children, who also worked in various capacities as house slaves. Eaton, the youngest of these, had only recently been brought into house service when coming of age. the light-skinned mixed breeds were routinely the ones dedicated to service in the house. Before that he'd been given some schooling so that he eventually could help James in the plantation's business office.

James had been a benevolent—affectionate, even—master. But he had died, and in the interim until the new master arrived, the plantation overseer, a rough Irishman, Edwin Hayes, had taken not only Hetty, but also her daughter, Betty, into his bed. Hetty now was too old to produce cash slaves for the plantation, but the overseer had bred Betty, now three months gone. He knew that the new owner would be pleased at the prospect of yet another slave to add to his holdings.

When naïve Eaton had tried to intervene in the bedding of both his mother and sister, he'd been whipped and sent to tend the pigs, although he'd been brought back into the house when word came that the new owner was about to arrive.

On a Sunday morning in June, they all, house and field slaves alike, were standing in a row, in their newest, cleanest clothes, below the front porch steps of the plantation house, looking down at the James River rolling by down to the ocean, awaiting inspection. John Matthews looked at each of them sternly, somewhat like assessing horse flesh, as Hayes walked him down the row, telling him the provenance, duties, and relative docility and trustworthiness of each of his newly acquired slaves. If Hayes told Matthews how closely these servants were related to the Matthews family, it wasn't during this ceremony. The new master stopped in front of Eaton and took a long look, which made Hetty hold her breath, before he moved on down the line. As expected, he looked questioningly at Hayes when he got to Betty and was proudly told that, yes, thanks to the overseer, Matthews had some new property on the way. Hayes made sure to establish that the father would be white; the child would be worth more.

Hetty had every reason to be concerned that John Matthews had looked at Eaton, a smaller-than-average and

58

delicately beautiful young, hardly chocolate man, the way he had. It was the same way that men had looked at her over the years. She too had been a great beauty until the overseer had fucked it out of her.

Eaton lost his virginity to the new master that night in the hut on slave row that he had once shared with his older brother, Mathias, but that now, conveniently for John Matthews, was occupied solely by Eaton. The young man, who slept in just a rough-cotton flour sack converted to a shift, was asleep, on top of his blanket, the shift having ridden up to his waist, when John, erect just from the thought of the delicate beauty of his brother's blow by, stole into the cabin, and came down, full length, on top of Eaton's back with his considerable weight. Surprised, but small and agile, Eaton managed to roll out from underneath the man. Matthews was up on his feet immediately, hunching in a pouncing mode, and standing between Eaton and the only door to the hut. Eaton gave him a terrified look, knowing that fighting with the man would get him killed or shipped south to the rice plantations.

Matthews's trousers were unbuttoned, and his cock jutted out in angry erection. Eaton looked down at the staff in alarm, and Matthews quickly closed the distance between him and the panting young man, his back to the log wall. With one blow of the bigger man's fist to Eaton's face, the small slave fell to the ground. Matthews climbed on the young man's back, pulling his pelvis off the ground with an arm slung under Eaton's belly. He mounted the young slave's buttocks, and, with a hand covering Eaton's mouth, was inside him and pumping before Eaton was fully recovered from the blow to the face.

Eaton struggled ineffectually at first, but he already was undone before he had any chance of saving himself from his new master—not that he would have any right to struggle anyway. John embraced him closely, latching his teeth on Eaton's neck like a cat subduing a kitten, and, moving just his pelvis up and down in an ever more frenetic pace and deaf to the moans, groans, and pleading of his young slave, he plowed and seeded Eaton's virginal ass channel deep.

It was not the shocking violation of Eaton that it could have been, as his thoughts had long gone to the magnificent bodies in motion in the fields of the black male field slaves rather than to the women. Matthews wasn't particularly long or thick—certainly not in comparison with what Eaton had seen in the fields jutting out of the male field slaves breeding their women and each other in hollows made in the corn fields, but he was the first one inside Eaton and was using little but spit for lubricant. Eaton went through a lot of pain before reaching pleasure, and the new master didn't finish taking his pleasure quickly.

Although painful, the taking by John Matthews was as much liberating as violating for Eaton. John sensed this as, at long last, he came close to loosing his seed—feeling it in the moaning Eaton was doing, how he slightly raised his buttocks to receive the thrusts, and in how he began to move his own hips in rhythm to the fuck and gave up his own ejaculation just before John came inside him.

At the last, young Eaton was bucking with the thrusts, grasping the wooden legs of his cot in a death grip, and crying out in passion, as hard, searching, demanding, his master rode him like a stallion covering and breeding a mare—and probably with little more moral concern than the biological necessity and privilege of ownership of the act of control, domination, and use.

A second coupling might have been much more satisfactory for both of them if Hetty had not arrived shortly after the moment of ejaculation, having feared precisely what was transpiring. She had a short whip with her and laid into John, who had little trouble wresting the whip from her and turning it on her—and also on Eaton when he attempted to come to Hetty's assistance.

Three days later, Hetty was sold south to a rice plantation outside of Charleston on the banks of the Ashley River. Betty was sent to the overseer's house as the housekeeper there, although the overseer kept her on his bed more than in his kitchen. Eaton spent the next three weeks in John Matthews's bed—the first few days, until he had become totally submissive to John, tied to the bed posts. Thereafter

Eaton became compliant to anything John Matthews wanted to do to him, which was most of what one man can sexually do to another. Matthews was a master of sexual positions and acts, and Eaton learned more in those three weeks of lying under him of the techniques of pleasing a man sexually than he would have learned in a year in a male brothel.

When not in bed on top of Eaton, John Matthews was occupied with finding a buyer for the plantation. He had no faith that the South would win this war of independence and Virginia was too much taken up with the fighting for Matthews to feel safe this far north. He wanted to realize what he could from this property and head back into safer territory down South as fast as he could.

He found a buyer for the plantation, who took most of the slaves as well. The price he got was almost laughable, but he felt lucky to have gotten anything at all. The remaining slaves were worth more than the land was, but they were bought by small farmers who would work them to death, hedging on getting their profit out of them before the marauding Union forces set them free. Betty was sold over into the Shenandoah Valley to a Scottish farmer, and Hayes was discharged and, seeing the writing on the wall, made his way north to join the Union army.

Of everything John Matthews would miss of his inherited property when he mounted his horse with his inheritance in a saddlebag and rode south, he would miss Eaton most. But eventually he sold Eaton for a tidy sum to a Thomas Temple of Richmond, showing his regret at parting from the young man—his biological nephew—by fucking him to exhaustion the night before sending him to the capital of the Confederacy.

By then Eaton was toughened up to lying under a man and had discovered that he could charm a man with his natural talents. John Matthews had given him a taste for it if not the roughest and most fulfilling of rides. Between the time of being undone and being sent away, Eaton found opportunity to walk out into the cornfields, to more than one black bull field slave he'd seen breeding other men, and discovered the pleasures of having a huge black cock churning in his channel and bathing his insides. Here also he learned that he could manage having several men inside him in quick succession. All of this was a valuable education for how he was to serve his new master in Richmond.

Chapter Two: Fleeing Richmond

Sunday, 2 April 1865, Richmond, Virginia

The nine-block walk west along East Broad Street from the First African Church at the corner of College and East Broad was strangely bustling this Sunday morning at 9:00 a.m. The previous Sunday had been quiet at this time. In fact, Temple's, where Eaton Matthews lived and worked, at Grace and 4th Street, had existed in a garden of quietude the previous week. There had been a period of frenetic evacuation of the Confederate capital by wagon and train during the previous two weeks, and then those determined to stay had hunkered down and remained indoors.

For some reason, though, the movement out of the city had started again this morning in earnest. Eaton wondered if the remaining residents of the city knew something he didn't. That didn't surprise him. He lived in a bubble in Richmond. He rarely left Temple's at all. The early Sunday morning service at the First African Church was virtually the only place he was permitted to go on his own. Any other sojourns outside of the house on Grace were limited-distance errands assigned by Thomas Temple. There were no physical chains on Eaton, but the psychological chains were a matter of clearly understood reality.

Eaton hadn't known any other life, nor could he imagine any other life, than slavery.

He preferred it when the streets were deserted for the nine-block walk along the main thoroughfare on a Sunday morning. He was always embarrassed and slightly fearful of the belligerence he was given by those he passed on the street. All of the sons of the Confederacy who were his age—barely nineteen—were out in the field, fighting the troops of aggression from the north. Those who weren't in regular units somewhere else now were down in Petersburg, twenty-three miles to the south, helping General Lee to hold the outer defense lines of the city. Eaton wasn't there, helping to defend the city. He was here, strutting, or so it seemed, down one of the main streets of Richmond.

What he felt like screaming at those giving him judgmental looks on the street—while knowing he couldn't possibly take that liberty—was that he couldn't fight for the Confederacy, even if he wanted to do so, which he didn't. He had nothing to gain either way; he had no choice in the matter. He was a slave. He had no choice in what he did. And few slaves were fighting for the Confederacy. They increasingly could not be trusted to fight for the Confederacy, and with slaves slipping off left and right, the work of those who remained had become a necessity for their masters.

The issue with Eaton was that he wasn't fully black. He was a quadroon—one-fourth black—and that one fourth was recessive. He was the spitting image of a young James Matthew, his natural-born white father. And his mother was the daughter of a black slave woman and a white plantation owner father. Eaton had been raised in the plantation house. For those on the street, he appeared to be a small, but very fit and attractive, white patrician. And thus he appeared to be a shirker of his duty to the Confederacy, a Confederacy that everyone in Richmond realized, but would not openly acknowledge, was entering its death throes.

In response, Eaton hurried his pace, dodging between people making trips from row houses in the Fan District to wagons at the curb, while residents decided what they needed to take with them when they deserted a city that they fully believed would soon be in flames.

He was flushed and nearly on the run when he mounted the stairs of the large row house at Grace and 4th and entered the foyer, where Thomas Temple was impatiently awaiting his return.

"Good, you are here. There is a young man here for you."

Eaton looked at the hands of the grandfather clock in the foyer to ensure that it not yet was 11:00 in the morning, a

Sunday morning. That was when his time, in the only morning that he had his own time before once more becoming fully chained to Thomas Temple's time, ran out. It was not much later than 10:00, but Eaton dare not point that out to Temple. There was, in fact, no time that wasn't Thomas Temple's time.

"Where is he?" Eaton asked.

"In your room, waiting for you. It's the cavalry captain who has asked for you before when you were not available. I doubt if he is patiently waiting."

"The city is on the move again," Eaton said. "I saw many wagons being loaded on my way from church. Could that mean—?"

"It's inevitable that Lee can't hold in Petersburg for much longer," Temple said. "It's nearly time for me to put the other flag out and put the photographs of my Philadelphia relatives out on the piano."

"We will be staying in the city?"

"Of course we will. Union soldiers are as much men, with men's needs, as Confederate soldiers are."

Eaton didn't dare mention that Union troops occupying Richmond would make a crucial difference in at least one regard—his own status. He doubted that Temple even thought that the fall of the capital meant the realization of emancipation for him. He would be free in fact, free of a master and of the obligations of his life between these four walls.

But then, as if Temple could see Eaton's thoughts in his face, he said, "When the Union troops get here, you can, of course, leave this house. But don't think you can leave this life. I can give you protection and limit the demands on you. If you choose to leave here and make your own life on the streets, you'd best give second thoughts to what you lose and gain. You may think that men in the North are fighting for your freedom, but they are men like any men and will use you like any other man would—they will either revile and beat you or they will cover and fuck you. This city will be laid open to their ravishing just as any conquered city is. What you give here in exchange for protection, food, and lodging will be taken from you in the streets without compensation."

65

He, of course, was right, Eaton knew. Although a black slave, Eaton had been educated and taught to think and to deliberately consider what his limits were and how he best could maneuver within them. He knew he couldn't just jump at freedom in a city under occupation by troops who had had to fight hard and had seen comrades die in the stubbornness of this city to give in. He knew that, if Temple could give him protection, his safest place until the city settled down again was here.

"I will go up to this cavalry officer now," he said, as he started up the stairs to his bedroom on the second floor, the most presentable of the bedrooms in keeping with the higher demand for his services by men in the wartime capital even than those of Temple's women prostitutes.

Eaton could tell that the man was agitated when he entered the room. He had already taken off his boots and his blue broadcloth trousers with the yellow stripe going down the leg and folded and placed them on a straight chair. Similarly his gray jacket was folded and placed on top of the trousers. He had shrugged out of his bibbed shirt and had his hands on the buttons of his underdrawers fly. He must have started unbuttoning those when he heard Eaton on the stairs.

He'd been pacing the room with nervous energy, and although the scent coming off of him was a manly musk, Eaton could sense something else in it—impatience and fear.

He was a young, handsome devil, much better put together than most of the men who visited Eaton's room. His chest was muscular, his waist narrow. His features were patrician South, his hair, including the tufts under his bulging pecs and on his forearms, were a sandy blond. He had unbuttoned enough of his fly for Eaton to see the same shade of reddish blond in his pubic bush.

"You have made me wait," the Confederate captain growled as Eaton entered the room.

"I'm sorry, sah," Eaton answered. "I was at church. I normally don't work on Sunday mornings."

"Well, don't make me wait now. Unclothe yourself and be quick about it and service me."

66

"Yes, sah," Eaton answered, hastening to strip down and sink between the man's spread thighs where he now sat on the side of the bed. The soldier had his cock out and in his hand. It was above average size and girth, able to stand proud against most of the black bull field slaves who had fucked Eaton in the cornfields for their and Eaton's pleasure. It was half hard when Eaton took it in his mouth and started to suck on it and to move his mouth up and down on it, encasing it a bit deeper each time he sank his mouth on it.

The man initially leaned back on his elbows and groaned his arousal and satisfaction with Eaton's technique in sucking the cock, a skill taught to him by John Matthews. Eaton could feel the soldier relaxing and becoming less agitated. After a few minutes, he rose back up off his elbows and leaned over Eaton's back, while the young slave continued to harden, lengthen, and thicken the man's cock with his mouth, taking the mouth off the cock from time to time to lick, swallow, and suck on two plump balls. The cavalry officer moaned at the latter attention and ran his hands down Eaton's back and his sleek flanks.

"You are good at the suck," he murmured. "How old are you?"

"Just nineteen, sah," Eaton answered as he moved from the balls back to the shaft. The man leaned farther over Eaton's back and ran his rough, calloused hands onto Eaton's buttocks as he knelt between the man's thighs. The soldier squeezed and separated the buttocks, the index fingers of both hands searching for and finding the rim of Eaton's ass entrance. Eaton groaned, shuddered, and trembled, not all of it feigned to please the client. This man was younger, more muscular, and more handsome than most Eaton was called upon to service.

He also was taking longer than most in the foreplay. Most of the men Eaton lay under could be on top of him, inside him, seeding him, and back out in under fifteen minutes.

Withdrawing from the tease of Eaton's entrance, the man's hands returned to gliding over and massaging Eaton's torso as the young man continued to alternate his attentions between the hard shaft and the man's balls.

"You have some darky in you, I surmise," the man muttered.

"Yes, sah. I'm a quadroon. My father is white as was my mammy's father."

"Raised on a plantation?"

"Yes, sah, Wellington Place, on the James, down toward Williamsburg."

"I know the place and the family. You are James Matthew's bastard then, are you?"

"Yes, sah."

"I knew him well. A good family. He teach you to suck like this?"

"No, sah. His brother, John, a preacher man."

The man laughed. "I can see the Matthews in you—except for the chocolate and cream skin. You are a right beautiful young piece. You learn to fuck good in your nineteen years? You are very young."

"Men seem to enjoy me, sah." Eaton gasped as he said this. The man had spat on the fingers of one of his hands, which he had returned to and had invaded Eaton's ass passage. The man laughed again. "You open right up to me."

"Yes, sah. You are a big man, but I won't give you any trouble getting in. I've been here at Temple's since the summer," Eaton answered, which the cavalry officer took as reason enough that the young man would open so quickly.

"Well, let's see what you have learned since the summer," the officer said.

He was lying on his back on the bed, his feet on the floor at the side of the bed, with Eaton, facing him, sitting on his cock, his arms slung back, his hands gripping the man's knees as he leaned back and rose and fell on the hard, buried cock, when there was a knock on the door. Without waiting for an answer Thomas Temple stuck his head in the room. What he saw didn't give him a second thought. It was what he expected to be going on in the room.

"Excuse me, Captain, but there is a courier here for you from the Executive House. You are needed immediately."

"Needed? Now?" Captain Charles Singleton answered through gritted teeth, having come close to ejaculation. He raised his torso off the bed, grasped Eaton's waist on either side, and began to pull him rapidly and brutally up and down on the cock to hasten toward the release of his seed. Eaton groaned deeply at the sudden increased demands of the thick, hard cock inside him.

"Yes, sir. The time has come." Temple stood there, watching the quickened pace of the fuck with no more concern or interest than the joy of seeing two beautiful bodies in motion and the money it would produce for his accounts. "President Davis sends word that Lee's defensive line in Petersburg has given way. The government must be away by 8:00 p.m., he says, or the government will be caught here."

"Christ almighty," Singleton declared, roughly pushing Eaton off to the side before his arousal was satisfied. He leaped up from the bed, grabbing for his clothes, and suddenly was all decisive action. "You have a wagon and a team?" he asked as he hurriedly dressed, the question posed to Temple.

"Yes, sir, of course."

"I am requisitioning it for the day. And this young man here. Is he your slave?"

"Yes, sir, he is."

"You know I am an aide to President Davis and speak with his authority?"

"Yes," Temple answered, all cooperation and subservience.

"Good. I have need for this man's service too. Have him bring your wagon around to the front. You may retrieve it from the Richmond and Danville rail depot on the river at 14th Street, below capitol hill, sometime after 8:00 tonight."

"Yes, sir," Temple answered, struggling to keep up with the captain's directions and impressed both that an evacuation plan for the government obviously already was in place and that this cavalry captain had a key role in it. In the flurry of activity he didn't ask if Eaton also could be retrieved at the rail depot that evening. Perhaps he should have posed that question.

* * * *

Captain Singleton didn't wait at the Grace Street entrance for Eaton to bring the wagon around. He entered the stable shed behind the house as Eaton was harnessing up one of Temple's two draft horses to the wagon.

"No, both of them, young man. They will have a heavy load to pull today."

"Yes, sah," Eaton answered. He had no idea why two horses would be needed, but he was just a slave; he knew it was no business of his to know white folks' business.

"And my name is Charles Singleton," the captain said. "I need to be able to communicate with you quickly. What is your name?"

"Eaton, sah. Eaton Matthews."

"Ah, yes, of course," Singleton said. "Now be sure to cinch those horses up tight, and bring fodder and water for them. They will be sorely taxed today. So will you and I."

"Yes, sah."

"Oh, and I'm not finished with you. I paid for release of my seed, and I mean to have it."

"Yes, sah," Eaton answered.

Singleton hadn't lied about it being a taxing day. As Eaton got the horses to pull the wagon out onto 4th Street and Singleton got in beside him, Eaton asked, "Where to?"

"Main Street. The Bank district, between Capitol Hill and the river," Singleton answered. Eaton saw the man take his rifle out of its case and lay it across his lap.

"We expectin' some trouble, Captain?"

"I hope not, but word will have gotten around the city of the break in the lines at Petersburg," Singleton said, a grim expression on his face. "There will be folks without wagons of their own in the mood to take someone else's today. They should have left days ago. The government as well, but they just didn't believe this would happen."

Sure enough, the mood was both frenetic and threatening once they got out to East Broad Street and started for Capitol Hill. More than once Singleton had to brandish his rifle to prevent panicked men from putting their hands on the bridles of the horses to try to commandeer the wagon. It was only eight blocks to the bank district, but the streets were clogged with panicking people, in wagons and on foot, coming at them, trying to escape the city to the west and south. Direct northern and eastern routes were already being blocked off by the Union Army.

Eaton had asked why Singleton's goal was the Richmond and Danville line rail depot, as that line went south, toward Petersburg, before turning west rather than the Fredericksburg, Richmond, and Potomac line headed west at the western end of East Broad, but the captain just muttered that there was a plan. "We have to follow the plan."

Progress improved within four blocks as they were met by a unit of soldiers who obviously were being sent to aid Captain Singleton. It became equally obvious that they were needed when Eaton was told to bring the wagon to a stop at Main and 10th Street, between the buildings of the Bank of Commonwealth and the Bank of Virginia. Soldiers and slaves, stripped down to their breeches, their muscular torsos slicked up with sweat from heavy work, already were here, at both banks, moving closed and locked leather boxes from the vaults in both banks out to the street. The Temple wagon wasn't the only one there that was being loaded from the bank vaults.

"Over there, at the Bank of Virginia. Help them load this wagon," Singleton commanded of Eaton, and the young slave moved to answer the command. If he had any question of what was being loaded into the wagons, that was answered when a slave, who was whipped and told to pull the case back together, dropped one of the leather boxes, which split, and gold bars and a mix of legal-looking papers spilled out onto the ground.

All during the afternoon and into the evening wagons were loaded at the banks, driven the few blocks down to the riverfront at the rail depot on 14th Street, and loaded into train cars. There were three locomotives, with a couple of passenger cars and three or four freight cars each, the fanciest of the trains not having been brought up until nearly dark—and much too near the 8:00 p.m. last safe departure time.

After cleaning out the vaults of the Commonwealth and Virginia banks, the wagons, including Eaton's, were sent over to the remaining two Richmond banks, the Exchange

71

Bank and the Farmer's Bank, where they engaged in a more hurried, less comprehensive transferring of the bank assets from the vaults to the wagons. It already was 8:00 p.m., the latest time that General Lee had told President Jefferson Davis he could keep the Union troops from reaching the southern bank of the James, in the town of Manchester, across the James from Richmond.

Eaton and the others were still loading bank assets into two of the trains when they saw Davis and his cabinet and their families arrive and pile into the lead train, the fancier one that had been brought up last. It was after 9:00 p.m. when that train entered the 14th Street railroad bridge over the James, headed south, and churned away, turning west once across the river and following the river bank out of sight. A smattering of shots pinged off the train as it reached the southern bank of the river and turned toward Charlottesville on its way to Danville.

The young quadroon still was helping to load the last of the three trains when the second one clattered across the bridge, meeting heavier gunfire from the other shore of the river than the first had, shortly before 11:00 p.m. His arms were aching and his lungs burning from the hard work that he'd been protected from all of his life. Like all of the rest, including Singleton, he was stripped to the waist and sweating profusely as he helped lift heavy leather cases up into the freight car. Singleton didn't just stand by and direct operations at the third train. He was everywhere, ordering and demanding and cajoling soldiers and slaves alike to get on with the loading and helping to carry cases himself.

Watching the god-like body of the young officer moving around in the uneven light of the rail yard, Eaton almost regretted that they hadn't completed their fuck in the brothel. Up until Temple had arrived, the captain had been taking his time with his cock inside Eaton, unlike most other clients, caressing Eaton's shimmering walls with the hard shaft's fat bulb, encouraging Eaton's muscles to make love to the thick rod. Singleton hadn't come yet, but Eaton had and was building to another ejaculation when they were interrupted. Even though it was a pay-for-service fuck, Eaton was looking forward to having it completed.

"Not all in the freight cars," Singleton demanded, as they got close to the last of the cases to put on board, and bringing Eaton's flagging attention back into the frantic here and now. "Line the far side of the passenger cars with cases up to the bottom of the windows as well." It was only later that Eaton realized why the captain had ordered that.

The last of the trains wasn't ready to go over the river bridge until midnight. By then they were able see the torches on the other bank. The vanguard of the Union troops was arriving.

"Time to go," Singleton called out. "You, Eaton, into the train. Keep yourself low, behind the cases below the windows."

"Me? You want me to go with you?"

"We have to unload at the other end—and I told you I wanted all that I paid for at Temple's. Don't question. Do it!" Singleton yelled, and Eaton dutifully climbed up into a passenger car with the soldiers and the slaves who were being commandeered. Once inside the train, he stood in the center of the car, confused. "I said get low," Singleton growled and pushed Eaton down onto the floor of the car behind the leather cases that had been stacked at one side.

They were only half way across the river bridge when Eaton realized why Singleton had ordered this. As they were coming into rifle fire range, bullets began pinging off the sides of the rail cars, with some entering through the windows. The soldiers were lined up, crouched on the sides, elbows and rifle stocks resting on the top of the insulating leather cases on the side toward the southern river bank, and returning fire. Eaton and the other slaves crouched down on the center floor of the carriages, praying for their lives.

At the other end of the bridge, the train came to a stop, and several of the soldiers piled out on the northern side of the carriages. The remaining soldiers maintained a withering barrage of gunfire into the Union positions to the south.

"Oh, Lord Jesus, the train is broke. We gonna die here!" a hulking jet-black slave who was huddled against Eaton wailed. This palpable fear was contrasted by his massive musculature, revealed by a hard body clad only in tattered cotton breeches, his chest gleaming with the sheen of sweat of having been worked hard all day and marked with African tattooing and whip welts.

The young man had no answer for that. He was almost immobile from fear and dread—and totally exhausted from the day's hard labor and how long he'd been pumping adrenaline already. He looked up into Captain Singleton's face, looking for guidance, understanding . . . protection. Earlier that day, the reddish-blond cavalry captain had been just another client, a man wanting to release his seed into Eaton, albeit one who had taken his time with Eaton and given the young man much pleasure in the process. Now, Singleton was Eaton's new master and, if that was possible, his protector and deliverer . . . and, Eaton could hope, the master of his body as well.

"We have to blow the bridge," Singleton said to Eaton as an explanation of why they were stopped. "They can't just waltz into Richmond across a railroad bridge."

At that moment, there was a loud series of explosions, and the jet-black buck of a slave grabbed Eaton hard and close and exclaimed, "Sweet Jezzuz, we all gonna get exploded to smithereens!"

Soldiers were piling back into the passenger carriage, and the train was starting out again. Singleton reached down and took Eaton's hand. "Don't worry, little one," he said, "We will get through to Danville. If you stay with me and lie under me willingly, I will protect you." Then he rose and left Eaton to give firing instructions to the riflemen lining the side of the carriage.

For some strange reason, despite not having any proof whatsoever that the captain could deliver on that promise, Eaton believed him, and his heart stopped racing in his chest as the train made a mad dash through the sporadic gunfire from the approaching Union troops. Singleton, still stripped to the waist and showing how hard bodied his torso was, had become a stud stallion to Eaton. The young slave's heart started to thump in his chest again, and with visions of writhing under the captain's strong, cut body, with Singleton's churning cock pinning him to the floor, going through his mind, Eaton found himself going hard. Unthinking who might be watching, he reached down to grasp his cock through the thin material of his trousers. The slave who had been huddled beside him and had cried out that they all would die was equally keyed up and pumped up with adrenaline after the day of back-breaking, frantic work to transfer the bank assets to the train.

He too was hard and obviously, from the way he was looking at Eaton, randy now. It was impossible not to notice both that Eaton was also randy and that Eaton was a fine piece of ass. The slave had seen how Singleton and Eaton responded to each other during the day and he knew that the captain was humping the fine piece of ass because he had just said so. He wanted to be humping him for hours too.

"It's good to be alive, ain't it?" he called out to Eaton, a big grin on his face, his hand reaching out to touch Eaton's cock through the material of his breeches. "A man should celebrate that."

Eaton took his own hand away and let the other man feel him up, jutting his pelvis forward to let the man know he was fine with it. The black buck's fondling became more possessive. "You want what I want?" the black stud asked. "You want Josiah's big one? I's a gonna stick it to you unless you cry to your captain for help." He was gripping Eaton's hard cock through the material of his breeches. Eaton didn't cry out to Singleton, who was obviously distracted with the problems at hand of escaping the Union troops. Nor did he object to the black bull feeling him up. He jutted his crotch up into the black buck's hand and moaned for him. He was no stranger to giving men what they wanted from him, and his mind went to the black field hand bulls on the plantation who had satisfied him like none of the clients at Temple's had done.

His captain was busy and Eaton was randy from the exhilaration of still being alive.

The man was tall, solidly built, and muscular—a field slave who had been worked hard and to hardness. He was a black bull. Eaton had noticed the tracings of the welts on his back. He hadn't taken to being a slave lightly; his tattooing indicating that he wasn't long from the wilds of Africa either, which Eaton found arousing, pulling a sense of primeval want from him. The black bull obviously was accustomed to using

75

the power of his body. He could have snapped Eaton in two if he wanted.

With Singleton and the soldiers occupied with firing outside of the train as it dashed for safety, the black bull, hunched down below the level of the window sills, dragged Eaton by his ankles across the floor of the carriage and behind a stack of leather cases. Jerking Eaton's breeches off his legs and tearing at the buttons of the fly of his own tattered breeches, he had Eaton on his back, a beefy hand clutching Eaton's throat to keep him quiet, and quickly pushed his knees between Eaton's thighs. The man was a stallion stud, hung as well as any slave Eaton had taken in the field, and he was hard as a rock in erection. Far from fighting him, Eaton arched his back, dug his heels into the rough wood of the carriage floor, and raised and rolled his pelvis up to give the huge cock straight access. The bull slid his cock inside, meeting little resistance from a well-used passage although still making Eaton open and stretch to him as he stuffed it in.

"Ass opens right up. You wanted me. You're a little man whore, ain't you?" the black stallion muttered. "Seen you goin' in and out of Temple's, ain't I? You can take it hard. You gonna git all of it."

"Yes, give it all to me," Eaton answered with a raspy voice.

And then Eaton, with a gasp and arching his back again, did get all of it. Deep and hard. Again and again and again.

The black bull was pumping in long, deep slides. As keyed up and randy and glad to still be alive as the bull slave was, Eaton was his match in lust. He threw his arms around the massive torso of the slave, holding the man's bulging chest into his own muscular, but slighter, one, the slave's taut nipples rubbing Eaton's hard nubs. With the slave emitting a deep, satisfied laugh, Eaton moved his pelvis with the rhythm of the fuck, moaning at how well and completely he was being plowed.

Eaton closed his eyes and imagined himself back in the cornfields of the plantation, being fully taken by one, two, or three of the field slave bulls in succession. He was being taken just as well now. There was no reason for him to have any inhibitions. He took four or five men a day, rarely as totally possessed and worked as this, though. He had been on edge when the captain hadn't completed taking him. This black bull was taking him masterfully, and totally. Eaton was taking the black stranger back, slamming his pelvis hard into the man's groin with each thrust of the cock, both of them grunting and groaning in primeval need, straining to get it in as deep as possible and then holding, tensed up, Eaton's claws buried in the black bull's whip-scarred shoulder blades and the slave's teeth pressing into the side of Eaton's neck, as the bull discharged—one, two, three prodigious loads, and, with a long sigh, Eaton ejaculated into the stud's belly as well.

They held there, unmoving and listening to the clack clack of the train wheels and the occasional murmur of a soldier and a rifle shot from across the stack of leather cases, the increasingly distant sound of enemy rifle fire, and the occasional ping of a nearly spent bullet off the walls of the carriage. All of that was another world. The two of them were alone, one unit, fused by the big, jet-black cock. Then, engorging again, the black bull stud started a slow pump, and, with a sigh, Eaton started to roll his hips again as well, undulating his passage muscles over the moving cock until, building up speed and intensity, they once more were frantically moving—pounding—against and with each other to a second ejaculation.

And holding there, both breathing heavily. The black bull covering Eaton's throat and chest with his lips and nipping teeth and Eaton waiting for a separation between them, a separation that didn't come. Although momentarily flaccid, the pitching and rumbling of the carriage floor under them kept the virile and needy black stallion's cock moving inside Eaton's channel. Eaton sighed at the pleasure of it sliding languidly inside him and laid back, arms akimbo. The heels of his feet rubbed the meaty calves of the field slave in invitation and surrender. This interlude was almost more sensual than the pumping inside him and the release of ejaculate. Almost. And only an interlude. Young, virile, full of juice still, strong, and rarely with an opportunity like this, the black stallion, knowing

77

the sweet, yielding little piece was fully open to him, hardened again and restarted the fuck.

Gripping, raising, and separating Eaton's buttocks wide to give himself maximum access, the black giant started pounding, pounding, pounding. Clutching him close, Eaton bucked with him for some moments, but giving up a weak stream of cum and having tired, although fine with the pleasure the stud was continuing to give him, he laid back, legs hooked on the black bull's hips, and reveled in how long the black stallion could remain hard, thrusting to yet another flooding of hot cum deep at his core.

The two, both grinning and satiated, rolled back, Eaton more gingerly than the stud slave, into the center of the carriage when they were done. Without, Eaton thought, Captain Singleton realizing they'd not been there all along. This thought was shattered a short time later, though, when Singleton came over to him, nudged him with his foot, and said, "Enjoyed the black cock, did you?"

Nothing more than that for the moment and then the captain was gone back to talking to and encouraging his soldiers. A few minutes later, though, he was back. "I watched you two for a while. You going to give it to me that good when I'm fucking you? You were holding back earlier today. I don't want you ever to hold back with me again."

This time he didn't wait for an answer before he left.

Chapter Three: Unexpected Problems

Tuesday–Wednesday, 4–12 April, Richmond to Just North of Danville, Virginia

The men in the train had barely settled down, a bit more than two hours after they had cleared through the skirmishes at Manchester, across the James River from Richmond and headed west along the river bank, before they pulled off on a siding in a forest near the town of Goochland.

Even though the men already were exhausted and had barely recovered from the fear of the close-call escape from Richmond, as soon as the train came to a stop, Captain Singleton was rousting the men out again.

"We'll travel only at night," he declared. "Now, I need every one of you off the train and cutting brush to lay over the rails spurring off from the main line and to hide the back of the train. Rocks and dirt over the connection as well. If there are Union scouts out during the day, we don't want them to find the train."

So, between then and the hour before dawn, the men worked hard to camouflage the train. The captain then told them all to get some shuteye into the light of day. "Get some rest," he said. "There will be work to do here in the daylight hours."

With that, he sent most of the men to the two passenger carriages in front of the freight cars and bade Eaton to come into the forward carriage with him. Settling himself and Eaton down on a padded seat at the forward end of the carriage with the other men in the carriage closer to the other end, he drew Eaton close to him and covered both of them with a blanket. When Eaton felt one of his hands being taken in Singleton's and moved to the captain's lap under the blanket, Eaton realized that he wasn't going to get to sleep for a while.

There was no question that he would give the captain the release from tension that he wanted. Eaton enclosed his hand over the engorging cock and stroked a groaning Singleton to an ejaculation. As he did so, he could feel the captain relaxing to his touch, with just a short period of tensing up before he released his seed, followed by a long sigh and a murmur by the soldier of, "I wish to do more, but we have a greater need for sleep in the time we have."

"I don't understand why the rail line follows the James River west by northwest if it goes to Danville," Eaton said as the two dozed.

"Ah, I forget you have been given some education," the captain responded. "The line doesn't go directly southwest to Danville. It serves Charlottesville to the west, as well, and then it goes south through Lynchburg. Tomorrow night we will be in Charlottesville. Then the long run to Danville."

"And then?"

"This train goes only that far. The government will reform in Danville and stay there if it's safe but go farther south, if it isn't. We go no farther than Danville, in any case."

"And the cargo we're carrying? Where is it going?"

"Sleep now, little one. There is much work to do in the coming day."

* * * *

After daybreak there were fewer men to do the work the captain wanted done than Singleton had thought there would be. When he rousted the men out, he found, to his great anger, that nearly all of the slaves he'd brought on board had evaporated in the night. To Eaton's disappointment, this had included the black stallion slave who had laid him so completely the previous night. And they had taken some of the leather cases containing the Richmond bank assets with them. The captain didn't discover this immediately, though. Before he could discover he had lost most of his black beasts of burden, he looked out of the window of the carriage after disentangling himself from Eaton to spy two of his own soldiers stealing away from the train and carrying one of the leather cases between them.

He was sluggish getting his rifle out of its case but spot on in bringing both of the men down with just two shots. He immediately gathered his most reliable soldiers about him, kicking himself that he had put them all in the first carriage rather than on watch dispersed among the other carriages, and made all of the remaining men stand at attention as the two dead soldiers were buried. He had confiscated all firing arms except for those his own trusted lieutenants carried.

After the burial, he announced that more shovels were to be dispersed among the remaining men and that they were to start to pull some of the leather cases out of the freight cars. He specified that twenty cases were to come out, and he designated where they were to be buried at a short distance in two different directions from the train there, just east of Goochland.

Only two of his most reliable men were with him as well as Eaton, who he kept within his sight at all times, when Singleton marked four trees in four different directions with symbols that were mysterious to Eaton. The burial complete, the small contingent returned to the hidden train. There Singleton charted the locations in some sort of code in a notebook he was carrying.

Afterward Singleton had the last freight car opened and five horses were brought out. He had the horses saddled and picked out four men to make up a scouting party with him. "I need to know if the Union forces have come this far up the river yet," he said. Before he left he took Eaton into the freight car the horses had come out of and chained him up, lying in the hay that had been spread for the horses and between hay bales, leaving little doubt that he didn't want Eaton running off like most of the other slaves had done. The other men were told to sleep until nightfall, when they would be required to clear the track so that the train could make a nighttime dash to the next stop, in Charlottesville. Leaving them under the guard of soldiers Singleton could rely on, he went off with the scouting party in mid afternoon.

About an hour after the scouting party left, Eaton heard the door of the horse carriage being rolled aside. His eyes were dazzled by late-afternoon sunlight for a brief moment before the door was slid shut again and he realized that three of the soldiers were in the car with him.

"Thought you might be lonely in here all by yourself," one said in a sneery voice.

"I know who you are—you're a male doxy from Temple's, ain't you?" the second exclaimed.

"And I know why the captain is keepin' you so close to him," the third added.

"He told us to sleep, but I'm not as tired as I'm horny," declared the first. "I can sleep better after a good fuck. You open for business as much here as you were at Temple's, ain't you?" He pulled some coins out of his pocket and tossed them in the hay beside Eaton's prone body. He turned to the other two. "Come on boys, ante up and let's keep this all business like. He has it for sale, don't you, boy?"

With a sigh, Eaton pulled his shirt over his head and unbuttoned his trousers. He saw no use in trying to deny them and it was, in fact, what he gave men who were willing to pay. There was no place for him to go anyway. He'd been chained here. They were white men. They could take what they wanted without paying him, if they wished. Once they saw that Eaton would surrender to them, the other two men were quick to add their coins to those the first man had dropped.

Eaton went on his back, his torso propped up on his elbows, his legs spread and bent, feet on the floor of the carriage, and a wad of hay under the small of his back, his pelvis rolled up and his hole open and winking at the three soldiers. "Who's first?" he asked in a weary voice.

The three took turns fucking him for two hours, in relay, both in the missionary and the doggie positions and fucking both his ass and his throat. They might have gone on for a third hour, if Captain Singleton didn't return from scouting, slide open the freight car door, and catch them in the act.

He would have shot the three soldiers there on the spot, if Eaton hadn't intervened. "I didn't deny them," he said, "and, look, they paid me. They are just men being men. And they did nothing to me that white men haven't done before."

"And colored men too," Singleton muttered under his breath, but he continued to look belligerent and stroked the trigger of the rifle he had pointed on the soldiers, Eaton said. "Don't you need these men for your mission here? Aren't they just taking what you want to have? Let them go, slide that door closed, and take what you want too."

Built up with denial of a completed fuck with Eaton the day before and with the adrenaline of all that had transpired in the day and night of the evacuation from Richmond, Singleton took Eaton the first time like a wild man, fucking him rough and deep and rapidly, his throbbing cock pistoning in and out, sliding easily through the accumulated cum of the three soldiers in Eaton's passage. Eaton wildly fucked him back, moving his hips in rhythm with Singleton's thrusts, opening totally to the man's kisses as well as the thrusting of his cock, digging his fingernails into the captain's biceps and shoulder blades.

"Good as you got from that slave last night?" Singleton growled.

"Yes, yes. Fuck me hard!"

The second coupling was slower, more sensuous, with Singleton kneeling and upright, embracing Eaton's small, more delicate body in his lap, and the two rocking back and forth to provide the friction of the hard cock in the channel that induced their mutual ejaculation.

When they left the carriage to join the men, they ate ravenously of the dinner that had been prepared in the twilight. Then, while the other men were clearing the track in the dark and before the train got under way again, Singleton carried Eaton out into the forest, lay his body on top of where they had buried one of the treasure troves, covered him full length, both men naked, and fucked him again in long, slow, deep slides into the quick of the sighing young slave.

After that Singleton accepted that no chains were necessary to bind Eaton to him. Eaton had been completely open to him, grasping the churning cock with his passage muscles and making caressing love to it—milking the cock and then holding Singleton close to him, inside him, and, with sighs and small cries of passion, milking it again . . . and again. Eaton couldn't get enough of the cock, and it was only the limits of time and the aching of Singleton's milked balls that brought them to a finish. It was clear that Eaton was bound by the need for the blond god's cock working inside him.

* * * *

"President Davis needs it to finance a new army. Some, as we did today, is being cached. But the two trains ahead of us are taking it where he can put his hands on it."

Captain Singleton and Eaton were huddled under the blanket just on the other side of the wall from the locomotive, as the train glided through the night as silently and slowly as it could toward Charlottesville to escape detection. The two were pleasuring each other with their hands under the blanket and Singleton was being surprisingly open in his responses to Eaton's questions about the captain's mission.

"Where can he put his hands on the money where the Union army can't get to it?" Eaton asked.

"The Union army isn't everywhere, and a great part of it is now bogged down in occupying Richmond. Lee's plan was never to hold the capital. He's racing his forces south even now in pursuit of Grant's headquarters. If he can capture the Union's commander, the northern forces will collapse."

Eaton wasn't that sure he believed that. The two forces had been fighting across Virginia for years. Someone in Eaton's position was able to hear unguarded talk by Confederate military men when they visited Temple's, having no idea that a servicing darky like him would have brain power enough to pay attention to and understand what they said. As far as he understood it, the South was being pounded into dust by a never waning supply of soldiers from the North—being ever supplied by immigrants from a starving Europe. He asked again where the assets to be used to raise a new army were going that was safe, whether that was where Singleton was headed, and whether Singleton was planning to take Eaton there as well.

"If the government can't stay in Danville—if Lee doesn't catch up with Grant and trounce him—President Davis is taking the government to Washington, Georgia, and is taking the gold on his train there with him. The second train is going to Charlotte, North Carolina, to what was the U.S. mint post there. That should be deep enough in the South to be out of the reach of the northerners. Yes, after I have cached the gold in this train, I am to go to Georgia. And, yes, I will take you with me."

Satisfied, as the very notion of a freedom that required him to take care of himself frightened Eaton, he snuggled down in Singleton's embrace, as the train crossed back to the north bank of the James River, and moved up to and through Charlottesville. The train didn't stop there, as the captain couldn't be sure which army held Charlottesville at the moment, but stopped on a siding just south of the town to be camouflaged as it had been the previous night. When daylight came, Singleton commandeered wagons and teams from nearby farms, loaded them with twenty of the leather cases, and took them up onto the ridge running along the southern edge of the town. He took Eaton with him.

Standing on the ridge top as men dug holes to hide the leather cases and after Singleton had marked a perimeter of trees with similar mysterious symbols to those he had done outside Goochland, he stood, with Eaton and looked down into the town. He drew Eaton's attention to the university buildings at the edge of the town and then beyond it to the ridge running east of Charlottesville and a small mountain upon which could be seen Thomas Jefferson's home, Monticello, untouched, thankfully by the civil war raging around it.

"Why here?" Eaton asked the captain as the soldiers and two of the slaves who hadn't managed to escape yet dug into the red-clay soil.

"A prearranged area," Singleton answered. "The ridge we're standing on is called the Hessian Hills. This is where the captured German troops who were British army mercenaries were brought to be interred when they lost the Battle of

Saratoga in the American Revolution. We selected memorable spots in our history that have generally been forgotten."

Emboldened by the captain having taken him into his confidence the previous night, Eaton asked about the symbols Singleton was marking on the trees.

"Have you heard of the Knights of the Golden Circle?" Singleton asked. "I wager not."

Eaton took a few moments to conjure up conversations he'd overheard in the brothel, but couldn't surface the mention of any such organization. "No, I haven't," he answered.

"The KGC is an organization of southern gentleman— and more than a few well-placed sympathizers in the North— who are concerned for the welfare of the Confederacy. I'm a member, as is President Davis. It was the KGC council's idea to salt some of the assets away, and, even more than historical sites, I'm burying parts of the treasury near where the KGC is in strength—secretly, of course. I'm marking the caches with the symbols they understand and am making a chart, which I will get into the right hands when our work is finished."

"So, there's a center of that organization here in what was Thomas Jefferson's town?" Eaton asked.

There was no indication that Singleton would have answered that question, but he wasn't given a chance to. As he gave his explanation about the KGC, he was using a telescope to survey the valley between the two ridges in which the town of Charlottesville was nestled. He suddenly growled an expletive, snapped the telescope shut, and declared, "I see a company of mounted soldiers down there, coming into the town from the north and wearing blue uniforms. We need to get back to the train now."

Within moments, the men were back in the two wagons and riding along the ridge to the south to where the train was hidden. When they got back it was to find that several more soldiers had deserted the train and had taken cases with them. There wasn't much Singleton could do about that at this point. He was losing control over who was loyal to him and his mission and who wasn't.

"What now?" Eaton asked him.

"We just have to continue with the plan," the captain answered. "Tonight we push on to Danville. We'll let President Davis decide what happens then. We've cached what I was directed to hide between Richmond and Danville. But for you and me now . . ." he said, turning a lustful eye on Eaton, who had no doubt that his "now" was going to be on the hay in one of the freight carriages, writhing under the captain.

Later, they were, indeed, in a freight car alone among bales of hay, with much of the hay having become undone and strewn around on the floor of the car. Eaton, naked, was sitting on a bale of hay, with Singleton standing between his legs, the fly of his trousers flared, his suspenders hanging down on either side, and his hands pressing into the back of Eaton's skull, as the young black took his cock deep in the throat at the manipulation of Singleton's hands. When he was ready, the captain reached down, grabbed Eaton's ankles, and pitched him onto his back on the bale. He then pressed in between Eaton's spread thighs, thrust inside his passage, and pumped him to an ejaculation.

Yielding totally to him, Eaton relaxed and opened his passage to take the officer's hard cock deep, raising his arms to run his fingers into the captain's blond chest hair and rub the man's taut nipples, while making little moaning sounds of total surrender in the back of his throat and murmuring, "Yes, yes, be good to me. Take me to heaven."

Singleton did just that, filling and fully possessing the young quadroon who was his slave in more ways than one.

When he was done, Singleton buttoned his fly and pulled the suspenders up unto his bare shoulders. He walked over to the sliding door to the carriage, turned, and said. "I need to be able to count on the loyalty of a few of the men at least. Do you understand?"

"I can see the need for that," Eaton answered.

"There are two who are my best—Lyle and John. I've seen the way they look at you when you are with me. They both lie with men. Do you understand how important it is for me to keep them with me—with us?"

"Yes," Eaton answered, dipping his head in submission.

"Do you understand what I need you to do for me?"

"Yes," Eaton said, not daring to lift his head so that Singleton could see the hurt and love in his eyes.

Singleton pulled the car door open and told the first man who passed by, "Find Lyle and John and tell them I want to see them here now."

"Yes, sir."

The two delighted soldiers fucked Eaton in successive turns, easily sliding their cocks in each other's cum inside Eaton as well, as what Singleton had earlier deposited there. Eaton lay there, the dutiful quadroon slave prostitute, receiving them as he had been trained to do so, legs bent and spread, arms outstretched in an attitude of openness and supplication, as the two rough soldiers plowed him hard. One crouched over where Eaton was on his back on the hay bale just as Singleton had been when the captain had fucked Eaton earlier and the other at the other side of the bale, holding Eaton's head between his hands, and arched back to give the soldier a straight slide of his cock into Eaton's throat. When the first one had come, the two soldiers, not believing their luck but ever grateful to their captain, who sat on another bale, stroking his cock and watching them, exchanged positions.

Thereafter, when it was convenient, Lyle and John were given sex privileges with Eaton—but only after Singleton had fucked him first. Their loyalty to Singleton was solidified.

There was no indication that Singleton was disturbed by this at all. Steeped in the culture of the South, he saw himself as both the master and the protector of Eaton, for whom he had a great deal of benevolent affection and whose servicing he enjoyed immensely. But Eaton was a slave, no matter what Abraham Lincoln said about it, and he was a prostitute. His lot in life was to take men's cocks, including Singleton's—to open his legs on command and pleasure and give release to men, and to serve Singleton as he was needed. Singleton's principle concern was that he get his release inside Eaton first—officers before soldiers. The randy little quadroon had made abundantly clear that he wanted men's cocks inside him. Besides, he was a slave; he really had no opinion to entertain in the matter.

Equally steeped in the culture of the South, in his own place in the order of things, and in a worship of Singleton that went beyond affection, Eaton didn't think any of this was untoward either—this despite the start of a hint in the back of his mind that changes were coming.

* * * *

"What is this place? We traveled on the wagon nearly two hours and came straight here. You knew where you were coming here, didn't you?"

Eaton was standing next to Captain Singleton while men were digging to place the ten leather cases they had hauled a good ten miles from the camouflaged train on a siding west of the town of Lynchburg. It was April 7th, the third day from their nighttime escape from Richmond. They were a day behind schedule, as the three trains had been set to meet in Danville on the 6th, but the third train had left Richmond several hours after the others.

Singleton stopped carving a symbol into a tree and looked through the trees and up to a low-lying brick villa in an octagon shape. "This here is Popular Forest, the retreat estate of Thomas Jefferson," Singleton replied. "And, yes, this is one of the set places where we were to hide the gold to be retrieved when the South needed it to rise again. A prominent leader in the KGC lives nearby, in Lynchburg."

"I understand this place as a recognized location—and what you said about the Hessian Hills above Charlottesville too," Eaton said. "But the first place—Goochland—I don't—"

"It seemed a sleepy small town near but not near enough to Richmond to have any import, didn't it?" Singleton asked, interrupting. "Looks can be deceiving. I told you of the Knights of the Gold Circle—the KGC. It has to center somewhere. Where better than a small, seemingly sleepy town near but not near enough to Richmond to seem to have any import? We have had contingency plans for some time for a resurgence, if our first fight with the Yanks didn't put them off. Goochland will probably always be a small town off the beaten

89

path—for those who don't know what is sleeping and waiting there. If Lee doesn't defeat Grant here in Virginia—and there's every reason to believe he will, being the better soldier of the two—we will have the means to rise again—from the center at Goochland. Maybe not this year or the next. Maybe not in this century. But memories are long and the determination of the sons of the South runs deep."

A soldier came over to tell Singleton that the burial was complete and the site had been covered with pine branches. The captain turned, completed the carving on the tree, and took one last, long look at the Popular Forest house, dark and brooding, no doubt mourning the pillage of the land around it by the interlopers from the north.

"Come, Eaton," he said, putting his arm around the shoulders of the young black man. "Time to go back to the train and to sleep eventually." At this he gave Eaton a knowing look and the young slave shuddered in anticipation of what new and fully satisfying invasion of his body the virile young army officer would perform on him following their dinner. "Tomorrow we will join up with President Davis and the others in Danville, and our mission will be completed."

"What then?" Eaton asked.

"Why, on to Georgia, I assume, unless we receive word of Lee's defeat of Grant. Then we will remain in Danville for a few days and return, triumphant to Richmond, I suppose."

"And unearth the treasury again, as we go?"

"I suppose that depends on how assured the sovereignty of the South is. I wouldn't put it past Lincoln to have yet another army to unleash on us."

"And me, when you go to Georgia?"

"I'll take you with me. Unless, of course, like so many of the other darkies have done, you wish to evaporate into the night. I won't shoot you if you do—as long as you don't try to take any of the gold with you. It is your decision. You have served me well. Do you wish to melt into the trees right here? Or closer to Lynchburg, when we return to the train? Or perhaps in the night, from the moving train as we near Danville? I wouldn't suggest waiting until Danville. I no longer will be in command when we get there. It won't be my choice how to respond to your deserting. Tell me, what is freedom to you and when do you want to grasp it?"

Eaton thought for a moment—not about what he felt but about what he would say. "Freedom is you—lying under you, with you deep inside me," he finally said. "I've never been to Georgia. I think it is time for me to see what Georgia looks like."

"Wise choice," Singleton said. "You darkies aren't made to stand on your own. As long as you serve me as you do—give me release as well as you do—I will protect you. It's wise of you to realize that you will always need a master and to be mastered."

"Yes, sah," Eaton murmured, lowering his eyes in submission, taking comfort in the memory of how closely the muscular captain embraced him, breathing heavily in his ear at the effort of moving as deeply inside Eaton's passage as possible, building up to fully possessing and seeding him. Eaton knew that he needed the master; but he also knew how much the master needed him.

"You know you give me great pleasure," Singleton murmured, nuzzling Eaton's cheek with his. Eaton was about to speak, to express his love for the white officer, when Singleton added, "No man's passage fits me like a glove as yours does." Eaton just smiled and said nothing, realizing that the two of them were speaking on different levels.

As the others returned to the wagon, Singleton took Eaton into his arms and they kissed before joining the others. When they got back to the train, they found that yet more of the soldiers and slaves had departed—and taken leather cases of the Confederate treasury with them. Less than half of the assets of the Confederacy that had been placed under Singleton's charge remained in the train. Still, enough had been cached to seed the resurgence of the South that Singleton fervently believed would happen.

* * * *

Singleton was stroking to the rhythm of the clack-clacking of the engine's wheels and the mesmerizing sway of the carriage as the train picked up speed in the night, reaching out for Danville with the goal of being past there before the break of dawn. The two men were locked in an embrace, Eaton pushed into the seat, his ankles on the top of the seat in front of him, as Singleton hunched over him, arms around Eaton's neck, lips plastered to Eaton's lips, and took long, deep thrusts up into Eaton's anal canal. The carriage had been cleared of all other men so that the couple need show no inhibitions in the visuals or sound of their fucking.

Two competing sensations were woven around the two groaning, grunting men. The sounds of the wheels and sway of the carriage were enough to dull the senses and send the men into a doze—which they undoubtedly believed would finally arrive—but Singleton was coming ever closer to an ejaculation, one that Eaton had already experienced, so the thrusting had become more frenetic and was beginning to double-time the rhythm of the wheels.

It was this more than anything else that made Eaton hone in on the application of the brakes of the engine in time to pull the captain, preoccupied by releasing his cum, down to the floor with him as the wooden wall behind the seat of the carriage shattered and the coal car came barreling over their heads, followed by the back half of the locomotive engine, which, miraculously surged up and over them rather than down on them.

The train teetered there for the longest second before turning on its side and sliding off the track and down an incline into a deep ravine.

Eaton, who had landed under Singleton, clutched the inert body of the captain as they slid across the aisle and under the seat on the opposite side of the carriage as it slid down the hill and came to a rest.

"Captain? Are you all right?" Eaton asked when he could catch his breath.

The captain obviously wasn't all right. He didn't respond. He lay on Eaton as a dead weight—a dead weight that, however, had protected the smaller man from blows from the collapsing seats around them.

"I smell fire, Captain. We need to get out of here," Eaton said, as he struggled up from under Singleton. The man had a gash in his head, but he was breathing. The wood of the carriage was alight with the flicker of flames, though, and the tender car had released coal into the carriage. The wood-sided car could go up in flames at any moment.

Finding strength he had no idea he had in reserve and climbing up sections of crushed seating, Eaton dragged the body of the captain straight up toward the windows on the opposite side of the carriage. With his last ounce of strength, after resting for a few seconds from the effort of pushing Singleton's body out of the window and onto the side of the carriage that now was its roof, Eaton pulled himself up beside Singleton. He raised his face to the sky and nearly let out a cry of Hallelujah upon the discovery that it had started to rain hard.

* * * *

Singleton came to shortly after Eaton had cleaned and bandaged his head wound. The surviving soldiers from the other two carriages—those who were able to move—had already started to bring order to the chaos. There had been remarkably few fatalities. Three of the horses had even survived the slide undamaged. One of the others had suffered a fatal broken neck, though, and another one had broken legs and had to be shot. One of the soldiers had worked his way back up to the tracks to discover that a barrier of logs had been placed across the line just around a bend. Looking down into the ravine, though, all he could see of the five rail cars and engine was the flickering of fire that the rain had not yet put out. Most of the side of the ravine the train had slid down was shale rock. There was no obvious snapping of large trees.

The rain lasted only long enough to aid the survivors in stamping out any evidence of fire.

"We need to spend the rest of the hours of darkness covering the train with foliage so it can't be seen from above," Singleton said, regaining command quickly. Eaton sat off to the side, shivering and wondering how he had managed to pull both of them from the train. In passing, the captain whispered to him, "I know what you did to save me," but he moved on then, all business.

The men groaned at the command and one even said, "The men who died. Shouldn't we—?"

"We all are likely to die from Yankee sharpshooter fire come daylight if we don't hide that we've gone over the side," Singleton retorted. "We can care for the dead tomorrow. Otis, you and Earl go see what you can do to reconstruct the barrier they set up so it isn't obvious something hit it. You, there, get up there and rake the side of the ravine so it's not so evident the train went over the side. The rest of you, cut branches . . . cover the side of the train."

"What about me?" Eaton asked.

"Tend to the horses. Quiet them down and feed and water them. Take care of the living first. And then see to the bodies. Make sure they're all out of the train and laid out at the side. Find something to cover them until we can get them buried tomorrow."

If any Union troops came by that day or the next five days while those at the train hid by day and buried their dead and a cache of the treasure by night, they hadn't seen anything amiss and raised the alarm. On Monday, April 10th, Singleton sent his two most trusted soldiers, Lyle and John, to Danville on two of the horse, the men's clothes changed for those of a couple of slaves who had died in the train wreck so that they wouldn't be recognized as Confederate soldiers if any Union forces were lurking about. They were to make contact with President Davis's government if it was still in Danville and request wagons to take away the rest of the treasury assets in the wrecked train.

Singleton had almost given up hope that they were going to return and was saddling the third horse to attempt the contact with Davis himself, when the two men returned.

"No sign of Confederate forces in Danville," one reported. "President Davis and the cabinet went farther south on the two other trains on the 6th, we're told. The town is defenseless and expecting Union troops to occupy it at any moment."

"Union troops occupy it? Lee's forces are—" Singleton responded.

"Defeated," the second soldier said, in a tremulous voice. "Surrendered to Grant at Appomattox three days ago."

Singleton stood there, stunned. His shoulders fell and he stumbled, leaning into Eaton, who helped him remain standing.

"Captain?" the first soldier said.

"What do we do now, Captain?" the second one chimed in.

Singleton hesitated, but only for a moment. He shook his head and said, "We need two wagons for what is left of the freight. Then we head out."

"South for Georgia to meet up with Davis?" one of the soldiers asked.

"No, Danville at first, among friends, to see if we are called to Georgia. If not, then across the Dan River and then east, to Henderson, to Warrenton."

"Warrenton?" one of the soldiers asked.

"Warrenton. My sister's plantation. What we need now more than anything else is refuge. I'll only take two . . . and Eaton, of course. And two wagons. If it's you two, that's fine with me. You are my most trusted men. If not, I'll take other volunteers. The rest need to tend to themselves now—to try to get to safety, if any there be. Our war as soldiers is over unless President Davis can find strength to rise again. Our trials are just beginning."

Chapter Four: Lost Cause

April and May, 1865, Danville, Virginia

The next two months were ones of hiding in the town of Danville among sympathizers whose loyalty had to be taken on faith and moving about, usually at night, to meet with other supporters and hear the news of the Union takeover of the state. The two loyal soldiers Singleton kept with him managed to find two wagons on loan, which held the remaining fifteen leather cases that had not yet been cached and that could be reached from the crumpled carriage cars camouflaged and increasingly obliterated by Virginia creeper vines. The boxes were hidden under bales of hay in a livery stable at the northern side of the town.

The men themselves were taken into one home after the other. The first thing they did was to burn their Confederate uniforms and clothe themselves in the garb of townspeople. What they couldn't hide, though, was that they were fit men of military service age. Therefore, they had to remain hidden in garrets and outbuildings for the time that Singleton had to wait for contact from the government. There were southern spies aplenty in the town, so he was at no loss for information. Unfortunately, he had to assume that there were Union spies about as well.

He was discouraged by the information he was receiving.

If he had expected a resistance movement to the signing of the surrender at Appomattox courthouse, he was sorely disappointed. The men were tired and defeated. Nearly to a man all they could think of was to go back to their homes to see if there were any homes to go back to. If the assets Singleton had helped to take away from Richmond were to raise a new army, it was clear to him that it would not be raised here in Virginia. Virginia had already given its all. It would have to be raised further south or from abroad.

The first shock Singleton was to receive when he established his credentials and started receiving reports in Danville was that the train that had preceded his had headed south with a much lighter load of precious cargo than it had arrived in Danville with. More than $200,000 in Mexican coinage had been separated from the rest of the cargo in the second train. But at some time during the train's stop in Danville, it had all disappeared. Singleton had let cases of assets slip through his fingers too, but nothing as massive as the loss of the Mexican coins. A few of Singleton's informants were of the opinion that the coins hadn't been stolen but had been hidden in the vicinity of Danville, but Singleton knew of no plan to hide any of the assets other than the ones that had been assigned to his train, so he was skeptical that they were still under Confederate control.

Then he learned that the bullion from the second train had been removed to wagons once the train had gotten well into North Carolina and split in two caravans, one going to the former U.S. Mint in Charlotte, North Carolina, and the other headed to meet up with President Davis and his cabinet in Georgia. As the first caravan approached Charlotte, though, they realized that the Union forces had already seized the mint compound. So, according to the spies, the treasure was packed in casks, barrels, empty ammunition boxes, and flour and sugar bags and sent in five different directions in five wagons—never to be heard of publicly again.

The biggest shock to Singleton came in the last week of May, when, trying to be quiet so that the family that was hiding him didn't know the relationship between him and Eaton— thinking Eaton was just his personal slave—Singleton and Eaton were facing each other, in an embrace, Eaton's legs encasing Singleton's hips, and the two rocking against each other to provide the friction of Singleton's hard cock moving inside Eaton's channel. Singleton barely had time to roll in one direction to a sitting position on the side of his bed and Eaton to roll in the other onto the floor, hidden at the other side of the bed, when the anxious voice of an informant was followed by a knock and an entrance without permission to do so.

"Yes, what is it?" Singleton asked, irritated and covering his erection with sheeting from the bed.

"Davis is taken!" the nearly breathless courier announced in a strangled voice.

"What is this? Davis captured?" Singleton cried out.

"Yes, sir. On May 10th by the Union cavalry in Irwinville, Georgia."

"The rest of the cabinet?" Singleton asked.

"Already dispersed by then. Some captured, I think. Others I know not about."

"The caravan from the second train? The treasury that was to meet him."

"It met up with him, sir, but it too is lost. The Union troops seized it and put what it contained in a local bank in Irwinville, but the bank was robbed on the 24th—just three days ago. It's vanished. Whatever gold there was is gone."

"Vanished. All vanished. The hope of the South vanished," Singleton murmured. And, as if awaking from a bad dream, he thanked and dismissed the courier.

"What now?" Eaton asked, coming up onto the bed, and reaching for Singleton, knowing there was only one way to console his master now and fully willing and able to do so.

"No reason to remain in Danville now," Singleton said. "Now we move toward the coast. What do you think of going in search of a new world?"

"Wherever you go, I will go," Eaton asked.

"For now, will you go on your back and open your legs to me?" the captain asked.

"Gladly," Eaton said, and did so.

Chapter Five: Race to the Coast

June and July, 1865

"What's the significance of burying a cache here?" Eaton asked.

The two wagons and four men were standing in a grove of trees in the back acreage of a deserted farm just east of Roxboro, North Carolina. It had been a night and a day since they'd crossed to the south bank of the Dan River from Danville in the darkest night, entered North Carolina, and headed southeast. The two soldiers who had remained with them had just finished burying a dozen of the leather cases, leaving three on one of the wagons, and Singleton had marked trees in four directions from the cache with the symbols of the Knights of the Golden Circle.

"Nothing is significant here," Singleton said. "Farther south, in Raleigh would have been better, the center of KGC activity in the Carolinas, but the Yankees hold that town already. They'll just have to use the chart I've made up."

Eaton had known that, indeed, Singleton had been making up a chart in some sort of secret language and using the same symbols he'd been carving in the trees—that he'd added to the chart at each location where treasure had been buried.

"There are still three cases," Eaton said.

"Yes. Lyle, John, gather around, boys. It's time to split up. We'll each of us take one of these cases. All hopes of keeping the treasury intact for the Confederacy are long past. We must look to ourselves as well. You two pick first and I'll take the last. This will be our payment for doing what we did. You pick first, John."

As the four men gathered around the wagon and the solider named John contemplated the boxes, no one remarked on why the slave, Eaton, wasn't getting a share. Each of them, including Eaton, still had the dissolving values of the South in mind as valid. None of them thought of Eaton as an equal even though he'd shared their trials and tribulations and quite possibly had saved Singleton's life in the train wreck.

Having chosen and taken a case off the wagon, John laid it on the ground, hacked the clasp off with two swings of a shovel, and went down on his knees as he opened the lid.

"Well, Jesuzz S. Christ," he exclaimed. "Paper. It's all paper."

Singleton and Lyle went down on their knees beside John and dug their hands into the case, all of them coming up with money certificates. Eaton stood off to the side, no part of the division of the spoils and knowing his place.

"It's Confederate war bonds," Singleton said.

"Worthless paper," Lyle exclaimed in disgust.

"Not if the South rises again," Singleton said, "but of little use for the moment, admittedly. Pick a box and see what you come up with, Lyle."

Lyle's box contained nothing but war bonds as well.

"Ah, this case is heavier," Singleton said, pulling the last one off the wagon. "You men should have lifted them before choosing. Let's see what I have."

All four of them stood over the open case, staring down into it. There was a pile of Confederate war bonds, to be sure, but nestled in the center of the case were twelve small bars of gleaming gold.

"Guess you're the lucky one," John said, standing.

Whether it was because he was a generous man, or that he denoted something threatening in the bitter tone of John's voice, Singleton quickly said, "Doesn't seem fair not to share it out. If you and Lyle bury the cases with bonds with the other ones you've buried, you'll get three bars each. I'll just take six of them for Eaton and me."

If any of the men caught the irony that Eaton now seemed to be in the count for a share—although Singleton didn't word it so that a share actually went to Eaton—none of the men remarked on it. The two soldiers obviously decided that three bars each was better than going against their raising and military training to shoot it out in hopes of taking it all. With grunts of agreement, they went off to bury the three last cases.

Singleton was taking off his trousers and bade Eaton to do so as well.

"Here? Now?" Eaton asked. Singleton had been a randy one, for sure, on this journey, but it surprised Eaton that they'd be doing it right at this moment and here.

"You'll find a needle and some thread in my bag," Singleton said. "I want you to sew two bars each into our trousers—just below the hips on either side. I'll keep two out in case we have an opportunity to turn them into something we can use." He looked at the changed expression in Eaton's face. "What, you wanted me to fuck you here and now? Can't get enough of me, can you?" Then he laughed.

It wasn't what Eaton had been thinking at all, but he couldn't disagree that he couldn't get enough of Singleton's cocking, so he just turned back to the wagon to find the needle and thread.

When John and Lyle returned, Singleton said, "To be safe, it's time for us to part company. Four men together on the road here would be taken as three too many by a Yankee patrol. You two take that wagon. There's a horse for each of you and the saddles from horses on the train. Head out any direction but east by south. If you part from each other, just make sure the wagon isn't left anywhere near here."

After thanking them for their service and noting, with regret, that they'd probably not be able to be in touch with him again unless—and until—the Confederate army was reconstituted, he and Eaton stood there and watched the two men ride off in one of the wagons toward the southwest.

When they had asked Singleton where he was going— there didn't seem to be any question that Eaton would be going anywhere Singleton went—the captain just said, "Better you don't know."

As the wagon went over the horizon, Eaton asked, "Where are we going from here?"

"East by south," Singleton answered. "We'll drive the wagon for a few hours and then switch to the horses. We can move faster that way."

"But to where? Where are we headed?" Easton asked.

"Better you don't know that either," was the only answer the captain gave. "It's enough for you to know that I'm taking you with me and will protect you as best I can."

* * * *

Charles Singleton pulled his horse to a standstill. "We're here."

"We're where?" Eaton asked, pulling his horse up to beside Singleton's.

"We're here. Our destination. On top of that hill. Warrenton."

Eaton looked to where Charles was pointing. The columned house had once been imposing but now it looked forlorn. All of the trees and foliage around it had been denuded and the stucco that covered it was yellowed, cracked, and peeling away.

Eaton's eyes kept glancing at Charles as they rode up to the house and he noticed that, with every stride of the horses, Charles' jaw set harder and his eyes seemed to sink deeper into his skull. Eaton didn't try to engage him in conversation as he obviously was reminiscing about Warrenton of the past and grieving for Warrenton of the present.

"Maggie, Toby," He said as they reached the steps up to the columned front porch running the width of the house. Two dark-skinned servants in mended clothes, obviously having seen the two men approach from afar and recognizing Singleton, had come out of the door and slowly descended the stairs.

"Massa Charles," the male—Toby—said, his eyes big and a grin spreading across his face. "The Lord be praised. You're alive and have come to us."

"Yes, Toby, I live," Singleton said. "Is Caroline here? And Tyler?"

"Miss Caroline, yes," the woman—Maggie—said, coming down the stairs and wiping her hands on her skirt. Both she and Toby had turned their eyes on Eaton—and narrowed them. "We ain't heard nothin' from Massa Tyler for some time, though. He's off at the war."

"Well, tell Miss Caroline I'm here, will you? We'll stable the horses before coming to the house."

But then the young woman, favoring the good looks and coloring of Charles Singleton to the extent that she had to be his sister, Caroline, came running out of the house, down the steps, and into her brother's arms. Half way through their joyous reunion, Caroline turned her eyes to Eaton. The expression in her face—one of interest and speculation—was quite a contrast from the view the two black servants had taken of him.

Shooing Maggie and Toby off to start a meal going, which Charles and Eaton only later learned involved chickens that had been held back for laying and the last of the flour in the pantry, Caroline took the two men upstairs to settle them into bedrooms. She flitted around, nervously acting the Southern belle, latching onto Charles as if he would melt away into the mist if she didn't hold him to the ground and fluttering her eyelashes at Eaton.

"You all take your rest now. Toby will see to bringing up some hot water for you, and if you have no clean clothes with you, Toby will help find you some from Tyler's bureau."

"Have you heard from Tyler?" Charles said.

"I'm sure he's on his own way home. Now supper will be at eight and feel free to rest until then. This is your bedroom, Charles. Mr. Matthews here can have the room across the hall, the last one at the back."

"Uhh, about that," Charles said.

"Oh, it will be so gay to have young men at my table again," she said, breathlessly, as she moved to the door. "Come with me, Mr. Matthews, and I'll show you where you will be."

Charles just shook his head as he found himself alone in his room. He wondered what Caroline would do when she found out about Eaton.

She found out between the main course and when fruit was to be served for desert.

During the first two courses, as Caroline chattered on in her Southern hostess mode and gushed over her two guests, Eaton more than Charles, Toby, who was serving, concentrated on giving Eaton the fisheye as he walked around the table. At the end of the main course, Toby asked a confused-looking Caroline if he could consult with her in the kitchen.

When they withdrew, Eaton looked at Charles and said, "I believe I should excuse myself and see about accommodation among the others."

"Yes, I think that would be best," Charles answered. "I will find you later."

When Caroline returned, subdued and no longer giddy, she was visibly relieved to see that Eaton no longer was there and acted as if he'd never been there in the first place. Charles said nothing either, realizing that Caroline would not have discerned that Eaton was a quadroon. Charles hadn't been treating Eaton as his slave and only close scrutiny—which Toby and Maggie automatically performed——identified him as nonwhite.

Charles quickly moved to change the subject. "I've looked at the fields, Caroline. They are fallow. They should be sown to wheat and corn now, shouldn't they? I know that it must be tough until Tyler returns, but—"

"I don't think Tyler is coming back, Charles. Do you?" Caroline's voice suddenly hard. "And, as for the fields, what we can do now is the kitchen garden and that's about it. And I do my full share in tending that garden. Did you look around and count noses? Did you see any darkies here other than Toby and Maggie today? They're gone. They're all gone. I wanted tonight to be a return—if only tonight—to how we grew up. And I couldn't manage more than just tonight. I can't promise we'll have eggs for your breakfast, because we ate layers tonight. I wanted . . . Oh, Charles, I just once wanted it to be like it was before."

Having finally burst her own bubble, she rose and rushed out of the dining room, leaving Charles with his own thoughts. He looked around the dining room, realizing that many of the fancy objects that had once graced this house were gone. He had known there was something different about the house when he'd gone through it earlier. Now he realized that it was what was missing—the whole world that had made the South gracious and refined had been stripped away by this war. Piece by piece his sister's life had been whittled down to one ruined evening of being unable to recapture the world she once had known.

He sat and thought for awhile, taking another sip of his now-cold coffee, just now realizing that what he'd just thought was badly made coffee wasn't really coffee at all. After a few minutes, he reached over and took up a sharp knife, put there to help him manage the less-than-tender chicken he'd been served. He slit his trousers, which he had refused to change from, at the hip, took out the small gold bar that had been hidden there, carefully laid it on the table, and rose and left the house, looking for Eaton. He felt no guilt in giving her a portion of the Confederate treasury. She and other women like her had given so much to the South. It was right, he thought, for the South to give a token back.

He found Eaton on slave row, in the first, now-abandoned cabin. Eaton had had his pick of nearly all of the huts on slave row.

"I'm sorry," Eaton whispered as Charles entered the hut and started to strip down. "I wouldn't have stayed in the house. I just didn't know how to bow out without upsetting your sister."

Eaton wasn't surprised that Charles was undressing as soon as he entered the hut. Eaton had stripped and waited, not knowing whether Charles would come to him or not. He just knew that he couldn't go back up to the house, to Charles, and that it was Charles' choice on whatever would happen. Eaton wasn't the master; Charles was.

"I understand," Charles said as he came over, sat on the side of the cot, and pulled Eaton's torso up to him. "I should have done something, but she wasn't leaving an opening for me to do so either. It all has settled down to be as it should, though."

It had settled down, he'd said. No questioning of the values of it in what the loss of the Confederacy meant at all— not from Charles and not from Eaton.

As they kissed, Charles stroked Eaton's flanks, moving to the young man's buttocks. Sighing, Eaton turned to facing down on the cot, raising his buttocks, and widening his stance, as Charles' fingers went to exploring around and then inside Eaton's channel. As usual, Eaton then accommodated whatever Charles wanted.

There was no speaking when Charles came up on the bed, mounted Eaton, slid deep inside him, and began to pump.

* * * *

There was no mention between brother and sister of Charles leaving a gold bar on the dining room table, but when Charles said he'd take Caroline into the nearest town with a bank if she wanted to go, she took him up on the offer. She was able to open up a line of credit at the bank, and over the following two weeks her holdings of livestock—a few cows, lambs, pigs, and chickens grew to enough to sustain Caroline and those slaves—now free servants—who had stayed on at Warrenton.

While Charles and his sister were adding to her livelihood, Eaton was helping Toby and Maggie expand the kitchen garden. Eaton never again went into the main house nor did Caroline cast eyes in his direction.

Charles and Eaton only stayed at Warrenton for three weeks before, in the waning days of June, heading east again. He might have stayed longer, but people were starting to notice he was here. One neighbor had even visited, thinking that Caroline's husband, Tyler, had returned from the war.

"You are too well known as having been part of the Confederate government," Caroline said. "I think that perhaps—"

"Yes, I agree. I think it's time that I moved on," Charles said.

So in the last week of June, Charles and Eaton mounted up again, their saddlebags now filled with enough food to last a couple of weeks, and off they went, winding up by the second week in July at the edge of the Great Dismal Swamp on the Atlantic coast of North Carolina.

"Why here?" Eaton asked.

"Just to gain more time from the end of the fighting," Charles answered. "When it settles down more, and the roving Union troops aren't in the area as frequently, we'll go somewhere else by ship—some other country for a while, with the hope we can return with the resurgence of the South."

"But why here, in a swamp?" Eaton asked.

Before Charles could answer, though, they had been surrounded by a motley collection of mean-looking men. Luckily one of the Confederate soldiers-turned-highwayman who had descended on them recognized Captain Singleton and convinced the others he was one of them. They looked less certainly at Eaton.

It was one thing not to accost the two but it was yet another to willingly take them into the thieves' camp to hide and wait. If Eaton thought that Charles might buy their way into the men's good graces with a bar of gold, he was sadly mistaken. Charles offered his own skills and abilities to help them in marauding about the neighborhood and holding up travelers—primarily northern carpetbaggers—from Virginia's Hampton Roads area down into the Carolinas. What really won the day, though, was that Charles identified Eaton as a male whore for a Richmond brothel, who would service the men who were interested in that in exchange for sanctuary.

There were very few women in the Great Dismal Swamp camps, so many men had turned to other men in their sexual needs, and the offer of Eaton's services won the day.

Eaton, of course, didn't assert his supposed new-won freedom. He recognized Charles as his master, so he lay on his back with his legs open at the pleasure of the men for the nearly month that Charles decided they needed to lay low before attempting to leave the country.

Similarly, when at last they rode down to Elizabeth City in North Carolina, with its docks for ocean-going vessels by way of the Pagan River, Most of their passage to Jamaica was covered by Charles offering Eaton's services to the captain of

107

the merchant vessel, *Helena*, rather than any part of the gold the two were carrying on their bodies.

All that Eaton cared, though, was that he was bound for someplace else and still was traveling in the company of Charles Singleton.

Chapter Six: Slave to Master

The light coming through the bay window in the captain's cabin at the stern of the *Helena* was eerie, as often is the case as dawn creeps in, but it was more peculiar than that. Clouds were scudding across the sky in ominous, dark formations, and the sea was unusually choppy. The captain said that this often was this way as the ship neared the Jamaica coast, and who was Eaton to question that?

The cabin was dark, but not so dark that the captain couldn't clearly be seen. He stood, naked in his stolid hairiness and pot belly, across the cabin beside the table fixed to the cabin wall where the ewer of wine was that he now was imbibing from while he scratched his low-hanging hairy balls and looked lustfully at Eaton. Eaton, also naked, lay on his back on the bed pushed into the windowed bow of the fantail, his young, trim body lit up by the eerie light coming through the window. His legs were bent and spread, as they had been through much of the night, as the randy, muscular ship's captain fucked him again and again.

The captain was obviously trying to get as much cocking in of the young man working off his passage and that of Charles Singleton to Jamaica as he could. The ship was due to dock in Kingston later in the day, sometime after dawn.

The captain was stroking his thick, half-hard cock as he swigged wine and watched Eaton fondling his own cock as Captain Huddleston had bade him do. The ship had increasingly been lurching and rocking all night as they approached the Jamaica coast. The pitching had been bad enough that it had kept Eaton confined to the bed, which was of no import, because the captain would not have let Eaton out of his bed this night in any event. On previous nights during the voyage, the captain had covered and held Eaton's body close to his in a powerful grip, mounted him in slow, relentless stretching of Eaton's channel with a particularly thick staff, fucked him slowly at great length to an ejaculation, and then turned over and went into a snoring sleep. Not tonight, though. Oblivious to the obvious building of a nasty storm, Huddleston had concentrated on getting every ounce of sexual pleasure he could get from Eaton's body on his last night of access to the young quadroon whore.

He had mercilessly ridden Eaton's ass to the young man's near exhaustion, a chore that had engaged the captain's total attention. Even now, when he himself, despite his long years at sea, was having trouble keeping his balance on the pitching deck. But all of his attention was arrested by the beautiful young body in his bed, Eaton's hand on his own cock, and the sight of the wide-bored hole that the captain simply had to fill one more time.

Huddleston lurched over to the bed, grabbed Eaton's ankles, wish-boning the young man's legs wide as he pulled Eaton to him, Eaton's buttocks resting on the edge of the foot of the bed. Eaton arched his back, scrabbled at the bedding with his fists for purchase, and groaned deeply, as the captain worked his thick cock inside him, once more stretching Eaton's channel walls to the maximum, coaxing them to open even more. Three hard thrusts and the captain was saddled deep inside Eaton and began to pump him with the aid of the lubricant of earlier deposits of cum.

They didn't speak. There was no reason to speak. Eaton was only there because he had a hole the captain's cock longed to fill. He was just a quadroon slave—former slave, but there was no reason for the captain to acknowledge the changed status as long as Eaton recognized one of the passengers as his master and the master was willing to hand Eaton over for the captain's pleasure. All the way down the Eastern Seaboard and into the Caribbean Eaton had appeared at the captain's cabin when summoned, stripped, lain on the bed, and opened his legs to the captain. The captain had mounted him and fucked him two or three times during the night, with Eaton leaving before dawn while the captain was still snoring away.

Eaton was writhing under the man's strongest, deepest, thickest onslaught of the night and the captain was nearing ejaculation, when someone started pounding on the door to the cabin and crying out, "Storm. Hurricane, Captain. The main mast is about to go!"

As the captain bounded away from Eaton and grabbed for his trousers, the sounds of the main mast, indeed, giving way could clearly be heard. What also was clear was that a hurricane had reached out to grab them and the captain had been too much taken with Eaton and the rest of the crew too drunk from the celebration of their last night at sea to have discerned the gathering storm and done anything to counter it—if, indeed, there had been anything they could have done at that point.

Eaton reached over the side of the bed for his trousers and pulled them on, knowing that he needed to help in doing something but having no idea what that might be. The captain had left the door of his cabin open when he'd rushed out, and the door was furiously banging back and forth, accentuating how severe the roll of the ship was. Eaton tried to stand up from the bed only immediately to be tossed back onto the covers.

Before he could make any other move, no matter how futile, the storm blew out the massive window above the bed in the bow of the ship, and Eaton was sucked out into the stormy sea.

* * * *

The first sensations Eaton became aware of as he was stretched out on the sand were the heat and something heavy being nosed off his torso. The latter sensation led him to think of a nose, as it was some sort of snorting beast with a wet nose. He tried to open his eyes, but the blinding light, which was producing the heat, made him close them again and build up strength to slit them open. It was a horse, and Eaton experienced the blurry sensation of a man coming off the horse and pulling the piece of wood the rest of the way off his body.

A hatch door from the *Helena*. That's what had been on top of him, protecting him from the red-hot rays of the sun baking the white sand Eaton was lying on. He had already figured out what it had been that had kept him afloat. And he remembered now that he'd watched the *Helena* breaking up in the hurricane. He didn't remember seeing anyone else in the water with him—no one holding onto a floating piece of wood as he had done. He'd been sucked away from the ship before it broke up and sank. Others were pulled down with the vessel.

"Are you all right?" The voice was a deep bass. Squinting his eyes, Eaton was able to bring the man into focus. His skin was a deep chocolate brown, and he was tall, with broad shoulders and a trim waist. His features weren't African, though; they were more European. A handsome devil. Dressed in fine, if serviceable, clothes—more as a master than as a slave.

"Here, sorry, let me feel for broken bones. Quite a hurricane. Did you come from land or sea?"

The man was feeling around on Eaton's arms and torso and then down his legs, on top of Eaton's trousers, which were all that he was wearing. The man's hands hesitated at the bump of the gold bars sown in just below Eaton's hips on either side, but he stopped there just a few seconds and then moved on. A hand brushed Eaton's crotch, and Eaton realized that he was going hard. He was looking into the man's crotch from where he was lying on his side and there was no doubt the man was hung—and hardening as well.

"Water," Eaton croaked.

"Yes, of course," the man said. He stood, took a water bag off the saddle of the horse, and crouched back down, putting a muscular arm under Eaton's neck, turning his body on his back, lifting his head, and putting the water skin Eaton's lips. "Slowly," he said. "Don't take too much. It will come back up. Good thing you were lying on your side. Any sea water came out rather than suffocating you. You came from the sea, didn't you?"

"Yes. The *Helena*. Bound for Jamaica from the Carolinas."

"Well, anything on the sea out there last night—anything that could have washed you up on the shore—is in the depths now. But you have reached Jamaica."

"Others? Have you seen—?" It came out in a moan, as the man had put the water skin down, had moved a large, brown hand around Eaton's pecs and down to rest on his lower belly. The man's crotch, still in plain sight to Eaton as the man crouched on his haunches, legs spread, was bulging even more than before. Eaton could clearly follow the line of a thick, long shaft nestled against the man's left thigh in his tight riding pants. Without a thought to what he was doing, Eaton raised a hand to the man's crotch, being awarded with a slight jerk. Eaton immediately moved to take his hand away, but the man covered Eaton's hand and held it against his crotch. He smiled down into Eaton's face.

The man lowered his lips to Eaton's and kissed him. He pulled right away, but they were staring into each other's eyes with so much mutual need that their lips met again and they kissed hungrily.

Eaton could feel the man going harder. His crotch was tenting as well. The man ran his hand under Eaton's waistband and slid his fingers into Eaton's pubic bush, two fingers running on either side of the root of the cock, the tips touching a ball on either side of Eaton's sac.

Eaton groaned, but he didn't pull away. Almost involuntarily he lifted his left hand to cup one of the man's buttocks cheeks.

The man spoke to him as if they weren't touching each other. "You're the only one I've seen along the beach. If you want to stay here and rest, I'll ride the beach and see if there's anyone else."

"Please don't leave me," Eaton whispered. "And please . . ."

"Please what?"

"I don't know; I'm not sure."

"Your ship was coming from the Carolinas? You're an American. You had family on the ship?"

"Just Mr. Singleton . . . my . . . my master."

"Your master? You were a slave? You have black blood in you?"

"Yes. I'm a slave."

"Not if you came from the United States," the man said. "The slaves there have been emancipated. And the Union has won. Just like we were emancipated here thirty years ago. You are a free man, son. Here you are completely free to do what you want. Is there something you want now, at this moment?"

"I don't know."

"I think you do know. And I think it's good that you have some black blood in you. How much?"

"I'm a quadroon, one quarter black."

"I'm a mulatto, half black, and because my father owned this land and because black men are free here, this is my land. I think it's good that you have black blood in you."

"Why?"

"Because I only fuck black men. Does it upset you that, when you've recovered, I want to fuck you?"

"No, not at all," Eaton answered breathlessly. With that, the man leaned down and took Eaton's lips with his with a possessive kiss again. Eaton didn't resist. Nor did he resist as the man unbuttoned the fly of Eaton's trousers and took possession of his cock. Eaton's experienced hands went to the buttons of the man's trousers and soon they were stroking each other—and eventually sucking each other off in a sixty-nine position.

"The house. We'll go to the house and get you cleaned up first and recovered enough to sheath me. You have had a man before, haven't you?"

"Yes, many men," Eaton answered. "Not many as big as you." Eaton was afraid that would make the man pull away from him, but it didn't.

"Then you must have time to rest, as I don't think I can be gentle with you."

"Nor would I want you to be. Not even now."

"Are you sure?"

"Yes, I'm very sure."

The man didn't wait for further permission. He pulled Eaton's breeches off his legs and unbuttoned and flared the fly of his own riding pants. Moving between Eaton's thighs with his knees, he wrapped an arm around Eaton's waist and raised the young man's buttocks to him. With Eaton's torso streaming on the sand and his arms stretched out in welcome and surrender, Eaton's rescuer worked his hard, horse-hung cock inside Eaton's ass. Murmuring, "I'm not sure you can . . . fuck yes, you *can* take me," and started slowly to pump him. "Am I hurting you?" he asked, solicitously, after several moments.

"It doesn't matter. Nothing else matters at this moment. Don't stop. Fuck me so that I know I'm alive," Eaton murmured. And then, in a weaker voice, he added, "Fucking is all I'm good for."

"What was that?"

"Never mind. Just don't stop."

* * * *

Jas Graham—for that was what Eaton's rescuer's name was—announced that he was going to come again and then did so after slamming his cock inside Eaton three more times, hard, as he covered and was mounted on the young man's ass. Eaton had eventually confessed that he was a male whore and was used to taking it. After that Graham wasn't being gentle with him—nor did Eaton plead that he be.

Eaton was on all fours on the thick mattress of the four-poster bed. Jas rolled off the younger man, taking him with him and landing on his back without disengaging the long, thick cock he had jammed tight up Eaton's channel. Exhibiting his muscular power, he wove an arm in and under Eaton's armpit and then pressed the wrist of that hand into the back of Eaton's neck, holding Eaton's shoulder blades close into his pecs. His legs wound around Eaton's, his ankles gripping Eaton's ankles and spreading the younger man's legs wide and lifting them and Eaton's pelvis up. He continued stroking inside Eaton's channel with a still-hard cock and stroked Eaton to an ejaculation with his free hand.

It was the third time the chocolate giant with the European features had fucked and filled Eaton with cum that night. Graham had told Eaton he could rest for as many days as he needed before they fucked, but Eaton had come to him that first night, after being fed and sleeping nearly the entire day away. Graham had put him to sleep by, first, bathing him in a copper tub in the bedroom Eaton was taken to, and then massaging the young man's body and stroking off his cock before, exhausted and satiated, Eaton slept.

Earlier, after Jas had let Eaton stand there, on the beach, looking hopefully out to sea for a couple of hours, Jas helping to support Eaton on his wobbly feet, the two returned to Jas' plantation house on the horse, Graham holding Eaton close to him in the front of the saddle and Eaton able to feel the big black's cock pressing into the small of his back.

They passed through sugarcane fields in which not only blacks, but Asians as well were working to cut and stack the cane. Eaton had never seen an Asian before.

"You have slaves? Some of them from another land?" Eaton asked nervously.

"There are no slaves in Jamaica—not for more than thirty years," Jas answered. "This is my plantation, but those workers work for wages. I provide them housing and sell them food cheaply, but they earn an hourly wage."

"So many aren't blacks," Eaton observed.

"This region was hard hit by what we call the Baptist War, or Christmas Rebellion, which was a massive slave rebellion thirty-five years ago. Some British plantation owners were killed, many in this area, but more slaves were killed before the British put the rebellion down. There weren't many blacks to return to the land and they were emancipated two years later and then many who had survived the rebellion didn't want to work the cane fields anymore. We had to bring in Chinese and Indian workers—from the other side of the world."

"We?"

"I was only seven upon emancipation, but my mother and I had already been given our freedom. My father, who was British, owned this plantation."

"And you inherited from him?"

"Yes, but not for many years later. My mother and I were emancipated in gratitude by my father right after the rebellion was put down. My mother hid him and fed him while the slaves rampaged. Theirs was a love match. He was nearly the only white man for miles around here to survive. The area is still blighted. The cane grows here easily and is a good cash crop, but few of the plantations are being worked. Working the sugarcane is backbreaking work. With so few workers, the British deserted this area of the island."

When they reached the house, a typically columned colonial-style building constructed of cut blocks of coral and plastered over, Eaton asked where the slave quarters were.

"Why do you want to know that?" Jas answered. "We built the workers better housing. The old slave quarters have been reduced to ruins."

"I presumed I'd be staying—"

"You're staying in the house with me. You need to understand and accept how it is in Jamaica. You aren't a slave here. You aren't a slave in the United States anymore either. You are a guest in my house, and, if you're willing, a submissive young man in my bed—but only if you want to be."

Eaton wanted to be. Although somewhat over forty, Jas Graham was a magnificently built man—in every way. Eaton had already discovered that he was hung like a horse too. And he was handsome and refined, and, truth be known, Eaton had not been covered in the comfort of a proper bed in less than furtive conditions by a black man before and was trembling in anticipation of being so.

Graham had not expected Eaton to come to him that night, but Eaton couldn't hold off any longer. He entered Graham's bedroom in a dressing robe he had been provided—and nothing else. Standing across the room, Eaton dropped the robe to the ground and dipped his head in submission.

"My god you're beautiful," Graham said, sucking in his breath. "Come let me hold you for a while. I promise I won't—"

"I want you to fuck me. Now," Eaton said in a tremulous voice. "I wanted you to fuck me again on the beach."

As it happened, Eaton fucked Graham first—after kneeling in front of him as the big black sat on the edge of his bed, and loving the older man's cock to erection. Then he pressed Graham onto his back in the center of the bed, lowered his channel on Graham's cock and slowly revolved around, rocking on the cock as well as rising and lowering on it. He took the cock deep and at length facing his host, facing to either side, and, at last, facing Graham's feet, with his hands clasping and unclasping his host's knees and Graham lifting him with a grip on either side of his waist and raising him and then slamming him down hard, and again and again, until both had come.

Almost immediately afterward, Graham was ready to go again and took Eaton in a missionary position, Graham erect on his knees, holding Eaton's legs high up under his armpits, and thrusting hard and fast inside Eaton's passage, with Eaton egging him on, wanting it harder, faster, deeper.

Lying stretched against each other, in search of sleep, then, Graham murmured, "You are an expert in this."

"So are you," Eaton answered. But then, after a while, Eaton said, "I don't want to mislead you. This is what I was used for in the American South—in Richmond. I was a whore boy in a brothel. Do you care?"

"I only care that you are so beautiful and so good at taking the cock," Graham answered. "Now sleep, if you can. I will want you again before morning."

"Good," Eaton said—and Graham did want—and take—him again before dawn—twice.

For the next three days, Eaton spent the day on the beach, looking out to sea, and the nights writhing under Jas on his bed. It occurred to Eaton by the third day that nothing was going to come out of the surf to attest to his most recent adventure—not Charles Singleton, his gold bars, or even the chart locating the bulk of the Confederate treasury that had been buried in Virginia and North Carolina. These were at the bottom of the sea, lost to the future for all time. The treasure had been frittered away to two small gold bars he had sewn into his breeches. For some reason, this made Eaton feel that a burden had been lifted off his shoulders.

For these journeys to the beach. Jas lent him a horse and left him to it until the third day. That afternoon, he rode up to the beach, got off his horse, and came and stood next to Eaton.

"This is the last time I need to come out here," Eaton said, turning his eyes away from the sea to the magnificent black stallion standing beside him—and he wasn't referring to the horse.

"Did you love this master of yours very much, the one you keep looking out to sea for?" he asked in a gentle voice. "I assume he was using your body."

"Yes I think I loved him. And yes he was using my body."

"And sharing you with others."

"Yes. At times it is how we survived."

"Do you still think of him as your master?"

Eaton gave that some thought. Did he still think of Charles Singleton as his master—as the arbiter of his destiny? He hadn't challenged that concept yet. But increasingly it was evident that Singleton was lost to him—at the bottom of the sea he was gazing at. And along with the captain, the chart to the financing of resurgence of the South's military had gone to the depths of the sea with him. But then, hadn't that treasure been filtering away for their entire journey? Hadn't the South he had known already begun to unravel and drift away? He was free. Was he only now beginning to realize that? But, no, maybe not. He had always been under the protection and control of another man. Wasn't that the role of a submissive?

"No," he answered hesitatingly. "I don't see Captain Charles Singleton as my master. I see you as my master now."

"Oh, no, I will not accept that role," Graham answered. "I will gladly use your body as long as you will lie under me. In those terms I will accept your submission. But I will only do so if you want to use my body as well. I believe I am giving you as much pleasure as you give me—that we are equals in this. In those terms, I will be submitting to you as

119

well. You are free. In Jamaica you are totally free. If you insist on being totally submissive to a man, I am not your man. You can go into Kingston. There are brothels there with male whores. You can be that, if you want. I won't stand in your way. I will help you get to Kingston, but I will go no further with you. I will visit you in the brothel and fuck you there. But I will pay for the use of your body and I'll not have you in my bed. I want a man who is giving himself to me as a free man."

"Fuck me. Fuck me now," Eaton said. "I want to use your body—your cock. Now."

Graham fucked him at the verge where the sandy beach ran into ferns and palm trees. He crushed the younger man to the ground under him, both men naked, with Eaton's ankles crossed at the small of Graham's muscular back and his arms around Graham's bull-thick neck, while the kissed and Graham punished Eaton's channel, ramming him hard, fast, and deep to a mutual ejaculation.

"So, do you want me to take you into Kingston?" Graham asked after they'd both come, but while they both were united as one.

"No, but what other option do I have?" Eaton asked. "If I stay with you and let you keep me, am I really free?"

"What were you planning to do with those two gold bars in the trousers you washed up on shore in?"

"You know about those?"

"Yes. Do you want to assert your freedom with those? You can buy one of the neighboring abandoned plantations with those and still have enough left over to start your own cane harvesting with a hired crew. We could take turns in each other's beds, fucking as equals."

"That sounds good to me," Eaton answered, almost laughing at this image of where the last of the Confederate gold that he knew about would wind up. "Fuck the Confederacy," he murmured.

"What was that?" Graham asked.

"Fuck the Confederacy!" Eaton howled to the tops of the palm trees.

The both laughed. "Yes, I think you now are finally free," Graham said, as he rolled Eaton over on his stomach, coaxed the young man up on his knees, mounted his ass, and fucked him again.

Fire Down the Valley

Chapter One: Down to the Schoolhouse

"Don't worry about that shed, Pa," Caleb said. "I've already talked to them up at Milo Mather's mill, and they should deliver lumber for a new shed sometime while I'm gone."

"Lumber? While you're gone?" Old Henry answered. He was sitting on the front porch of the house, rocking, and pulling on his pipe. He'd already put in eight hours on the garden behind the collapsed shed and the sun wasn't far beyond its zenith yet.

"Remember, Pa? I told you about it yesterday. They got word to me from down in Hayden that a couple of more buildings were being put up. They need my help. It will mean cash enough to pay for the lumber from the mill."

"Regular boom town they got for themselves down in Hayden, I reckon," Henry said.

"Yes, Pa. A regular boom town." They, in fact, were always putting up more buildings in Hayden. It wouldn't be long before they'd talk about making a town of it. It had started to take off as soon as they decided to put that road to the West, going over the mountains from Denver, right through the center of the settlement. They were talking of trying to get the town incorporated for the centennial of American independence, but that was only two years off, and Cal couldn't see any Colorado politician down in Denver moving that fast for anyone on the west side of the Rockies divide.

It wasn't really construction Cal was going down the valley, across the Yampa River, and into Hayden to do, but he'd be getting the money they needed to pay for the lumber, and his foster father never needed to know how he'd gotten it. He knew he wouldn't be more than a couple of miles away from the spread before Henry forgot he'd even gone.

"John and Harv will take care of the sheep while I'm gone. I've already talked with them—and they'll help us raise that shed when I get back. I should be gone two weeks, maybe a couple of days more if they need me longer in Hayden. And you stay near the house, you hear? Don't be going to that section you've fenced and are trying to farm while no one else is here to go with you."

"Hayden. Quite a boom town they got going for them down in Hayden," Henry said, stopping to take a couple of puffs on his pipe. It was like he hadn't even heard Cal's admonishment. "Used to be that up at Slater was where we'd go for excitement, but now it looks like it's Hayden—since they put that road through."

Excitement, Cal thought. Yes, it was excitement of a sort that was taking him down to Hayden. He was afraid it wouldn't be that long before they'd have all of the excitement around here that they could handle, though. He could smell it in the air. The danger. Ever since they'd passed that law back East in Washington that settlers could fence their land, you could feel the tension in the air. Something just waiting to happen. Having the sheep people move in—people like Cal's foster parents—had raised the tension, what with the cattlemen claiming the sheep ruined the pastures by close cropping and slowly being pushed out of valleys like this in search of better grasslands. Now folks could fence their land and farm it too. Even Old Henry was starting to make the transition. Cal didn't think the cattlemen would give into that without a fight. And he was afraid that fight would come before the farmers arrived, while the cattlemen could take out their ire on the sheep men.

Cal had already decided he'd leave the valley to do something else once his foster father had passed, but it looked like Old Henry's brain was going to give out before his body did. It had come to a head over that shed. When it caved in, Cal had told Henry that it was a sign, a sign for them to sell out to a farmer, to sell the sheep, and to move down to Denver.

124

Old Henry had taken Cal's hand and walked him out to that little stand of trees up on the hillside in back of the house. They'd stood there beside the graves of Cal's foster mother and of Henry's and her two little daughters, and Henry had said that he was going to be buried there too in the not-too-distant future, and that he wouldn't be leaving his family as long as he had breath.

Cal had lost the question of whether the shed would be rebuilt, but it had been a bad winter. They'd lost sheep. There wasn't any money for lumber for a new shed. That was until the tinker had passed through, coming up the valley from Hayden, headed for Slater, selling wares off his wagon. He'd been given a message from Levi Yost down in Hayden to deliver to Cal. Samuel Forster at Levi's place in Hayden had business down in Denver for a couple of weeks and Cal was needed to temporarily take his place. He'd done this once before. The pay was something Cal couldn't turn down, not at a time like this. So he would be going down the valley and across the Yampa to Hayden for a week or more.

"Guess I better be going," he said to his foster father. "I'll take the mule. John and Harv will need the horses to check on the sheep."

"Be home for supper, will you?"

"I'll be gone for a couple of weeks, Pa. I'm going to Hayden for a couple of weeks. John will be fixing your suppers. You've always said his cooking was better than mine, so that should make you happy."

"Be sure to say good-bye to Lizbeth and the girls."

Cal's eyes teared up. After two years, Henry still couldn't talk like his wife and daughters were gone for good. He still talked to Lizbeth and included her in the day-to-day activities on the sheep farm. Cal turned and walked around the house and started up the hill to the graveyard under the trees. He would have stopped to say good-bye to her anyway, he supposed. But he sure as hell hoped she wasn't in a position to know what he'd be doing down in Hayden.

When he came back around the side of the house with the mule, the old man was standing at the top of the porch steps. He was holding a couple of wooden dolls in tiny colorful

125

dresses and carved horses in his hands. Cal almost teared up again. Of all the things for his foster father to remember it was to remember to carve those things. It was one of the last things Lizbeth had asked Henry to do. It was before she died but it was while she was caring for Mary and Sally in their last lying-in.

"Henry," she'd said, "I don't suppose the girls will need the new dresses I made for their dolls now. We'll keep the dresses on the dolls they have; the girls will probably prefer having the familiar clothes on their dolls to take across with them. Perhaps when winter sets in you could carve another set of dolls for these dresses, and we'll send them down to the girls at Mrs. Thornton's. You might make something for the boys down there too."

Mrs. Thornton was the widow woman down the valley at the schoolhouse, where she was the teacher. She'd taken in several orphan children. She'd been married to a sheep man who had run afoul of some big-time rancher at the southern mouth of the valley and been killed for trying to show spunk. Warren Savage, Cal thought the powerful cattleman's name was.

And Cal's foster father had remembered to carve those dolls and a few horses too. Cal wondered when he'd done that. He'd spent most of the winter just sitting at the window and looking up at the graveyard as far as Cal could remember. He must have been spending some time working the wood with his hands too, though.

"You'll be going past the schoolhouse," the old man spoke up from the porch. "Could you drop these off at the Mrs. Thornton's for those orphan children?"

"Sure, Pa," Cal answered, taking the toys from Henry's hands. Now suddenly, the old man was lucid, Cal thought. On the way down from the graves, Cal had been thinking that he could get his foster father moved from the homestead and the old man probably wouldn't even know it. But there were the lucid moments like this that defeated any thought of that yet.

At the front gate he turned and looked back at the house, but Henry was already back inside. Cal knew he'd be sitting at that back window already, gazing up the hillside at the graveyard.

Looking up above his head, at the cross bar above the gate opening, Cal saw the weathered chunk of wood on which he'd carefully carved the word "Paradise" when he was no more than twelve. Looking beyond that, up the length of the valley and then even higher, up the flanks of snowcapped Hahn's Peak, his heart went zing as it always had at the first glimpse of the sun rising in Antelope Gap. Heaven. That was what his foster father had wanted to name the place they'd homesteaded. But Lizbeth thought Paradise best, and her husband gave in with an indulgent smile and without a fight, neither of which was normal for him. And so Paradise it was— at least until there was no one to argue with Henry; everyone in the valley called it Heaven now, but no one had bothered to change the sign.

It hadn't turned out to be much of a paradise for Lizbeth or his foster sisters, Cal thought—and it sure didn't seem much of a paradise to him either. And it sure as hell didn't seem like heaven either. More like hell.

Before he nudged the mule to set forth down the valley, he looked up at the sign one more time, remembering. He had made it because Mrs. Thornton had said that the Cowdens would like it and that he should do something for them for taking in an eleven-year-old boy, especially one who had been raised as he had been.

* * * *

It was a good two hour's hard mule ride down the dusty road to Mrs. Thornton's place at the schoolhouse. When he'd been at the school, Cal had lived there during the week and only came back to the ranch on the weekends—except when he was needed at the ranch and then he just would be skipping school. The road was not much more than a trail, along the lowest point of the valley that ran down inside the Rocky Mountains, with the towering Hahn's Peak to the east, from Slater on the Snake River that divided the Wyoming territory in the north from the brand-new state of Colorado to the south. On the western side of the valley was the high ridge, which would be thought of as mountains anywhere else in the country, with the sheep-shipping center of Craig beyond.

From the southern mouth of the valley, a good two-day's ride from Heaven, Cal would follow the Elkhead River for half a day and then drop down due south to the Yampa River for another half day, arriving in Hayden on the southern bank of the Yampa late in the night. The Yampa would pose no problem in crossing. The snow melt had come and gone, and he figured he'd be able to ride across what little water was running in the Yampa without getting more than his boots wet.

It had been a lonely ride to Mrs. Thornton's. Usually there'd be some traffic along the road, as this was the only track in the valley that carts could easily navigate, but on this day Cal didn't meet a soul. The two hours alone, if he didn't count the mule's presence, and he didn't, gave Cal more than enough time to carefully not think of conditions in Heaven—his foster father's ranch—and how close the inevitable decision to leave was, not just because Henry couldn't hang on there much longer but also because of the rumblings of the cattlemen building up to something nasty.

They had rampaged through the valley before, burning homesteads and slaughtering sheep. The sheep men had held on, but they hadn't recovered the strength they once had had. They probably couldn't even withstand having farmers move in and fence the land, Cal didn't think. And more of the sheep men in the valley were, as Henry was starting to do, turning to fencing the land for farming themselves. In terms of needing an open range, the sheep men and the cattlemen were more or less of the same opinion. But whereas the sheep men would be content to coexist with cattle, the cattlemen showed no such willingness to share the land with sheep—or to tolerate fencing of the range.

Instead of worrying on the Henry and Heaven problem, Cal turned his thoughts to where he was headed today. He would be spending the night at Mrs. Thornton's. He'd be lucky to be able to leave there the next day to continue on to Hayden. It was inevitable that she'd have this or that to fix that she and the children living with her—some students and some orphans she'd taken in—couldn't handle. Cal couldn't tell her no to fixing anything he could.

Cal had been one of her orphans. Although Lizbeth and Henry Cowden had been the only parents Cal could remember—and they'd been as good as any parents could be—they weren't Cal's real parents. He hadn't gone to them until he was nearly twelve and Mrs. Thornton decided that some family would be willing to take him because he'd grown to be a good and sturdy worker. He'd be giving more to any family he went to than he'd be taking from them, she decided. In many respects, Mrs. Thornton had allowed, she was sorry to see Cal go. She had said she felt like he was the son she'd never had, and he had been her star pupil, her biggest success. Not having the colloquialisms of the insular valley family engrained in him from birth, for instance, she was able to teach him to speak almost as properly as she did. In this valley that was no mean feat.

Cal had come to Mrs. Thornton at what everyone figured was the age of eight. He'd been a wild one—literally. Only Mrs. Thornton had the kindness and fortitude to take him in at the time, and he was left to her by a U.S. cavalry unit as it rode down the valley from having just helped round up and subdue the Arapaho tribes to the east beyond both Hahn's Peak and Mount Zirkel. It had been a messy and bloody roundup, and the tribes were being force marched south to reservations in southern Colorado and also down into what was to become the Oklahoma territory. Cal, his blue eyes and blondness identifying him obviously as not being Arapaho, was found in an Arapaho camp and otherwise was as native American as any of them. Along with a few other obviously white people, mostly women, he was separated from the tribe before it was marched off. A white woman old enough to remember who she was before being captured by the Arapaho had said that Cal had been in the camp before she arrived there and she understood that, as a baby, he'd been the sole survivor of a wagon train wiped out by the Arapaho.

It had taken all of the four years Cal had been with Mrs. Thornton for her to cajole most of the Indian out of him. She had done it with love and kindness, and although Cal still remembered his life with the Arapaho as natural and good, he had only appreciation for Mrs. Thornton's kind reordering of his life. He felt the same about the Cowdens. There was a time when he thought of the Arapaho as his people, but there no longer was a moment that he didn't think of Mrs. Thornton and the Cowdens as his family.

He had made no stops on his way from Heaven to the schoolhouse. Henry had suggested that he stop in and check on the widow, Hattie Anderson, who, by herself, was scratching out a mere existence with a small herd of sheep. Her small spread was on the trail between Heaven and the schoolhouse. But as he rode up to her gate, a bullet whizzed over his head, and Cal figured that Mrs. Anderson didn't want any company. She got along fine with his foster father, but Cal was receiving the welcome that most passing by her place got, so he just rode on by, yelling out a "Good day to you, Mrs. Anderson."

There were all kinds of folks living in this valley, he thought. He'd miss them all, even Hattie Anderson. But even if nothing exploded in the valley to change life here, Cal knew that he'd have to leave. This wasn't the life for him. Even if folks from around here never discovered his secret.

While he was at Mrs. Thornton's, mending a fence near the house before his breakfast the next day, Cal found out why he hadn't encountered anyone on the road the previous day. The sound of the clattering of metal on metal made him look up to see that the tinker who had dropped him the message that he was needed in Hayden was making his return trip south on his cart from Slater. Mrs. Thornton heard him too and came out on her porch and watched Cal and the man talk briefly before the tinker moved on down the road.

"That was Mr. Gifford you were talking to," she said as Cal sat down to his breakfast.

"Yes, it was."

"You two were talking pretty seriously."

"He told me why there hasn't been traffic on the road. When he entered the valley up south of Slater, he ran into a barricade."

"A barricade?" Mrs. Thornton put the kettle back on the stove and sat down hard in a chair at the table where Cal was sitting. A few of the children were gathered around the door into the kitchen and she shooed them off by assigning tasks for all of them to do. Giggling and shoving each other, they were off. They had gathered, really, to see Cal, who was somewhat of a hero to all of them—the former student and orphan who kept coming back to do chores for Mrs. Thornton.

"It's the cattlemen, isn't it?" she asked when the two of them were alone.

"Yes, Mr. Gifford was told there was a barricade at the southern end of the valley now too. They let him pass, but they took his rifle and the pistols he was peddling away from him."

"Took his guns?" she asked with a distressed voice. Her hand went up to her mouth. Nothing was more serious out in this country than parting a man from his firearms.

"They told him that no firearms were to go into the valley. And . . ."

"And what, Cal? What could be worse than that? You've told me the worst now, but there's more, isn't there?"

"Yes, there's more. And I'm not sure I've told you the worst. They aren't letting any men, anyone between sixteen and sixty in or out of the valley."

They sat there in silence for several minutes, each thinking individual thoughts of what it could mean, both arriving to the same conclusions, but neither wanting to voice them.

"That means you'll have to go back to the ranch, then," she said dully.

"No. I've got to go to Hayden."

"But they'd take your rifle."

"Nobody's taking my rifle," Cal responded with a set jaw. "It doesn't matter anyway. They wouldn't let me pass. I'm nineteen."

"Oh," she said and then, "Oh, so you are. I keep forgetting that you've grown. But what will you—?"

"I'll go up on the slopes of the Hahn's Peak. There's a road up from here to Milo Mather's mill—and then there's a track beyond that I know of. I won't go on the valley road; I'll go through the mountains."

"Through the mountains?" There was a touch of fear in her voice. "You know of a track south on the slopes of the mountains to the east?"

"Yes."

"That you learned of when you were with . . . when you were with the Arapaho?"

"Yes."

"But there are still remnants of the Arapaho up in there, braves who escaped from the relocation south."

"Yes, I imagine there are."

"You're not one of them anymore, Cal. They won't see you as anything but another white homesteader, just one of the white men who brought tragedy to their people."

"I realize that. Nonetheless I need to go to Hayden, and I can't get past the barricade and I won't give up my rifle. I'll use the mountain path."

Chapter Two: The Mountain Path

The track up from the valley floor to Mather's mill was comparatively easy going. Wide-berthed and heavily laden Lumber carts regularly came down the path that ran alongside the narrow, but rapid-running Slater Creek. The deciduous trees were thick here—still, after more than a decade of lumberjacking. The trees along the stream bed were mainly cottonwoods, unfit for any use in building. The undergrowth at this elevation was thick and the other trees were mostly soft wood. The mill camp had been built farther up the slope of Hahn's peak precisely to put it in the middle of the tall and straight stands of fir trees, the mountain pine. You could make longer, straight boards from these trees. And you could make telephone poles to accommodate the telegraph lines snaking west from the "civilized" East Coast.

The mule didn't object to the rise of the road at this point, but Cal held it back, knowing that there was much rougher, more objectionable and rocky terrain to follow.

Mrs. Thornton had fixed him a full breakfast and had offered to fix something for him for the midday meal, but Cal had turned her offer down, knowing how scarce food was for her and how many mouths she had to feed. He was accustomed to bringing her foodstuffs, not taking them from her. He planned to eat with the men at the mill. He had been a favorite of theirs the year before he went to the Cowdens. He'd gone to the mill nearly every day and helped wherever he was needed. The work toughened him up, and Milo Mather always had foodstuffs to give him to return to the schoolhouse in the dark of the evening. It had been a good arrangement all around. It made him feel like he was giving back for what Mrs. Thornton had given him.

When he arrived in the mill camp, he was surprised to find that it was deserted. He had timed his arrival for mealtime, and the loggers should have been in for their midday repast and those working the saws to trim the wood into planks should have been shutting down operations and moving toward the dining hall.

But no one seemed to be there. The silence was eerie, and for several minutes Cal thought he was completely alone. But as he rode up to the dining hall, he saw that old Hiram, one of Milo Mather's original loggers, who had nearly cut his arm off in the first year of operation and who was too old to work the lumber now anyway, was sitting in a rocking chair on the building's porch and sucking on his corn cob pipe. Milo Mather hadn't just sent Hiram packing when he no longer could work the timber; he'd found odd jobs for him to do around the camp and had given him the title of "caretaker," even though the camp, to Cal's recollection, had never needed someone to take care of it.

That apparently had all changed now, because Hiram was the only one Cal found at the camp.

"What's happening up here, Hiram?" Cal asked as he rode up to the porch. "Where are all the men?"

"They'se all gone, Caleb," Hiram answered. With a little jerk, he'd taken the pipe out of his mouth and collapsed into a phlegm-filled coughing fit. Hiram had always called Cal by his full given name, thinking that it gave the young man who had come to the camp as an orphan from an Indian raid some dignity. Some of the white men never would fully trust Cal after knowing he'd spent time with the Arapaho. "A few went into Hayden, but most to Denver and beyond," he continued in a strangled voice when he was able to. "It's gonna be a mite hard for Milo to pull together a new crew. But I guess they's always men in the valley needin' work."

"Bad cough, Hiram. You need to do something about that."

"God will provide. But if you have a bottle of somethin' there in your saddle bag, that might be a big help too." Hiram cackled at his own joke, which only served to set him off coughing again.

"Sorry, the Cowdens don't drink anything you might want."

That "God will provide" sounded so familiar coming from Hiram's mouth. It was the saying Cal had always attached to Hiram, and Cal guessed that maybe God had provided for Hiram. But it seemed, on the surface observation, that it had mainly been Milo Mather who had taken care of Hiram. "Why and what are you doing here alone?"

"I'se caretaking as I'se supposed to. Old Mr. Mather didn't want me to stay, but I said that he could either let me do my job or let me go. I didn't want to leave from my job at the first sign of trouble."

"The first sign of trouble?"

"Jah. That would have been from the men from the Double O ranch down on the way to Hayden. Mr. Savage's men. They came ridin' in here three days ago and told Old Mr. Mather to shut down operations for a while if he didn't want to get mixed up in what was happening."

"Happening? What did they say was happening, Hiram?"

"They said no farmers would be comin' into the valley and that they were going to take care of the problem of the sheep at the same time. They didn't have to say any more than that. Mr. Mather, he don't want to take sides in any of this. He just wants to cut and sell lumber. So, all the men are gone for a spell and I'se here caretakin'. You come for some supplies for Mrs. Thornton down at the schoolhouse? 'Cause if you are, I know that be fine with Mr. Mather. You go on into the kitchen and take anything you need."

"Thanks, but I'm just passing through, Hiram. I'd appreciate a little something for myself for a midday meal, though."

"Passing through?"

"Yes. I'm taking the mountain paths to get into Hayden. Got business there for a couple of weeks."

"Why the mountain path?"

"The cattlemen have the passes into the valley at both ends blocked off. Taking rifles and not letting men pass."

"Ah. Then it's started, has it? You go on in and get you some grub."

"Thanks, Hiram. You might think of leaving too."

135

"I imagine everything will be just fine up here, Caleb. The cattlemen need lumber too. I figure that Mr. Savage ain't stupid. He may stop the work for a spell, but he don't want to end it altogether. And he won't find no sheep or farm fences up here. He just wants to keep the lumbermen out of the mix."

Cal figured that Hiram wasn't stupid either. After scrounging something to eat in the mill kitchen, he started out again, this time on a logging trail, but not too long after that turning onto a track that only his training with the Arapaho told him was a trail. The mule, of course, wasn't Arapaho and didn't believe there was any trail there, so the going not only started to get steeper, toward the higher elevations beyond the stands of pines, but the mule also got harder to move.

In late afternoon, mule and rider broke out of the pines above the timberline. The peak of the mountain looked almost near enough to touch, but Cal knew that he was barely half way to the top in elevation. From here there was a stretch up the slope of barren rock and hard soil, but the line of snow, even this late in the year, was not too far above him. From here the path followed the timberline. Even the Arapaho hadn't wanted to be too exposed at this elevation. There had been tribal clashes even in the centuries before the white man arrived in the area. He'd heard many a story around the campfire of the wars between the Arapaho and the Utes. And this was the domain of the large, aggressive animals such as the bear and the timber wolf as well. Even the Arapaho had traveled trails that would permit them to melt into the pines at the first sign of danger.

The mule obviously felt safer here, in the more open terrain and on the surer path, even if Cal himself went on higher alert. It wasn't just the big animals he was watching for but also for maverick Arapaho braves who had escaped the forced relocation to the south and were existing alone or in small bands in the mountains. He would have been surprised, though, to find marauding cattlemen at this elevation. Cowboys didn't like the mountain, and there was little to draw them this high. Cal imagined that, to a cowboy, the mountains were too much like the hated fences. That was what Cal was counting on by taking the mountain path. Completely oblivious to the dangers at hand, now the mule wanted to get on with the journey at a faster clip than the ever-vigilant rider did, and Cal continually found himself reigning the mule in.

It was about the time that Cal broke into the timberline that he had every reason to be worrying. He presence hadn't gone unnoticed. Tracking him now was one of those solitary Arapaho braves Cal was watching for. Cal, however, wasn't anywhere near as able to detect the young brave following him as the Arapaho was in tracking his prey.

Not long after breaking into the open, Cal came upon a turbulent mountain stream taking snow melt down into the valley and knew that he was half way to Hayden now and that he could start looking for someplace safe to camp for the night, which was quickly approaching. He followed the stream back down the mountain, looking for and picking out a good place to cross, and then continuing on for a bit to find a glen in the forest next to a pool of water below a waterfall to make camp. This, he reasoned was as safe a place to spend the night as any.

His was a false sense of safety, though, the Arapaho brave followed him at a distance down the stream and climbed a tree as they neared the glen, knowing instinctively that Cal would set camp there, and attentively watched Cal's every move as he made a campfire, set up a lean-to tent, and boiled coffee for an evening meal of hard bread and smoked trout.

* * * *

Ilesh clung to the branch of the tree, almost motionless, for more than three hours, watching Cal prepare and eat his dinner, check to ensure that the mule was safely staked out, inventory what he had in his saddle bags, douse out the fire, strip down to his underlinens, and crawl into the lean-to he'd constructed against the protected side of a rock outcropping.

The young Arapaho brave was well versed in being one with the tree, and he had the strength to perch there, motionless for as long as he needed to. In the years since, as merely a boy, he had eluded the American soldiers who were rounding his people up and shipping them off, Ilesh had lived up to his name, which translated as Lord of the Earth in Arapaho. He had grown lithe, yet muscular, and straight and strong. And he had learned to steel himself against the elements, clothed only in a breechcloth and leather leggings and moccasins, in all but the coldest weather.

He waited there until the dark of night before silently slithering down the trunk of the tree. The mule knew he was there and moved nervously away as far as its tether would permit. But Ilesh came closer to the beast and put his hand its muzzle, stroking it and keeping it from whinnying its fear. Having calmed the mule down, Ilesh reached down and pulled his breechcloth away, freeing a long, thick knife. Taking this in hand, he slowly stole toward the lean-to, entered it, and landed at a full stretch on Cal, who was lying on his back.

Ilesh had the element of surprise and he was a stronger man than Cal. The struggle was fierce, with Ilesh having the advantage of hold from the beginning, as Cal was just waking up. Slowly but relentlessly, Cal was tiring within Ilesha's full-body embrace. The Arapaho brave forced his knees between Cal's thighs and spread and raised them. The brave's knife was long and hard and sharp. It sliced into Cal again and again and again. Cal thrashed about, but he couldn't withstand the relentless attack of the Arapaho brave for long.

Cal lay there, limbs akimbo, and head turned to the side, limp and totally finished. Ilesh rose up on his knees, prodded the body under him without obtaining response, and nudged Cal's body over onto its stomach. Straddling the young white man's hips then, Ilesh thrust his knife—his hard cock—inside Cal's channel and enjoyed a victory fuck inside his prey.

* * * *

When Cal woke up, it was morning, but not fully light yet. Still, it was later than he had planned to be up and on his way. He stretched his limbs, working out the kinks. He still felt hung over from the night's activities. The Arapaho brave had taken him twice more in the night after that first assault.

This led to the thought of where the brave was now. Had he just attacked and then run? With a groan, Cal sat up from the horse blanket that had covered the ground underneath him in the night and stumbled up and out of the lean-to tent. He was surprised that the canvas covering of the lean-to hadn't come down on them in the night while they were thrashing about. When he managed to stand up from the crouch that had brought him out of the tent, he saw that there was a fire going and a coffee pot brewing. But no Arapaho brave in sight.

He looked around and caught the glimpse of movement out in the stream, under the waterfall, and moved cautiously in that direction. The brave was in the pool of water, naked, and magnificently formed. He was showering under the waterfall. Cal shivered just to watch him, knowing that the water must be icy cold. The brave was acting like he didn't have a care in the world and could take all the time he wanted in the water. Cal crept up as close to the pond as he dared, hiding himself behind a bush inside the tree line.

"I see you, little Jivin," the brave called out in Arapaho. "Come into the water. I can make you forget how cold the water is, and you stink."

"All white men stink to you," Cal said, with a laugh, as he rose and walked out from behind the bush. He stood there, smiling at the man who had been raised as his campmate, the only man for a long time who had referred to him as "little"— or, for that matter, had called him by his Arapaho name, Jivin, which had been given to him as a baby. The name translated as "To Give Life," and the Arapaho had given it to Cal and called him that as a reminder that it was they who had let him live rather than killing him along with all of the others who had been in the wagon train with his parents—and possibly his siblings. Cal would probably never know if he was an only child.

But he hadn't been raised as an only child. He had been raised in the same communal group of tents with other Arapaho children. Among those had been this sturdy Arapaho brave, Ilesh, standing so magnificently under the waterfall and wagging his hefty cock at Cal. For years, Cal had thought that he and Ilesh, a couple of years older than he was, were actually brothers, and at some point, as Cal started to become aware of his sexuality, he regretted that this was the case. It was only when the American soldiers came and his paternity was questioned that his Arapaho family revealed that he wasn't Arapaho as well—one with a different look about him. He wasn't even fully a member of the greater communal family around the common fire. There were other blond and blue-eyed people in the camp, mostly women, and some with both Arapaho and Caucasian features. No one having told him otherwise, Cal just assumed that Arapahos came with various different traits.

It had been a revelation to him that Ilesh and he weren't related, even of the same human grouping. This had made him look at Ilesh a whole new way, thinking of the times Ilesh had touched him and given him a strange sensation that had disturbed him, thinking that he and Ilesh were related. He had seen men taking men in the camp and the surrounding brush and forest, and he'd been curious about it and perhaps a little more than curious. Little was private in an Arapaho village, and the practice didn't seem to have any taboos in that culture. But no sooner had he learned of this nonaffiliation than he had been taken from the Arapaho and deposited with Mrs. Thornton at the schoolhouse in the Slater Creek valley.

But Ilesh had known they weren't related. And Ilesh had known what Cal was learning about his sexuality and his preferences. And Ilesh had the same preferences and had an affinity for Cal.

The previous year, while Cal was at Mather's mill on the lower slopes of Hahn's Peak, Ilesh had come for him. He fucked Cal in a glade almost within sight of the mill camp, pinning Cal on his back on the ground between the spreading roots of a giant tree, with Cal's knees hooked on Ilesh's hips and his pelvis rolled up to give Ilesh maximum entry, while the Arapaho pounded, pounded, pounded Cal's channel and made his former campmate his. Cal had welcomed Ilesh's attentions, having ached for him for over half a decade before the Arapaho maverick brave had come for him, not knowing that

Ilesh had not been force marched down to the Oklahoma territory with the rest of his family.

For the past year they had met nearly monthly during Cal's regular visits to Mather's mill to gather food to take down to the schoolhouse for the orphans who had become his family after the Arapahos had been taken from him.

"You are getting sloppy," Ilesh called out from under the waterfall. "It could have been any stray Arapaho brave who pounced on you in your tent last night, one with a real knife rather than a cock like mine wanting to mate with you."

"I knew the instant you picked up my trail. Soon after I left Mather's mill," Cal called back, with a laugh. "I never felt safer than the moment I knew you were there. I knew you were tracking me, and I knew you were lying on that tree branch up there and watching me. If you had not come for me when you did, I would have come out of the tent and asked you why you were taking your time."

"I enjoyed watching you being a white man, of the modesty you showed even when you thought you were alone. I can see little of the Arapaho in you now."

"I'm sorry to hear that, campmate."

"Don't be. I know our time is past, that to survive you need to be a white man. I don't want you to be taken for a renegade as I am."

"The time may be neigh that it is no better for me to be what I have become in my latest life than living as you do, where you go and live," Cal answered simply. "At least there is an honesty and lack of greed in the life of an Arapaho." And then, at the raising of Ilesh's eyebrows, Cal told him of the cattlemen and of the inevitability of trouble in his valley.

"I must watch over you more closely then," Ilesh said.

"You mustn't put yourself in danger," Cal answered. "Don't come into this, campmate. All parties will oppose you."

"But not you?"

"No, Ilesh, never me."

"You could come with me now."

"I go to Hayden. There is a job for me there for a short time. One making good money, money we need at the ranch."

"You could come with me now. What good is money in a festering world as you have described?"

"I can't leave Mr. Cowden. Not now, not yet. He is not well—not in body and not in the head. I don't think it will be long. But he took me in when few others would. I can't abandon him."

"I understand," Ilesh said. Then he grinned. "But you understand that that is a value you learned from the Arapaho, don't you—not from the white man? This is the Arapaho in you that is speaking of this call to loyalty."

"Yes, I understand."

"Well, then, it is time for you to get the stink of a white man off you. Come to me in the water."

"It's too cold."

"I will make you warm. I will make you hot. Moving fast up and down on my cock will warm you up. I will come and get you. But, if I have to, we won't be back in the water for a while."

"Fuck you."

"No, fuck you." And that's what Ilesh did. He was faster than lightning and reached Cal on the bank of the pool of water before Cal could—or even tried to—escape.

Ilesh dragged Cal on his back to the edge of the pond and then, kneeling in the water himself, he slapped Cal's thighs open, lifted the young man's legs to rise up his muscular chest, forced his cock inside, and began to pump. Cal raised his pelvis to his lover and started a counterpistoning rhythm.

Long before Ilesh finished, he had dragged a shivering Cal out into the water and under the waterfall and fucked him standing in the water, with Cal plastered to his pelvis.

In the makeshift camp, with both of them drinking the coffee Ilesh had brewed and Cal checking the saddle bags that he had repacked with his camping equipment, Cal spoke first after a long period of silence, during which both were thinking about how long they'd have to wait before another meeting and how dangerous such meetings now were becoming. "I guess this is good-bye for now," he said. "I think it's too dangerous to meet again for a while."

"I will follow you farther on your journey today. And, as for the future. If you need help, just come to the mill camp."

"You can't stay near the mill camp, Ilesh. It is too close to those who would do you harm."

"If you need help, just come to the mill camp. Continue on through and come up the same path from the logging track that you did yesterday."

"And it's too dangerous for you to follow me farther toward Hayden, too," Cal continued. "The cattle ranchers have men out. I might not be shot on sight. You most certainly would be."

"Then go in peace, little campmate," Ilesh said. He rose and melted into the forest with no more of a farewell than that.

With a sigh, Cal started off along the mountain slope toward the south. Dark was already approaching when he started to descend, at an angle, the slope to the plain leading to the banks of the Yampa River and, across that, the lights of the growing little town of Hayden. He made sure he went well past where the southern mouth of the Slater Creek valley was before coming down on the plain. Once on flat land, the ranch hands of the Double O cattle ranch he had to cross to get to the river wouldn't readily identify him as with the sheep people rather than the cattlemen.

Unbeknownst to him, however, Ilesh didn't stop shadowing him after he had started off from his makeshift camp, but followed him almost the entire way as Cal descended toward the plain just north of the Yampa River. Cal heard the rifle shot behind him as he reached the plain, but there was only the single shot and it was at a good distance behind him. He had no reason to think that it had anything to do with him or anyone he loved.

Chapter Three: En Route to Hayden

"Havin' a good time with that there Double O calf, are you?"

Cal looked up. The guy wasn't much older than he was. Some sort of half breed, but on him it looked good. Probably some Mexican in him. But not all that much, just enough to give him sultry dark looks, deep-tanned skin, more than the sun alone would do and more uniform too, and black, curly hair. Maybe a day's growth on his chin. Steel gray eyes. The eyes looked more amused than threatening now, but a rifle was being held loosely across his body, at the ready.

Cal looked over to the mule where his own rifle was holstered. Not a chance of making it there.

"As you can see, the calf slipped down this embankment and was caught in the brambles. I was just helping it get free before it thrashed about enough to do real damage to itself." The calf's cow was standing on firm grounding nearby, not showing that much concern for the plight of her little one.

"Sort of like what would happen in a wire fence of some homesteader's lot," the young cowboy said. He uncocked the rifle, but he didn't remove it from the ready. Cal was quite sure the guy knew exactly how far Cal would have to move to get to his own rifle.

Cal also understood what the cowboy's remark meant. It meant he was testing Cal out on what side of the cattlemen vs. farmer divide Cal was on. He wouldn't fall for that one. He was just glad that he hadn't been pegged for the more hated sheep men faction—not to mention his background as an Arapaho. He'd be shot on sight for that. This was Ute territory down here, and they still hadn't been successfully rounded up and shipped off. They were as fair game for the cattlemen as a wolf would be. And Arapaho or Ute, it would all be the same to this man.

Cal took another hard look at the young man but decided that the mix in him was Mexican, not Ute.

"Yeah, this bush looks like it could do about as much damage as a wire fence could. I about got the calf free. It's gonna kick a good bit when I do, though. Think you could come down here and give me a hand getting it up to its momma? Seeing as how it's your ranch's calf if you're from the Double O."

It was a ploy to neutralize the tension of the situation, of course—to get that rifle lowered. And it was using what Cal thought needed to be established—that he wasn't making a claim on this calf. The calf hadn't been branded yet, that Cal could see—although the cow certainly was. The law of the West on this was that Cal could walk away with it before it had been branded as someone's property if he could manage that. He wanted to dispel any notion that he was making any such claim or had any such intention.

It worked. The rifle uncocked and at the cowboy's side, the half-breed slid down the embankment to help Cal with the calf, which now, indeed, was free but without any sense of what else needed to be done to reunite it with the cow. Cattle aren't famous for their brilliance, no matter how old they get. The two men, huffing and puffing to get the calf moving in the right direction, worked together, straining their muscles, coming into contact, a contact that was arousing Cal, who had assessed the other man as desirable from first sight. He was fairly blushing and trembling when they got the calf up the embankment. The cow slowly moved over and took possession of the bawling calf as if she had never been worried and had done all the work of freeing it herself.

Cal had gone hard and hoped to god the young cowboy couldn't tell that. He turned at an angle from the dark, handsome young wrangler, both to put himself in a vulnerable, nonthreatening position and so that the cowboy couldn't see that the Confederate-issue thin woolen pants he was wearing were tenting and straining at the crotch.

Everything about the young man was bigger than Cal—his height and heft, which was invested in muscle rather than fat. The reach of his arms, the size of his calloused hands. The thickness of his lips and the white toothiness of his smile. The mound at his crotch, emphasized by being framed by the chaps on the cowboy's legs. All of Cal's experience in being aroused was based in the other man overpowering him and being able to manhandle him at will. Cal hadn't moved far from wanting to have it taken from him rather than seeking it out. Ilesh understood that, and it remained an element of their lovemaking.

The rifle—the phallic symbolism of it not escaping Cal—remained at the man's side, and he too was angled away from Cal, looking in the northwestern direction, the direction in which Cal's mule was standing. "Where'd you come from and where you going to?"

The question sounded friendly enough, but Cal knew that he was still under scrutiny. He was on the Double O's range. Assuming this was one of the ranch's hands, it was his responsibility to make a determination on any young man crossing the ranch, especially in these troubling times. And if it wasn't a Double O ranch hand, it likely was someone who shouldn't be on Double O land, which made him twice as dangerous and skittish.

"On my way to Hayden," Cal answered, trying to keep his voice casual. "I'm from up at Milo Mather's mill." It wasn't a lie he'd be caught in any time soon; he, in fact, had come from the mill. "We were told to clear out for a piece and so we did. I've been over at Crawford's ranch in Steamboat, east of here, and now am going to Hayden to do some work." His explanation was getting more dicey here, but it still was well within the realm of possibilities that a Double O ranch hand would know. Hiram had said that it was Double O men who had told the mill workers to scatter, while not targeting them for anything. In identifying Steamboat and the Crawfords, Cal brought into play a known family settled where a town was forming to the southeast but still on the northern side of the Yampa—thus well away in direction from the Slater Creek valley that had been blocked off.

146

"Well, thank you kindly for freeing the calf then," the man said. He tipped his broad-brimmed hat and moved toward his horse, which was standing off a bit to the west of the gully. He turned at the horse and said, "Maybe we'll meet again."

Cal swallowed hard, seeing the possibility in the man's smile and the look in his eyes, making him wonder if he was overassessing what the young man might be suggesting in what he was saying, but knowing that if the cowboy walked back to him now, Cal would lay down and open his legs to him.

Then the cowboy was in the saddle and slowly trotting off to the north, maybe, Cal thought, to help man the barricade at the south end of the Salter Creek valley—and probably not meaning anything at all except neighborliness in the "see you again" remark. Cal probably had no cause to think there was any more than that—it probably was just him thinking on what lay ahead for him in Hayden.

Cal momentarily regretted that the two obviously were on opposite sides of something so much larger than either one of them. Then he too went up the opposite embankment, pulled his reluctant mule down and up the gully onto the western side, and started riding down to the banks of the Yampa.

It was dark before he saw the lights of Hayden on the other side of the river. It hadn't gotten dark enough, though, for him not to have noticed that the sultry young ranch hand had been scouting him throughout his journey down to the Yampa and then along it, west, toward Hayden. Cal wasn't too worried, though. If the ranch hand had wanted to do him harm, he could have shot him at any point during the ride, and Cal would have just lain out on the range, being reduced to blanched bones and then to dust, without anyone being the wiser.

And if the ranch hand had wanted to fuck him, he only needed to have said so—to ask Cal for it, or better yet for Cal's arousal, just tell him they were going to fuck. Cal was sure he hadn't hidden his interest very well. Out here on the range, with few women around and men being randy no matter where they were, men could be direct about what they wanted and no one took umbrage at the suggestion even if it was off in figuring—well, most didn't, anyway. Those who did didn't act without having the upper hand, and at no point during Cal's contact with the young cowboy did either one of them misunderstand who had the upper hand. That, in itself, had been arousing to Cal.

Cal was more worried that the Yampa was in higher flow than he'd anticipated and that it would be far into the night before he'd find a good place to cross.

Chapter Four: Hayden's Saloon

"It's just for ten days—until Samuel gets back from Denver."

"I realize that," Cal answered Levi Yost, the owner of the Hayden saloon.

"This is Samuel's job. It's his when he gets back."

"Yes, sir, I understand that."

"Although I'll own that he's gettin' a little long in the tooth and some would like you instead. They'se tol' me as much. So, it's not like it won't happen . . . someday."

Cal didn't see that there was an answer needed to that, so he kept his mouth shut. He wanted to say that he wasn't looking for it permanently, that he was only doing it to pay for lumber for a shed that likely would be burned down as fast as it was built, but he didn't want to close any doors. Besides, for a short period of time it scratched an itch he had. Truth was that after he'd done it before he realized he wanted more of it. Who was to say that he wouldn't want to be doing it more here in this saloon?

"This is your place, right here at the end of the bar on this stool," Yost continued. "Where you can get a full view of the room. Anybody come in here, they should know the stools at the bar are for you and Sadie, Katie, and Faye. Everyone else at the bar stands. They give you trouble on that, William there behind the bar will put them right. Don't you go gettin' into any fights now, ya hear? Keep that face handsome."

"Yes, sir."

"Now we done a little rearrangin' upstairs since you were here last. Two rooms for you, the big one on the east front and then the smaller one behind it. I say when you go up there and what room you are to use, got it?"

"Yes, sir."

"You use the small room to sleep in too. You order the best drinks you can think he'll pay for when it's on a customer's tab. And you drink anything you are given and act like it's the best."

"Yes, sir."

"OK, then. It should liven up here in an hour or two. Maybe you should go take a nap till then."

"I'd appreciate that, thanks. It was hard finding a river crossing," Cal answered. "And it was a rough ride down from the valley. Had to go around the regular road."

"I heard that was the case. Sort of surprised you made it at all. Use the smaller room."

"Yes, sir." Cal rose off his designated stool at the end of the bar, which was right in front of the staircase to the upper level. He wearily reached down for his saddle bags and stood and looked at the steep, rickety staircase—this was about the only two-story building in Hayden as yet. As tired as he felt, he wasn't sure he even could make it up the stairs. And he was more than a little leery about stairs and upper floors anyway. He knew it was coming to Hayden, the taller buildings. But it could hold off for a while as far as he was concerned.

"And, Caleb," Levi answered, putting a hand on Cal's arm to arrest his movement, "I really am sorry about what's about to come down. You best not talk anything but cattle in this town while you're here, though. And I meant it about this bein' Samuel's job permanent like, but you decide you can't go back to the valley, I'll find somethin' for you around here. We'll take care of you. You got value here. There's some private work possible."

"Thanks, Mr. Yost," Cal said, with a sigh, as he looked up at the challenge of the stairs again.

* * * *

Cal lay there, still exhausted, a two-hour nap not having been enough to erase the bone-weariness from the nearly three-day journey from Heaven. Wanting to be anywhere but here just now, he concentrated on listening to the monotonous squeaking of the bed springs and felt as much as watched the loose brass head- and footboards bend in with each thrust and then jerk back as the man was on the rise. The headboard thumped against the wall of the small bedroom while the smelly cowboy, probably straight off three days on the range, crouched on top of him and pounded his ass. The man was scrawny and weather-beaten, his teeth—those that he still had—were stained with chewing tobacco, and his dick was nothing to challenge Cal, but he had stamina, Cal had to give that to him. He also wanted it bad and was taking it hard and fast. And Cal was addicted to cock. It was enough to keep him aroused that the dick was hard, was inside him, and moved fast enough to heat him up with skin-on-skin friction.

This was in contrast to Cal's first, rather hesitant customer, who had stood by the bed, still fully clothed except for his dong hanging out of his fly, while Cal sat on the bed and gave him a blow job. That middle-aged man—or maybe not that old, but certainly worked hard—had come quickly and then was too embarrassed to demand more. Cal had to speak soothing words of encouragement to him to put him in the frame of mind to come back in a few days and plunk his money down again for a "real" fucking. Cal didn't think the man would be ready for a real fuck even then, but as long as the man believed it—and paid for it—that was all that mattered.

Whereas the one riding him now, Cal felt, would have to be told that when he came the first time, that was it for the money he'd paid. More than once Cal had thought the man would come but he seemed able to hold it off to gain more time inside Cal.

Cal wished that the men were told they had to bathe before they could get their lay. There was a tub in the larger, much-better appointed front room. But Cal knew that wasn't going to be required—or permitted—for the basic fuck price.

Cal hoped that sometime tonight he'd get a young, big man who would give him a fuck he could think about until he had to start this all over again. There were enough such men around. One should be along soon.

It was a busy night, a Saturday night, and Cal assumed it would get busier. He permitted his thoughts to go to the rhythm of the headboards bouncing off the walls up here on the second floor of the saloon. Not just his; he could tell that all three of the women were entertaining as well. He worried a bit whether the building was strongly built enough to take this jarring but decided that was Levi Yost's problem. For now, he needed to concentrate on making this grizzled long-endurance cowboy come.

Cal moved his heels to the backs of the man's calves and rubbed them, snaked one hand between their bodies and rubbed one of the man's nipples—he was still wearing his shirt, but it was open, and other than that he was just wearing his wide-brimmed hat and his boots. Cal had made him take off the spurs; the man obviously wasn't going to think of doing that himself. Cal's other hand went to the man's buttocks and squeezed one cheek, he started calling out that the man was killing him with his giant cock—a great exaggeration—and that Cal had never had it that good, and he began squeezing his channel muscles in a steady rhythm on the thrusting dick.

The man didn't hold off much after all of that started. He shot off, and, with a groan, rolled off to the side of Cal in the three-quarters-wide rope bed.

"Fuck, you're good. Really sweet," the man said. "Maybe we can—"

"Don't think there's time," Cal quickly interjected. "I think we've gone too long now. I lost count of the time because you were doing me so good. But, yeah, I want you inside me again sometime soon. Maybe you can come back. It'll be hard waiting time till you're fucking me again. A real man's man you are. I like it especially good when a man knows what to do with his dick and can keep on giving it good."

That seemed to please the guy. He slapped Cal on the butt and then let his fingers enter him and come back with his own cum and rub it around on Cal's buttocks."How long you gonna be here? Sam gone now and it's you?"

"I'm just here for a little more than a week. Samuel's in Denver on personal business."

"Don't tell Sam I told you so, but, damn you have a sweet ass. And you're a real looker. A lot fresher than Sam is. I'll be back next Saturday night."

"I'll count on it. Can't wait. You're a great fucker," Cal answered, almost automatically, although he tried to sound sincere. He told them all they were the best. He'd even found a way to tell the reticent premature shooter he was the best. They all believed it, because they wanted to believe it.

He was making money. But usually there were one or two who made the sex worthwhile—who were all muscle and manhandling and who gave him a big-cocked ride that he felt all the way to the quick. That hadn't happened yet. But it was early and he'd only taken two so far this evening.

* * * *

The evening was still early and Cal was on his designated stool, now hoping that business would pick up because if he was going to do this thing, it needed to be profitable. He'd taken two guys, but only the last one was in any way taxing and that was from the man's vigor and stamina more than challenging endowments. He sensed that he was being watched. Well, he was being watched by more than a few guys, but not that intensely. Most of the men here were zeroed in on Sadie, Katie, and Faye, who were doing brisk business. Most of the men who were looking at him were doing so more out of curiosity. It was a curiosity borne of thoughts a lot of guys would have out here in the West, where they might be out on the range for long periods of time with only guys to look at and be with. Thoughts they wouldn't have had in the more urban areas of the East—or, if they had them, they wouldn't act on them as readily.

But Cal sensed there was one guy . . . and he scanned the crowded barroom, trying to pick him out. When Cal saw him, he did a double take. It was the sexy half-breed cowboy he'd had the encounter with in freeing the calf in the gully.

A half-breed. Cal had hardened right up for him when they were working together, saving that calf—Cal was hardening up even now. And Cal melted to the Arapaho, Ilesh, too. He got hard for these two faster than he'd ever done for a full-blooded white man. Maybe it was because emotionally, if not physically, Cal was a half-breed himself—those first eight years with the Arapaho.

Seeing that he'd been caught looking, the man rose from the table he'd been sitting at with hard-drinking—from the look of the empty bottles on their table—other young cowpokes and moved slowly toward Cal. Cal was sure that they'd just be touching base from recognizing each other out on the range. But he thought that with a tinge of regret. The man was sultry and arousing. Cal's eyes went to the curve of the young guy's basket and he caught his breath. His trained eye picked out the long, thick bulge of the cock snaking over on top of the man's right thigh under the tight material of his britches. The leather chaps he was wearing, exposing the basket between them at the midsection, put the focus on the man's crotch. Cal felt himself go even harder and he had to restrain his hand from moving to his basket as the young man walked toward him.

"So, this was where you were headed," the half-breed said as he slipped in between Cal and an older man in a suit, indicating he was from the town, who was chatting up Katie at the bar. "Not just Hayden but Yost's saloon."

"You knew where I was heading," Cal answered. "I noticed that you followed me practically to the door of the saloon."

"Only as far as the river. You'd done the Double O a favor; I didn't want to see you get into any trouble from any of the other guys out on the range. But was I that obvious?"

"I don't think you would have been to most." Cal didn't mention that he'd been raised with the Arapaho and therefore trained to track and notice tracking in ways the white men never perfected. "But you were noticeable to me."

"You wanted to know where I was? What I liked?"

"Something like that." That brought a smile from the guy.

"I was that obvious back there, when we were helping that calf?"

Cal wasn't sure how to take that, so he let it pass.

"My name is Frank," the young man said, and held his hand out to offer a strong shake. During the shake his thumb moved between their palms and he rubbed it back and forth. The West was rough and the men working in it were rougher and were prone to violence, so men interested in men out here—which were a quite high proportion as women were scarce and the sex drive didn't respect the restrictions of location—had developed some secret signals to identify each other. In the scheme of such a handshake, a top would rub the palm with his thumb and an interested receiver would grasp the other man's thumb before they came out of the handshake. It took no more than this to establish interest and willingness, and a contract between a bottom and a top. Another top would push the hand away; a man interested in going both ways would move his thumb between the hand palms to join the other and rub against it. A man not knowing what was being signaled would merely end the handshake, maybe with a bit of a confused look.

Cal merely ended the handshake—not from lack of interest, but because Cal wasn't in the world of white men who were signaling each other this way. He had no idea it was a signal. The Arapaho were much more direct. In the Arapaho camps, they managed the man-on-man by keen observation and the top isolating the bottom in the forest and fucking the stuffing out of him no matter what pretense of not wanting it that he exhibited. That's what Ilesh had done with Cal the first time, with Cal crying out that he didn't want it while Ilesh was wrestling him down, and then demanding that it never end after Ilesh had gotten his dick inside him. As far as Cal had any idea of how this worked out, if Frank had wanted him, he would have taken him out there on the range. Cal would have let him. That's where Cal had done his tentative signaling.

Even another white man, a burly lumberjack up at Mather's mill, had done the same the previous summer as Ilesh had done—lured Cal into the forest and fucked the stuffing out of him. Perhaps it was Cal's upbringing—the naturalistic views of the Arapaho and that neither Mrs. Thornton nor the Cowdens were Bible thumpers—but he saw nothing unnatural about a dominating man manhandling him and fucking him. Ilesh had made him aware that he liked to be fucked, and the hierarchy of size and power seemed natural as far as he was concerned. There was nothing in his mind that made him think that he should only let one man fuck him either. He hadn't sought it out from a specific man—at least yet. It had been that lumberjack who had told Levi Yost of how enticing Cal could be for a man—and that, once subdued, Cal was a firecracker bottom in the fucking.

As Cal released Frank's hand, he smiled and said, "I'm Caleb, but folks mostly call me Cal." Levi had told him he should make up another name to give these guys if they asked, but Cal had forgotten to do that with this Frank, he was so besotted with him.

Nonplused by the lack of reaction to his signal, Frank seemed confused and almost stuttered out, "You do know who's stool this is you're sitting on?"

"Samuel's in Denver for a week," Cal answered, not realizing that this wouldn't be seen as a clear-cut answer. This just confused Frank more. He was saved from pressing the question further, and Cal was left thinking they were just casually chatting and that Frank may not have any idea what Cal was here for, when Levi sauntered over and pushed himself into the conversation.

"You men just having a friendly chat, or do you want to talk business, Frank?"

Cal had no idea how Levi Yost knew Frank's name— although it stood to reason that, as a ranch hand with the nearby Double O, the young man probably frequented the saloon a lot. But having uppermost in his mind not wanting a straight Frank to know he was part of the sex service in the saloon, Cal nervously answered before Frank could say anything. "He was just passing the time with me, Levi. We met out on the range in passing as I was riding into Hayden, and we were just introducing ourselves. We'll just—"

"Yeah, we can talk business, Levi," Frank said. "I'll buy an hour."

"I've heard an hour with you is a hard ride, Frank," Yost said. "I'd have to add 50 cents to the rate to do it on time rather than a one-time finish."

"I said I'd buy an hour," Frank repeated. "The time. Not a one-time finish."

"The small room, Cal," Levi said, as Frank counted out money in Levi's hand—with Cal being so set on edge that he didn't consider that Frank didn't have to ask how much the hour would cost at the base of the extra being demanded.

It was too noisy to talk as they slowly mounted the rickety stairs, being very careful about the strength of the boards as they placed their feet on them. They were following the man at the bar in the suit and Katie, who he'd been chatting up at the bar. The pair were starting the foreplay on the stairs, so they were moving slowly and seemed threatened to go over the banister on every other step. This didn't help with the jitters Cal was feeling. Was he really going to be fucked by this hunk? He knew what they had been dickering over. Most men came once and that was it. In talking about time or finish, Yost was indicting he knew that Frank was a fast multiple shooter. Call was wondering why he was melting in anticipation of this more than he did for any other man, other than Ilesh?

At the door to the small room, Cal turned, finding Frank very close behind him. "You know you don't have to pay . . . just for us to talk. I can return your money and we could just meet somewhere else . . . to talk . . . if you'll still be in town tomorrow morning." Not even Cal knew why he had proposed this. He still wasn't clear that he didn't want Frank to fuck him here—and to pay for it. He wanted Frank to fuck him, just not here, but somewhere where it wasn't a financial transaction. Could it be that he was after something purer, more concerned with mutual giving and taking? He just didn't know. He did know, though, that he didn't just want to talk. He wanted Frank to fuck him. He was so hard for it he couldn't walk straight.

"This is on the clock," Frank said, with a bit of amusement showing in his eyes. "I want to fuck you twice—I'm aching to take you swift and hard, but I want something else too. I wanted to fuck you out on the range but didn't know you'd do it—and that's a tall order to get done in one of Levi's short-changed hours. You don't think I can't see that you're hard for me?"

"I was hard for you on the range," Cal murmured.

"Then we're wasting time here."

He pushed Cal into the room, hooking an arm around the younger and smaller man's waist while he slammed the door behind them, and pulled Cal to him in a deep kiss while his hands stripped off Cal's shirt and unbuttoned Cal's fly. He quickly went to his knees and had his mouth on Cal's cock, with Cal moaning and digging his hands in the sultry half-breed's thick black head hair, before Cal could even start to gather his thoughts. "God, I wanted to do this out on the range," he growled as his lips came up to Cal's trembling belly and then went back to suck Cal's balls into his mouth cavity.

"The bed, the bed. Fuck me," Cal whimpered, completely off the script he'd memorized to handle customers.

"That bed's got more fleas on it than that old hound out on the porch of the saloon," Frank answered. "We'll fuck standing up. At least I ain't goin' on that bed ever again. Too much noise in thumpin' against the wall, anyway. And I always think the damn thing is gonna collapse when I get into a good fuck."

Cal was too taken up with what was happening to him and discovering, by feel, that Frank was horse hung, to latch into how Frank would know about the condition of this bed. But then it sank in. "You been here before?"

"Lots of times. Maybe twice a week. Most of my money goes into Sam's ass. I've got lots of practice at this. I'm gonna fuck you three ways from Sunday. Can't wait to get into somethin' fresher than Sam."

Cal moaned and relaxed in Frank's arms. "Fuck, do me now. I can't wait for it."

Within minutes they were beside the bed, and Cal was leaning down on the bed on his elbows and trying to widen his stance as much as he could as, behind him, Frank, his shirt open but not off his back and his boots and britches, covered by the leather chaps, still on his legs with the fly flaired out on each side, huffed and puffed to get his dick stuffed up Cal's ass.

"Oh, shit," Cal called out as he was being penetrated. This was it. The big one of the night that would hold him over to the next evening, reminding him that he was doing this for more than the money. "Oh, fuck, yes," he exclaimed with a moan as the big cock started to plow him.

Once mounted, neither young man spoke other than the occasional "oh shit" and "fuck yes" as each worked to get as much out of the fuck as possible. Not even Cal's Arapaho lover, Ilesh, had a dick this thick and long, which made up for Ilesh's better technique—but not a whole lot better. And there wasn't a damn thing wrong with Frank's technique. Cal was luxuriating in the fuck. This was why he was willing to do this—because of the possibility of a man coming along who could scratch his itch deep like this Frank guy was doing.

"God, yes, you've had a lot of practice at this," Cal said, with a groan.

"Told you. Never had an ass this sweet, though. Jack yourself while I'm doin' this. Try to come together. Shit, I wanted to do this out on the range. If I knew what I'd be gettin', I woulda done you out there."

"You would have saved the money out there," Cal whimpered.

"I woulda been willing to pay for this out there. God, your ass is sweeter than Sam's was when he was a baby."

A long slide in and a long slide out, powered by Frank's strong, calloused hands on Cal's waist, ending in a gulp from Cal. And then four, five, or six, fast, deep plunges, never the same, to keep Cal off guard, and Cal gasping and begging for more of it. Each time.

Half way through the fuck, Frank turned Cal so that Cal's shoulder blades rested on the bed and his legs were wrapped around Frank's waist. They each fired off in this position, Frank now having taken over jacking Cal's cock and the two coming almost simultaneously, and then Cal raised his torso and flung his arms around Frank's neck, at Frank's command, and the half-breed backed up and sat in the straight chair that was just a few steps away in the narrow room. Cal sat, facing Frank in his lap and on the cock in its momentarily flaccid condition, as they kissed and talked dirty to each other in low voices, coaxing Frank to go hard again, which he did well before the hour was up, giving them time for a second fuck.

"You said you'd be here for a week?" Frank whispered when they were cooling down in the last minutes of their time with each other, Cal still sitting on the cock in Frank's lap.

"Nine more days after this," Cal answered.

"Ah, a couple of days longer. I might—"

"That would be nice. But any morning . . . anywhere you can come. Just tell me when and where and I'll be there. I'd like it better if it weren't on Levi's clock."

"I understand. You then could keep every—"

"No, you don't understand. I'd like it better without money involved. I want you to take it from me by right . . . by the right of the biggest, best cock in the West."

"Well, when you put it that way . . ."

Cal could feel Frank starting to grow to the "biggest in the West" dimensions.

"Oh, shit," Cal said with a groan.

"We got six minutes. And I got money for another half hour beyond that," Frank murmured, already starting to raise and lower Cal's channel on the cock. "And I ain't gonna stop now for no one. Even if you wanted me to stop, I wouldn't."

"That's exactly the way I like it," Cal answered. And he wasn't just sweet-talking the customer with this admission.

"You mean you like it harder and rougher? Harder and rougher, like this?"

"Oh, fuck yes. Oh, fuck yes. Oh, Fuck YES!"

* * * *

"Good work in getting' him to buy another half hour. Want you to go in back and scrub down now and take a clean change of clothes. Then wait in the smaller room upstairs. You'll be going to the bigger room."

Cal had barely had time to settle—gingerly this time—back on his stool. He was still watching Frank stride off toward the saloon entrance from the back and thinking that he hadn't seen Frank bare-ass naked yet and wanted to, when Levi Yost came over and told him to be on the move again.

"An important customer?" Cal asked.

"Would I ask you to clean yourself and go wait to go to the big room otherwise? I'll be losing money here, while you are sittin' around doin' nothin' but playing with your dick. But don't you go doin' that unless the customer asks for it. Don't want you wearin' out the goods. And remember what I said about you not wantin' to start fallin' for any of these guys and givin' it away for free. Only a damn fool would hurt himself— and me—in the money making to be doing that."

Cal fought hard not to blush. Was Levi giving him a knowing look? Was Levi listening at the door when he and Frank were fucking? Of course that was a possibility. Or could he just tell by how Cal watched Frank move away? Frank wasn't revealing any special feelings for Cal when they came downstairs. Frank had just banged him hard and treated him rough that second time and been all business. Well, that was OK with Cal. He wanted big-cocked muscle men who used him hard. No deeper entanglements for him other than with Ilesh.

"Yeah, that would be stupid," he answered Yost. "Out back, did you say? The shower stall," he said, trying to get out of this dangerous area of discussion.

"There's a pipe and fence around it in back. When there's a petticoat hangin' over the fence, stay away. Don't want you wearin' out those goods either—unless you want to buy time for yourself. Otherwise you are free to sluice yourself down there whenever you want. The hired help does the laundry, so you can get into clean clothes whenever you want too. Evenings you'll probably decide just not to have underlinens. They just get in the way. You're just a bit smaller than Sam, so you should be able to get his clothes on. Do it right and you won't be in the clothes long anyway. Sam hasn't worn them out, and he has some pretty snazzy duds. Gettin' clean is up to you except for customers using the big room. For those you come in clean unless he asks for otherwise. Some men get excited about the smell of other men on their doxies. That's their call."

"You want me clean for this guy, though?"

"Yeah. And it will be your last customer for the night. I don't think you'll be up to taking on any more anyway."

161

As far as a sore and well-reamed ass, Cal didn't feel like taking any more tonight after Frank, but he didn't tell Yost that. Yost obviously was nervous about and intimidated by this next mystery customer.

And then Levi was moving off. He stopped half way across the room to talk to what looked like a town guy who was looking Cal up and down real good to give the guy the bad news that Cal was booked for the rest of the night.

Feeling clean for the first time since he bathed under the waterfall on the slopes of Hahn's Peak with Ilesh in what seemed to be a lifetime ago, Cal took the back stairs to the second floor and the small room assigned to him. He pulled on a pair of tight woolen britches and a billowy sort of white cotton shirt he'd found in a drawer in the small room and he was going to just rest a bit on the bed, but he went to sleep almost immediately and it was dark in the room when the house boy came to tell him he was wanted in the big room at the front of the building.

The room wasn't all that big, but it was set up more like a parlor than any of the other rooms he'd seen. He assumed that the girls had a room or two like this for important customers. The walls were covered in a red velveteen-type wallpaper that wasn't torn or smudged in too many places. There was a big braided rug on the wooden-plank floor, which insulated the room a bit. In other areas of the upstairs the gaps were big enough to see movement down in the saloon and you could hear the honky-tonk piano going and hubbub of the boisterous men below nearly as well up here as you could downstairs.

There were two Victorian armchairs set off to one side with a marble-topped mahogany table between them. The four-poster bed with red velvet curtains dominated the room. What was most prominent, though, to Cal, when he entered the room, was that there was a big brass bathtub set out in the middle of the room, and in the bathtub reclined a huge-boned man, bullet-headed and bald, with a craggy face with a scar slicing down from the edge of his right eye to his chin. The size of him made the bathtub look small, and it wasn't small. He had a cigar in one hand and a bottle of whiskey in the other.

One of the serving girls was sponging him down when Cal entered the room, but when the man saw Cal, he waved her away and out of the room and told Cal, in a booming, bass voice, to come take over the sponging.

Cal walked over to the side of the tub and pulled up the sponge from the surface of the water where the serving girl had dropped it. After he got his hand on the sponge, though, and before he could lift it, the man gripped his wrist in his fist, managing to hold both Cal's wrist and cigar, and held it there, glowering at Cal until Cal gave the man his full attention.

"Just so you know, I'm gonna fuck you into the next county," the man growled.

Cal didn't need to pretend to shudder at that declaration and the manner in which it was delivered. The man freed his wrist then, though, and Cal lifted the sopping sponge, pressed it into the man's neck, and moved it down over a bulging bicep. Everything about the man bulged. He was stocky. He wasn't fat; it was all hard muscle. But he was built in oversized proportions. Cal could see through the soapy water that the man's dick was standing up from a patch of red hair with gray streaks. Other than the hair here, though, the only other patches were between his bulging pectorals and in the pits of his arms.

He wasn't a handsome man. His face—and his body too, judging by the scars—had been in too many fights. His nose had been broken and was tilted off center, and his right eye drooped, which called attention to the angry red scar there, obtained most likely in a knife fight. He exuded an aura of command and meanness and, when Cal looked at the scar, he shuddered at the thought of what the other man who caused that must look like—most certainly he was six feet under. This man didn't look like he lost fights or forgot grudges.

He was a thug through and through and Cal was already having fantasies of being held captive in his arms and being fucked hard.

The man's age was indeterminate, but it must be somewhere between forty-five and sixty. Cal would have thought he was on the high side of that except that his body was still hard as a rock.

His cock was hard as a rock too. It didn't look super big on the body he had, but Cal reasoned that it likely would look well over average on a man of regular size.

"Put these over on that table and come back here," the man growled. He handed Cal the whiskey bottle and the cigar and Cal took them over to the table between the two Victorian chairs. There was a dish there where he could put the cigar. He went back to the side of the tub, where the man encircled his waist with a wet, beefy arm and unbuttoned Cal's fly with the other hand. He fanned out the sides of Cal's britches, pulled the young man's cock out, gave it a couple of jerks, and then grabbed Cal's balls and jerked them down a couple of times too.

Cal grunted and gave a little cry of surprise and pain. The man laughed and, while alternately pulling Cal's balls and cock again, slapped him a couple of times on the rump.

"Take them off."

"Both? The britches and the shirt?"

"Yaw, just the britches. I like the shirt."

Cal stripped the pants down off his legs and tossed them aside. When he turned back to the man in the tub, the man grabbed his ass again with one hand and his balls and dick with the other and went back to prodding and pulling. He slapped the ass hard and Cal went up on the balls of his feet, gasped, and almost tumbled into the tub as the man pushed his index finger up into Cal's ass canal.

"You like this, boy?"

"Yes, sir, I like it fine," Cal answered, his eyes watering. But his dick was hard.

"Hard for me already, are you? I like that, boy. Levi tells me you're new. Still tight enough for a man to enjoy?" He dug around with one finger and inserted another. He was grunting and Cal was writhing in his grip and gasping and tears were welling up in his eyes. He was fighting for his balance, but the man wasn't helping him any there, and, with the man laughing in deep tones, Cal was pulled into the tub on top of the man.

"You want me to fuck you hard, boy?"

"Yes, sir. Please fuck me. Fuck me hard."

The man managed to reverse Cal on this body and dug the fingers of one hand in the back of Cal's head.

"Suck it," he commanded. He pushed Cal's head below the level of the water and was pressing the head of his dick into Cal's lips, which dutifully opened to him. The cock pushed up into Cal's mouth cavity, under water, and the man thrust up three times before pulling Cal's mouth back out of the water. Cal came up gasping, water streaming out of his mouth and down his chest. His shirt was soaked, a transparent film now, glued to his heaving chest. The man did it again. This time after Cal was allowed up to take a breath, the man thrust his hips up out of the water, following Cal's head up, and pumped up into Cal when Cal thought he would have his passageway open to breathe. He sputtered and gagged and the man laughed again, obviously very entertained by this.

But then they settled down for several minutes, with the man holding his pelvis up to the surface of the water so that Cal could work the cock above the waterline. At Cal's other end, the man was roughly eating his ass out and making sounds of pleasure.

Just when Cal thought they had settled into a rhythm, though, the man turned to his side, pushing Cal over and moving their bodies so that Cal was belly down in the tub and the man was on top of him. Pinning Cal's hips between his strong knees, the man, again with a grab hold on the back of Cal's head, pushed Cal's face under the water, again and again and again. Cal came up sputtering, all but the last two times, when he came up half drowned, with water shooting out of his mouth and over the raised back end of the tub.

Satisfied that Cal was totally subdued and half gone, the man pulled Cal's chest up over the end of the tub, with his arms dangling down the outside of the curved surface, mounted Cal's ass with a thrust upward inside the young man with his hard cock, gripped the sides of the brass tub with his fists, and plowed Cal hard and fast for twenty minutes to his ejaculation deep inside Cal's channel.

Cal just lay there, floppy and totally subdued under him, and moaned and groaned.

He was nearly unconscious when the man finally lifted the weight of his body off him and sloshed out of the tub. Cal lay there draped over the end of the tub, his arms dangling, without the energy available to move a muscle, and watched the man towel himself off. His body looked even more massive and muscle bound with him standing up on the floor than it had seemed in the tub. And on this frame, the cock and balls, if anything, looked slightly undersized. But Cal had had the cock inside him and could compare it with other men. He was no Ilesh or Frank, but he was close.

Everything about the man exuded anger and meanness—even his attempts at smiles were more like domineering sneers. The red bush at his groin and between his pecs and the red slice of a scar on his face supported that impression.

And it became clear that the rough assault on Cal in the tub hadn't calmed the man's demeanor down. Cal watched with tired, dull eyes but with his brain screaming fear and concern—and, dammit, arousal and anticipation—while the man walked over to the foot of the four-poster bed, fiddled around in the red drapes at the top of the posts on either side, and pulled down black leather restraints. From a bedside drawer, the man extracted a short, multithonged horse whip.

Tossing the whip on the bed, the man turned, with an evil grin on his face, and moved toward the tub. Cal whimpered and whispered, "No, please. Oh, god, no," as the man reached him and, ignoring Cal's plea, pulled him up from the tub with the strength of an elephant. Cal was carried over to the foot of the bed and trussed up by the wrists in the restraints, his arms spread wide, and his body sagging on the bonds.

The man ripped off Cal's sodden cotton shirt, now clinging to his body, and the flogging began. It wasn't too onerous, but Cal's back, buttocks, and thighs were criss-crossed with welts, a few bleeding in driblets, before the man released him, tossed him up on the bed, turned him on his back, spread and raised his legs, rolled his pelvis up, and fucked him hard for another thirty minutes.

Cal had remained hard throughout the flogging, much to the man's voiced amusement.

"It's what you like, isn't it, boy?"

Cal murmured, "Yes, sir, it's what I like." It's what he had to answer. He had no idea what the truth of the matter was, though. Nobody had ever flogged him before.

"Fuck me again, sir, please."

This also went over well with the man, but he didn't comply. After he had bathed again, leaving Cal to moan and to breathe wheezily on his back on the bed, and had dressed and left the room, a serving girl and the house boy came in and helped Cal over to and into the tub. He was asked—a couple of times before their words got into his brain—to turn over in the tub, and the serving girl applied salve to the welts on his back.

He looked up at the sound of his name. "Did you manage all right? Yes, I see that you're fine."

Levi Yost was standing in the room.

Cal certainly didn't feel fine, but somehow he felt that, as mean and nasty as the man had been, he'd been holding back. Cal felt like the man would have drowned him without the slightest remorse and that the whipping hadn't been with anything of the full force the man was capable either.

"He said you did very well. He's pleased," Levi said.

Cal felt like saying something nasty, but he needed this money and he'd been warned that some of the men would be rough. He hadn't equated that with cruel, but he knew that was his own naiveté. What he managed to mumble was, "Will he get rougher than this?"

Levi seemed to be pleased by the response—the acknowledgment that, the man being pleased, he likely would be coming back again before Cal left the brothel—and that Cal knew it and wasn't fighting it. "Not unless he becomes dissatisfied with you—or, perhaps, feels that there will be no further visits with you. I haven't told him that you are temporary. And, as I said, he was very pleased."

"And it's important that he is pleased? Who is he?" He watched as the serving girl and house boy stripped the bloodied sheets off the four-poster bed. His blood. He winced.

"Oh, I didn't realize you wouldn't know. It seems everyone knows. That was Warren Savage. He owns the Double O ranch, the biggest ranch in these parts."

Oh, Cal thought.

"He's also the silent partner in this saloon. He gets what he wants here."

Oh shit, Cal thought.

Chapter Five: The Double O Ranch

Warren Savage only visited the Hayden saloon and required Cal's services one more time during Cal's temporary work there. He was a bit more demanding and rough than the first time, and Cal sensed that this was something that would build in intensity until something gave—probably Cal's life. Thus, although the totality of the taking attracted Cal on some level, and he was forced to say it was what he wanted, which only egged the man on, he was relieved that he was only at the Hayden saloon temporarily and thus didn't have to worry about where it was going.

Despite Levi's advice to neither become attached to any of his customers nor to give his favors away for free, Cal met Frank more frequently. Never in the saloon again, but three times, in the morning, across the Yampa on land of the Double O ranch. They met in a lean-to in a gully Cal could get to on foot that was there as an emergency shelter in case one of the men was out on the range in the winter and was overtaken by a storm before he could get to one of the more permanent buildings scattered about the ranch.

Whoever got there first stripped and lay on blankets under the low, sloping roof of the lean-to. They would embrace and kiss and grope each other as soon as they met, making full use of every minute available to them. Whoever had arrived first would start off on the bottom. The first time Cal arrived first and Frank, stripping off outside the lean-to, came down between Cal's spread legs and lifted his knees with his own knees. He leaned over Cal's body, his hands around Cal's neck, his thumbs stroking under Cal's chin, and his forehead plastered against Cal's forehead, the two of them locking eyes to fully capture the effect of the coupling on each other. Cal's hands moved between their bellies, and he stroked both cocks together as they engorged. Then he rolled his pelvis up and guided Frank into him, giving a little cry at the thickness and strength of him—and then at the length of him as Frank pressed in and in and in. He stroked slowly at first, and Cal moaned deeply, a sound that was cut off by Frank's lips finding his.

Innnn, and outtt, slowly at first. Then increasing in speed and intensity. Cal grabbed Frank's buttocks and dug into the flesh with his nails as Frank pounded him, both of them lost in the fuck.

The second time Frank was there first and Cal straddled his pelvis and rode the cock.

The third time Cal almost left before Frank finally arrived, thinking that perhaps he had the date or time wrong. And when Frank did arrive, he seemed disconcerted and he fucked Cal roughly, in a more primeval, businesslike way like their first copulation rather than like the previous two hot, and almost romantic, couplings in the lean-to.

"Is something wrong, Frank?" Cal asked. He felt he knew what it was. Cal's time at the saloon was coming to an end. Frank would be wondering where, if anywhere, the two went from there in what could become more than casual fucking.

He was completely surprised and dismayed by the answer, which wasn't something he'd been prepared to hear. Once hearing it, though, he knew that he'd been stupid and shouldn't be surprised.

"I've seen Andy Reeder from up at the lumber mill on Hahn's Peak. You know Andy Reeder, don't you?"

"Oh," was all Cal could say. Yes, he certainly knew Andy Reeder. He knew him from Milo Mather's mill; they had worked side by side on more than one occasion. And he'd seen Reeder just two days previously—in the Hayden saloon. Like the other mill workers, Reeder had left the mountainside until tensions between the cattlemen and the sheep men and homesteaders settled down. Reeder had seen Cal in the saloon, and he'd found out what Cal was doing in the saloon.

For the life of him, however, Cal had not imagined that Frank and Andy Reeder would ever meet up and, even if they did, that they would have a reason to discover that they both knew Cal. Now he could see that that had just been wishful thinking.

"Reeder tells me you live in the Slater Creek valley—that you are a sheep man."

"I live there, yes. And I live on a sheep ranch, yes. But I was adopted. I have no stake in the sheep; I'm just living with an old man there who is no threat to the cattlemen. I doubt he'll have an opportunity to be a threat to anyone very long."

"I can't be consorting with no sheep man," Frank said. "If Savage found out, I'd be a dead man. So would you. This has got to be the end."

Cal processed this and sat on it for a minute, but then he answered, with a sigh. "It would have been the end, or close to it anyway, Frank, wouldn't it? I finish in Hayden and go back to the valley in a couple of days."

"They won't let you back in the valley."

"I got out of the valley when they weren't letting anyone in or out. I'll get back in. I can't just leave the old man there."

"What's the name of this ranch you live on?"

"Round and about it's known as Heaven; but it says Paradise on the signpost. But it's neither, Frank. As soon as the old man can be convinced to leave or . . . or dies . . . I'll be moving on. Maybe into Hayden."

"To be a fuck doxy?"

"Maybe and maybe not. That's how you found me, Frank. That's how you've used me. Does it matter so much now?"

Where was this coming from, Cal wondered. Frank had always been so impersonal about their fucking, giving the impression that he was just taking his pleasure on Cal's body—for free now. Cal was getting what he wanted out of the coupling, and it's true that he was having feelings for Frank. But Frank hadn't shown any indication that it was more than just a good fuck for him.

Frank didn't say anything. He just moved away from Cal and reached for his trousers and shirt.

"Or does what matter is that I live with the sheep men? Would it make it even worse if you knew that before that I lived with the Arapaho? That I was raised by them? That I'm no better than a half-breed. You're a half-breed, Frank. How do people look at you? As who you are, inside, or do they only think of you as a half-breed?"

"I don't think there's any more to say," Frank said angrily, as, standing outside the lean-to, he buttoned up the fly of his trousers.

The last time Cal would see that lovely horse-hung cock. The last time he'd feel it inside him. Nothing else was said. Frank turned and strode toward his horse. Cal watched him go, his heart sinking. The man was magnificent, even from the back. Back in the saloon that first time they'd fucked, Cal had fantasized on what Frank looked like naked. Now he knew, and the reality was much more arousing than the fantasy had been. But now it was over.

After he'd had time to be angry and sad and to mourn the loss, Cal gave a sigh and became resolved to how this had turned out. It would have only been a matter of days before they had parted anyway. He would have hoped that it wouldn't be because Frank had learned of the great divide between them—something that was larger than either one of them; something that, Cal believed, was silly nonsense.

But maybe a sudden, sharp break like this was for the best. Levi Yost had been right. There was nothing but folly in having feelings for men who bought your tail for their personal release. He turned his eyes to the south, toward Hahn's Peak. Three more days and he'd be moving out in that direction again. He missed Ilesh. Perhaps he'd take an extra day or two. Linger at the timberline above the mill, spend a day or two with Ilesh before returning to the drudgery and frustration of Heaven.

* * * *

The break with Frank wasn't as clean as he had tried to establish. Frank dogged Cal's trail all the way back to the southern slope of Hahn's Peak, where Cal picked up the Arapaho mountain trail that would permit him to bypass the cattlemen's blockade of the southern end of the Slater Creek valley. Frank had hung back far enough to think he wasn't observed by Cal, but Cal was aware of him—and was inwardly glad for the protective gesture. When he was close to the mountain, though, Cal evaded Frank as best he could. Frank was with the cattlemen. Cal didn't want to reveal to the cattlemen where the Arapaho trail started.

Also from the moment that Cal felt he had lost contact with Frank, though, he started to ache for him. But that was working to a dull ache. Just another disappointment to add to the others in his life.

Cal camped out for two days where the Arapaho trail branched off at the Hahn's Peak upper timberline to drop down from the western slope to the wider logging trail leading out of Milo Mather's lumber mill. He was waiting for Ilesh, who had told him to come to this point if he needed the Arapaho brave. Cal felt he needed Ilesh badly—to help him recenter himself if nothing else. He had fallen for Frank. He was able to admit that to himself after the break. It isn't what he wanted. It was as much a disaster for him to fall for a cattleman as it was to Frank to fall for a man living on a sheep ranch. And then, as another reason to camp a few days before returning to Heaven, there were the bruises and welts that Cal had to nurse and endure from his second visitation from Warren Savage.

Added to this was how, despite the roughness of Savage's fucking, Cal was increasingly aroused by the man. This was not the sort of domination that Cal wanted to fall under, but he could see that it could happen—that he could succumb to the sexuality of the man even while Savage was beating him.

But Ilesh didn't appear. The Arapaho brave had been so insistent that he would be here if Cal needed him that Cal hadn't even considered that it wouldn't happen. But why had he counted on that, Cal thought—just because Ilesh had been so positive and Cal hadn't ever known him to fail in what he wanted to do? Ilesh was a hunted man, continually on the move. There was no reason Cal should expect the brave to know that Cal was waiting for him there. And Cal couldn't afford to wait for another day.

His heart was heavy as he pushed the mule to descend to the logging trail and then north to the lumber mill camp. Being alone as he had been for four days on the trail now, he had the time to think on whether what he'd had to do, to give of himself, in the Hayden saloon was worth what he had received. He was coming home with more cash than he'd ever seen before in his life, that was for sure. But what was it for? It was to rebuild a shed to please his adoptive father, to allow him to live the false hope that life in the valley wasn't irrevocably changing—when, in fact, it was ending for sheep men like Old Henry. And until the mill was back in operation, the shed couldn't be rebuilt anyway. Was that worth what Cal had put himself through?

Other than that he had enjoyed being fucked, of course, having men wanting to be inside him. Even knowing that they were willing to pay for it had a little thrill of its own. He could do this, what Samuel was doing, more than just occasionally, he thought. It was another option for him. And he didn't have many options in life.

By the time he was riding into the lumber mill camp, he had decided that, yes, it was worth it. Henry and Lizbeth had taken him in and given him everything they could in life. What was happening in the valley was going to happen no matter what; it was bigger than any of them. Cal had to just keep on being a son to Henry as long as he could. The big issues would just have to take care of themselves.

For now, Cal had a new problem, a new concern. The mill camp was truly deserted this time. Not even Hiram was there, and it didn't look like anyone had been there for several days. All of the perishable supplies in the kitchen had gone bad and had not been removed. He already had been disturbed before he got to this point, however. Next to the logging trail as it entered the camp was the camp's graveyard. Fatal accidents were an occupational hazard in a logging and lumber mill operation, men working here didn't tend to have family nearby, and the mill was isolated from most of the civilized world. So, it was natural that there would be a graveyard near the camp. But it wasn't natural that there should be a freshly dug grave—dug sometime while Cal was on his journey to and back from Hayden—there. And yet, there was a freshly dug grave. And it didn't have an improvised wooden cross stuck in it as there would normally be.

So, Cal was steeled against some tragic mishap when he rode into the deserted camp.

There wasn't anything here for him other than supplies, so Cal didn't dawdle. He picked out the biggest logging dray that he was confident the mule could pull with a load in it. On this he loaded lumber still around in the mill yard that he thought could be used to start the building of the shed at Heaven. He would settle with Milo Mather later; he did have an order in for the planks and their mutual trust would make this an easy transaction. On top of this he loaded all of the nonperishable foodstuffs that he could find in the camp's kitchen. He left a note for Hiram to that effect in case the man was just away from the camp. Hiram wasn't very mobile, though, so Cal didn't think there was much of a chance that Hiram had strayed from the camp on his own. Chances were good that he'd come to his senses and somehow gotten down to one of the ranches in the valley—or that someone down there had come for him and convinced him to leave the camp.

That was if the freshly dug grave wasn't his. And if it was his, who had dug his grave?

The answers, Cal, hoped were waiting for him down in the valley. If anyone would know what had happened, it would be Mrs. Thornton, at the schoolhouse where this path from the mountain joined with the valley road. The school—and Mrs. Thornton—were where all the news of the valley gathered.

Cal's first stop in the valley would be the schoolhouse anyway to leave off the nonperishable provisions he was bringing from the mill camp.

* * * *

Nobody told Cal that they knew anything about what had happened up at Milo Mather's mill in the past two weeks. Hiram either didn't come down into the valley or he didn't linger around the schoolhouse or any of the places to the north of that up to Heaven long enough for anyone to mark his presence. As soon as he guided the dray into the homestead compound, Cal went up to the graveyard and buried the money he'd gotten in Hayden between the graves of Lizbeth and one of her young girls.

"Glad to see you giving your respects up on the hill first thing when you get back," Old Henry said, who had come out to the front porch when Cal returned to the house. "Looks like you got enough money for the lumber for the shed, though it looks like the shed will need a mite more than that."

"It's all the mule could manage, Pa. Yes, I got enough laid by for the shed lumber. When I've used these planks, I'll go back to the mill for more." Henry was already half way in his own fantasy world. Cal saw no reason to disturb his thoughts further on how things really stood around here.

And he did what he could to continue to let Henry drift along.

Cal was out nailing boards to the corner posts of the shed he'd sunk in the ground when three riders trotted up to the front of the house. Cal recognized cattlemen when he saw them and made it to the front of the porch by the time Henry had come out of the house. Henry was carrying his rifle. Cal hadn't thought to keep his with him by the shed. He moved quickly to stand between Henry and the mounted men.

"You Cal Cowden?" One of the riders asked Cal as he came around the corner of the house.

"That's me," Cal answered.

"We've come to fetch you. Mr.—"

"Can we discuss this off a bit?" Cal asked, giving a gesture toward the old man on the porch in a way that only the riders saw him. "Don't want to be making anything out of this that isn't necessary."

The cowboy gave him a hard look and then shrugged and said. "Yeah, I guess so. We were told not to put any holes in you. Way we heard it, you're the one with a hole to be plugged." Both of the men sitting on horses behind him gave a snort. Both had their hands on their holstered rifles, though, and Cal didn't doubt that one or both could get off a shot before Henry could get his rifle lifted and pointed.

So this was what this was about, Cal thought. No killing needed to happen today if he kept his wits about him and didn't fight the inevitable. "Just some men from Hayden, Pa," he turned to Henry and said. "Something about the job there, I think. I'll talk to them."

When they'd pulled off a bit, the lead cowboy said, "Mr. Savage sent us to bring you back to the Double O. He wasn't pleased when you weren't at the saloon the last time he visited. So, he thinks you should be at the ranch now."

"I was only at Yost's temporarily," Cal said. "He'd have known that if he'd asked Levi Yost."

"Well, Yost didn't tell him, and Mr. Savage isn't happy. He wants you to visit him at the ranch."

"I have work to do here . . . and how did you know to find me here?"

"Frank Barlow told us he'd heard you came from a ranch named Heaven in the valley. He didn't tell us it would be a sheep ranch. But I guess we could figure that out for ourselves. And maybe Mr. Savage don't care. Maybe you could make it worth our whiles not to tell him."

The men were looking at Cal with faces full of speculation. He didn't know whether it was money or tail they were after, but he figured he'd find out soon enough.

"Frank? He's not with you."

"Said he wouldn't come. Said he didn't feel well this morning, so we came without him. You gonna give us shit about this? We could shoot the old man and burn the place and you'd still have to come with us."

"You plan on doing that anyway, the way I hear it," Cal said.

"Not today. Not if you come with us quiet like. And if you make sure that old man doesn't do anything stupid."

Cal turned toward the porch. "There's some more construction needs done in Hayden, Pa. I need to go help with that. The shed'll have to wait."

"You'll have to take the mule again if you have to leave right away, then," Henry answered. "John and Harv have the horses out at the other end of the spread."

"That'll be fine. I don't think I'll be gone long," Cal said. Let the old man live his illusions as long as he could, Cal thought. For Cal, though, he didn't think he'd ever be back here again. Or still be living for long, if it came to that. Especially now that Warren Savage knew he was from the sheep folks.

It was a two-day trip back down the valley and onto the Double O ranch. When they stopped for the night, Cal found out it wasn't money that would buy these cowboys' silence about finding him on a sheep ranch. Each of the men had him in succession bent over a saddle by the fire and in more than one round through the night.

* * * *

Warren Savage took Cal immediately from astride his mule to his bedroom in the big house when they arrived at the Double O ranch and kept him there through to the next morning. Cal had seen Frank from a distance when they'd ridden up to the house, but Frank, looking miserable, just turned and walked unsteadily off. Cal didn't see much of anyone for the next three days. He was kept in a small bedroom in the ranch house with a serving girl tending to his welts and bruises.

Savage had indeed been angry Cal had been taken from under his nose at the Hayden saloon and he also had a much larger collection of toys in the ranch house than were kept in the big room on the second-floor, front of the Hayden saloon.

On the fourth day, Savage visited Cal in the small, locked room Cal was being held in and informed him that he hadn't been brought to the ranch for Savage's exclusive use.

"I'm tired of the men having to go into Hayden to get their entertainment," he said. "I've already brought Faye out and she's in her own cabin for the use of the men who want that. I've put the men who don't want what she has in a bunkhouse all their own because they are too disruptive when mixed with the other men at night. You're going into that bunkhouse, and your job will be to keep them happy. I'll send for you when I want you."

"You can't keep me here," Cal said in a weak voice. It was just an act of desperation, and he knew it.

"I can do whatever I want with you. You're lucky. If you'd stayed in the valley, you'd probably be dead this time next week. Being here, you should last longer. No guarantees on that, of course."

"Within a week?" Cal asked with a shudder. Savage didn't answer. He just turned and motioned to a couple of the men who were standing in the hallway, turned, and left.

The men carried Cal, only barely able to walk yet, slung between them, out of the ranch house and across a dusty yard surrounded by several other log houses. Out beyond these to the south were some sheds and a horse barn.

Four other ranch hands, all burly and licking their chops, were waiting in the bunkhouse Cal was dragged to. Those that weren't naked got naked quickly, and Cal was gang fucked by the six of them on one of the bunks.

"Great idea Mr. Savage had," one of the men growled. "Said we don't even have to pay for it; we've just got to keep our work up to his satisfaction."

"Just part of the herd now, sweetie," one of the other men said, slapping Cal on the bare rump. Cal was lying on his belly on the narrow bunk, with his arms dangling down each side and a glassy look on his face.

"Just like one of the cows," a third man said. "Just another Double O animal meant for breedin'."

"Hey that gives me an idea," another of the men chimed in. The men who were speaking were gathered around watching the sixth man take his second turn. He was straddling Cal's hips and fucking down into him. Cal was well past the groaning stage.

"What's that?" A man asked.

"He's Double O property now. What do we do with Double O cattle to make sure they come back if they just wander off?"

"You mean we could—?"

"Sure," the guy with the idea said. "When Dan's done with him, we'll take him out to the branding shed."

This did make Cal moan and protest, but if any of the ranch hands heard him, they didn't make like they had.

"But won't Mr. Savage—?"

"He'll think it's funny. He'll probably also think it's a good idea. We took him off a sheep ranch. It's not like we'll be keeping him long."

"A sheep ranch?" Cal said, with a groan. "You know that I—?"

"Everybody knows you came from a sheep ranch," the man answered before turning and spitting derisively into a bucket. "Your life ain't worth a plug nickel around here. As soon as we wear your ass out, you're for wastin'."

They'd done it, Cal thought miserably. This wasn't one of the men who had come to take him away from Heaven. They'd told everyone on the ranch—probably Warren Savage too—where Cal had come from. He knew then that it was just a matter of time. They didn't value his life any more than they did a single steer on their range.

They hustled Cal across the yard and over to the branding shed. The iron was being heated up and Cal was stretched out over a branding frame and struggling weakly and objecting in a low, exhausted voice, when Frank appeared around the corner. He was carrying a rifle, trained in the direction of the clump of men, none of whom had come away from the bunkhouse with firearms or much in the way of clothing, for that matter. Most even were barefoot.

"First man who moves that iron anywhere close to that young man's ass is gonna get plugged," Frank said. "And it won't be somewhere that you're gonna recover from in this lifetime."

"Ah, Frank, we're just having—"

"Mr. Savage sent me down from the big house to tell you that if any of you does any more harm to this man, he'll flay you alive. He's just lending him to you. He's to be in good condition with Mr. Savage needs him. A festering brand on his rump isn't good condition."

"Sorry, Frank, we—"

"Leave him there. Mr. Savage is in the smoking shed. He wants to see you all there. Now."

Sheepishly the six men moved ahead of Frank, still holding his rifle, even further to the north of the ranch compound and over a hillock to where the smoking shed was. It was a strong-walled, well-insulated log building to serve its purpose. It also had only one door and no windows, and the door was a strong one, with a heavy bar on the outside. When the six men were inside and trying to pick Warren Savage out in the darkness, Frank put them in total darkness, pushing the door shut and lowering the bar.

He hurried back to the branding shed.

"Do you think you can walk on your own?" he asked Cal.

"I don't think I can do anything on my own for some time to come. What are you doing, Frank?"

Frank stood there, as if in indecision for several minutes. Finally he said, showing some regret, "Well, fuck, I guess I couldn't explain you escaping this way anyway. Come with me. Your mule's in the stable, whatever you brought, clothes and such, is still in the saddle bags out there. I guess I knew this was the way it was going to be. I've got my saddle bags loaded too. Come on, I'll help you there. We're leaving."

"You're going with me?"

"Not like you might think, but like I said, it wouldn't be too healthy for me to stay. We can get a head start if none of the other hands see us ridin' out of the stable or what direction we went in. The guys in the smoke house will be settled for a while."

"But my mule. It won't move fast."

"You came with the mule; it's yours. My horse is mine. If we take another horse, they can shoot you on sight as a horse thief—not that they'd have to worry much about shooting you on sight anyway. But we'll go back north and lay low for a while. Maybe in the lean-to we were meeting in. I can take the rides into Hayden and stable them there and walk back to the lean-to. Once they get a party rustled up, they'll assume we're headed for the valley or Hahn's Peak."

"You told them I'd used a trail on Hahn's Peak. And about me living at the Heaven ranch?"

"I couldn't help it. Savage beat it out of me. He'd been told that I'd been with you."

"So he knew even then that I was with the sheep men."

"Yes, I think he's always known. Yost probably would have been too scared not to tell him as soon as Savage revealed that he was partial to you. And Savage must be partial to you, or you wouldn't have lived this long."

It was only then that Cal noticed the bruising on Frank's face and that he wasn't moving real steady himself as they hobbled to the stables.

After four days hiding in the lean-to and eating cold hard tack and coffee because they couldn't chance a fire, Frank decided it would be safe for him to retrieve the horse and mule from Hayden and to ride to the start of the trail Cal knew on the northern slopes of Hahn's Peak.

At the trailhead, Frank held up.

"You're coming with me, aren't you?" Cal asked.

"No, at least not now," Frank answered. "I know the cattlemen are about to make a move on the valley, and I'd best try to find out more about that. It just ain't right what they're fixin' to do. But even then, maybe it's best that I just head west, where there's less of all of this."

"Including less of me, I suppose," Cal said in a small voice. They had not fucked in the four days they were huddled together in the lean-to. Cal would have been willing, but Frank held back. And both of them were beat up enough that it would have been pretty painful.

"Yeah, I guess that's right. You be sure not to linger in that valley. You said you had something to get from there before you could leave, but then you leave, you hear?"

"You could stay here and we could meet up when I came back out," Cal said. He was just fooling himself. He knew he wouldn't walk off and leave Henry if there was going to be an assault and burning in the valley. But his wants were somewhere else. "We could both go west."

"Yeah, maybe. I'll think about it."

But it didn't seem to Cal to be something that Frank really was going to think about. "Well, good-bye then. And thanks for saving me back there." He turned the head of the

182

mule toward where only he could tell that a path up into the mountains started.

"Cal," Frank said in a strangled voice. Cal turned back and Frank grabbed his head between his hands and brought their faces together in a deep kiss. And then, with a sob, he released Cal, turned his horse south, and galloped off.

Chapter Six: Fire Down the Valley

Cal nosed the mule under the bar as he turned into Heaven. Looking up, he saw the weathered chunk of wood on which he'd carefully carved the word "Paradise" when he'd first come to live with the Cowdens. Looking beyond that, up the length of the valley and then even higher, up the flanks of snowcapped Hahn's Peak, his heart went zing as it always had at the first glimpse of the sun rising in Antelope Gap. Paradise. Looks were deceptive. Neither Paradise nor Heaven any more. He wished he had time to change that sign to "Hell." It had been one of the few things that Lizbeth and Henry had struggled over—whether the name was to be Paradise or Heaven—and even there it was more banter than fight. Paradise it had been—at least until there was no one to argue with Pa; everyone in the valley called it Heaven now, but Cal hadn't bothered to change the sign. He thought now, that it was his way of agreeing with Lizbeth. She always got the short end of the stick living here. She might as well have naming rights. He'd refer to it as that from now on except to those who already knew it as Heaven.

"Don't know what the fuss was all about," Cal muttered to himself—as he so often did as he entered under the name plaque. As he saw the deteriorating farmhouse and the shed, only a third done and he was nearly out of lumber already, bitter bile rose in Cal's crop, and a shiver of fear and dread—and of deep regret for what was unfolding—ran up his spine as his eyes came down from the majestic heights of Hahn's Peak. His attention moved, caught by movement, to the glitter on the slopes of the upper valley that he knew could not be explained by the fingers of sunlight peeking through the gap and glinting off the roof of the Estes place—and then up the dirt track to the weathered wooden, slightly leaning family house. And his gaze moved at last to the old man sitting, leg propped up on a flour barrel, rifle across his lap in the old rocking chair of granddad Isaiah's that Lizbeth and Henry brought all the way out from Pennsylvania on the wagon.

"Damn stubborn old coot," Cal groused under his breath as he cantered the mule, foaming at the mouth and shuddering at the withers after the mad dash up from Hattie Anderson's, where Cal had been helping round up the livestock, what was left of them. It had taken him far too long getting Mrs. Anderson out of the house. And then even more precious time aiding in herding sheep and the old woman alike up the shale-sided shanks of the western valley wall, toward the hidden wagon trail through Mint Creek gap that had been hooked into the road down into Craig just for this possibility. It was a trail that all of the sheep ranchers and homesteaders had carefully kept secret from the cattlemen. Or at least they hoped they had. Cal, in turn, had kept his own route to the east on the slopes of Hahn's Peak as his own secret escape track.

Craig, in the northwest corner of the new state, was a center for the sheep trade. It was about the safest place any of the sheep people and homesteaders could go now until the federal troops arrived—if those troops ever got sent here. For all Cal knew, it could be like the Indians. The government might just leave it for the strongest to do the whittling down and then just come in and put its stamp of acceptance on a deed already done.

Cal tried to stare the old man down as he approached the porch. Riding the fences of the land he'd had plowed, thinking he might switch over to farming, and at his age. And his feeble mental condition. Just like Cal had told him not to do when he'd gone down to Hayden. Henry had done that while Cal was at the Double O ranch. Cal would never have let Henry go out to the fenced field if he'd been here. Of course Henry would break a leg. And at the thought of the word "fences," the bile at last surfaced, and Cal leaned over and spat it out on the dusty dirt that had once been his playground. Fences. It was all because of the fences. And that Homestead Law. They'd all managed before that—not all that fine, but they'd never come close to anything like today.

Cal was beyond the end of his rope on any of this business.

"Hope you're not thinkin' of sittin' there and restin' that mule all day, son." The voice was raspy, old—rough, but his foster father's affectionate tone, not the one he used when he wanted to get your attention real fast. The dust of forty years of hardscrabbling sheep herding in his throat.

"Sorry it took so long, Pa. Mrs. Anderson had to be pulled out of there clawing and scrathing, the old biddy."

"Always did like that Hattie," Henry said with a low chuckle. "That girl had spunk."

"Pa, don't you think it's time to . . ." The mule shied and Cal had to reach a soothing hand down on its neck to calm it. The mule's nose was twitching, not liking the scent on the breeze wafting down the valley, bringing images of smoke and heat—and fear and death.

"The widow Thornton down at the schoolhouse will be needing help, Cal. That passel of young ones she's got are probably running in all directions. And best you get a move on. Not much time now." This caused them both to look up the valley. Pockets of flame—mere small bonfires from their perspective—dotted the sides of the valley slopes. They both knew better, though. The Estes place. It hadn't been sunlight.

"The widow Thornton? The schoolhouse and the orphans?" Cal answered with a snort, tearing his eyes from what he didn't want to see. "They wouldn't. Surely they couldn't—"

"Never can tell. Not when blood is on the rise like it is today, son," Henry responded. He grimaced and loosened his grip on the rifle he had been holding tightly across his lap. Then he reached out and rearranged his leg on the flour barrel top to a more bearable position.

"Damn cattlemen," Cal growled. The mere thought raised more bile, which, leaning out from the side of the mule, he spat out on the ground.

"Don't curse them, son." Henry's voice was stern. "And not in hearin' distance of the house. Your ma never could abide no cursin' this damn close to the house. No, cattle and fences don't mix. The cattlemen always had a point there."

Cal had very reason to curse the cattlemen, but that wasn't something he was going to tell Henry about. "Then fuck those interferers down in the capital," Cal persisted. He'd kept it in too long. He was to the bursting point.

"Them neither, Cal. They done what they thought was best."

"But why, Pa?"

"Sometimes there ain't a good answer to the question 'why,' son. Farms need fences just as much as cattle and sheep need open range. And the cattlemen claim the sheep shear the pasture too close for it to be any good to cattle. The three just don't go together. And there're more folks movin' in from the East all the time. And they have to eat every day; they can't wait for the end of a cattle drive to get their next meal. They need the farms and lamb to eat when the cattle are needed to produce cash. Cattle have been king around here, but time and need bring changes no matter what we like or don't like. Passin' a law requiring a homestead claim to be fenced just gave point to the inevitable. If anyone is to blame for that, it's the claim jumpers. The cattlemen knows the fences change the balance. It's man's curse to think he can fix everything. Sometimes life is just too big for mere man."

"Where are John and Harv?" Cal asked, wanting to change the subject—wanting to change everything, in fact, but helpless in the wanting.

"I sent them out an hour or two ago. Up over the Mint Creek divide."

"Well, I'd best go around and fetch the wagon, and then we'll go on to the schoolhouse and be on our way after we gather up Mrs. Thornton and the children," Cal said after giving Henry a hard look.

"I sent John and Harv in the wagon, son. They needed it for Lizbeth's fancies."

"Lizbeth's fancies?" Cal was incredulous, nearly overcome with frustration and powerlessness.

"She'd never forgive me if those got scorched."

That had done it. The flash of an image of the unspoken future. Actually putting reality in that one word, "scorched." Cal's shoulders went down in defeat and tears welled up in his eyes. There was no hiding, and the options were all floating off in the ash-scented breeze. It was like Henry wanted to slam shut all of the trap doors.

The two faced off there, hopeless and seemingly helpless for the longest moment—Cal barely hanging onto his perch on the increasingly skittish mule and the old man motionless in his rocking chair, grimacing at every twitch in his shattered leg.

The moment was burst when Cal saw Henry's gaze move off his face and to the left over his shoulder, up the valley. Cal turned to see the unmistakable flicker of flames in the uncomfortably near distance. "The Greiners?" he whispered, denoting a sheep ranch not more than five miles south of the schoolhouse.

"I reckon so," Henry answered in a dry voice.

Cal slid down off the mule, tied the reins around the porch railing, and mounted the creaky porch stairs, headed for Lizbeth's rocker on the other side of the doorway from where Henry sat. When he'd come off the mule, he'd pulled his rifle out of the saddle holster and carried it up onto the porch in the crook of his arm.

"What are you doin', son?"

"I figure I'll sit and rock with you for a while, Pa."

"Don't you sit down there now. I asked you to go help Mrs. Thornton and her children. You never disobeyed me before. Don't make this the first time. And take the mare. That mule there looks spent—just like I feel."

"But the mare's yours, Pa. You've never let anyone else ride her after Ma—"

"Until now. I don't think Lizbeth would want her here either. The mule's fine with me now."

Both stubborn as all get out, Cal thought. He had never heard such a deep and trembly voice from Henry before. Henry had always been in control. A rock.

"Pa . . ."

"Don't you argue with me now. Lizbeth would never forgive me if I let you . . . if we didn't do this charity for Mrs. Thornton and her children. Don't forget who saved you and raised you well enough for us to take you."

Cal was beyond exasperation. "Lizbeth's dead, Pa. She's been gone nearly these three years now. She's dead and buried up there in the cottonwood grove, Pa."

"Don't . . . you . . ." Henry was angry now, angrier than Cal had ever seen him be. But as sudden as it had come on, it was just as quick to dissipate, and Cal watched his foster father age twenty years before his eyes.

"She's not dead to me, son. Lizbeth's alive to me. She's more and more alive to me with each passing minute . . . now. And more to the point, she's alive in you. Just because you didn't come out of her don't mean that she didn't put all that was good in her into you too. And I want it to go on bein' that way."

"It ain't worth it, Pa," Cal persisted. "This little piece of scrub here in this valley just ain't worth it."

"All of our lives, Lizbeth and me worked hard to get to heaven son, and this is it. This is our heaven. I'll not be cursin' or spittin' in the wind, but I'll not be givin' up on Heaven, either. Don't deny me this dignity . . . or bring more grief to me than is necessary. Mrs. Thornton needs our help—your help. And time is runnin' out. Now, you go on to the barn and bring out the mare. I suggest you not try to take Mrs. Thornton by the canyon road toward Dixon. There's somethin' nasty waiting for any folks trying to come out of the canyon—just like there is at the southern mouth of the valley. And you can't use the hidden road most of them took across the western ridge to Craig either."

"Why not?" Cal asked.

Henry lifted his rifle barrel and pointed it toward the western ridge. "Looks like the burnin' has already come past where that trail starts over the ridge. Best way I can think of is straight up Slater Creek to Milo Mather's mill. I don't think they'll go that high. But best keep on movin' from there. There's a logging trail from there meetin' up with the new trail over the gap toward Hayden. Go on now. Make me proud, as I know you can."

Cal knew all about that logging trail, and Henry knew he did—when Henry was all here. But Henry was slipping away from Cal. He was already drifting off into the world where he could meet up with his Lizbeth.

It was the hardest tug Cal had ever had on the commandment to honor your pa and ma for him to bring out the mare, guide her under the Paradise sign, and not look back to catch the tears in Henry's eyes.

Just as Henry had thought, the widow Thornton was beside herself with useless action when Cal got to the schoolhouse—not that she would be useless in her own action, but the children had no concept of impending disaster and were giving her fits. But just seeing salvation coming down the road on his mare was enough to put her action to better use in gathering up the children and figuring out at last how to yoke the old gelding to the wagon.

"Here, let me help you up into the wagon," Cal was saying as he heard the rifle shots echoing off the mountain walls and noticed Mrs. Thornton's attention go up the valley and her eyes open wide.

"Isn't that . . . ?" she muttered in a tremulous voice.

Cal looked around, and he almost collapsed against the wagon at the sight of the flames rising above the knoll just over two miles away. Since his youth he'd been able to locate his family's homestead from any point he happened to be standing in up and down the valley.

"Yes," he managed with a clutch in his throat. "I think that's Heaven." God, he thought, they are coming down from the north too. He must have made it on the road just before they got to Henry's place.

"Heaven," Mrs. Thornton said, drawing the word out long as if it was the last word she expected to be hearing that day—which, no doubt, it was. And then they both took in the full view of the valley stretching out to the south of them, from the sun on the rise to the east, its radiant beams glittering off the snowcap of the majestic Hahn's Peak and then sinking down into the deceptively beautiful, green valley, its slopes and undulating floor dotted with a hundred bonfires of the dying homesteads.

"I had never thought I'd actually see it," Mrs. Thornton said in a small, awe-filled voice. "But there it is, yes. Heaven. Heaven descending into Hell on earth. But why?"

"Why?" Cal asked, his voice choked with tears for the paradise that was lost. "A stubborn old coot once told me that sometimes there isn't a good answer to the question 'why,' Mrs. Thornton. Sometimes life is just too big for mere man. I reckon he knew what he was talking about."

"I just don't know, Cal," she said. "It makes a person just want to sit down and let it wash over them."

Cal's thoughts went back to Henry. That's exactly what he'd done.

Mrs. Thornton must have read his thoughts, because she then said in a voice with a catch in it, "Henry?"

Cal gave her a look that told her all she needed to know. Then the two boys of the six children they had in the wagon began scrapping and this brought Cal back into the world.

Mrs. Thornton staggered back and she leaned into the tail of wagon, her shoulders going down in defeat. Cal gently reached over and pulled her back onto her feet.

"You've got these children to get to safety, Mrs. Thornton. You've taken care of them so long already that it would be a waste not to get them out of here. Up in the wagon with you, now, and let's head on up the slope to Mather's mill."

Half way up the track to the mill, they met Frank riding hell for leather down from the mill. He pulled his horse up short a few yards from the wagon.

Cal's hand instinctively reached for the stock of his rifle where it was sheathed at the side of the saddle. Frank equaled cattleman in his brain. But he just couldn't do it. If this was it, he wasn't going to fight.

But Frank sat there on his horse, not pulling his rifle out either.

"Frank. I thought you—" Cal started to say.

"It's just not right, Cal. This just ain't right. I came to see what I could do."

"We're trying to get these children out of the valley," Cal said. "This doesn't have anything to do with them."

"Then let's do it," Frank said, turning his horse around to move back up hill.

They made it up past the lumber mill camp and onto the logging trail before Frank's horse reared up, and he started to pull his rifle out of his saddle holster.

Cal almost was too late in raising a hand and crying out. "Wait. Frank! Don't. He's my campmate."

"Your what?" Frank exclaimed. Although the declaration was enough to keep him from pulling the rifle—at least for now. It helped that Ilesh looked like he wasn't carrying a weapon of any kind and he had an arm in a sling.

"I was raised with him among the Arapaho. He is as one with me. I can't explain it any better."

"Jivin," Ilesh called out from the opening to the Arapaho path up the mountain from the logging trail. "You're safe. I was coming for you."

Despite everything that was happening, Cal's spirit soared. He wasn't alone. Two men who meant a great deal to him had come for him.

Mrs. Thornton had thrown herself protectively over the children when she'd first seen the Arapaho brave half hidden in the trees, but she relaxed noticeably at Cal's explanation of who Ilesh was, fully aware of his story and having heard that all was not a trial in the life Cal had led in the tribe.

"I told you down near the ranch, when we were in the lean-to, that I had been raised in my first years in an Arapaho tribe, Frank. Ilesh is my Arapaho campmate. All of the children of the tribe are raised together and grow close to each other. But what has happened to you, Ilesh? Your arm."

"It's the shoulder, Jivin, and it is healing. It was a clean wound. I was shot from a distance on the mountain near to where you left it to travel over the plain to the town you were going to."

"You followed me? I told you not to."

"I had to know you were safe."

"The new grave at the camp," Cal said. "I thought that maybe—"

"I came into the camp and found the old man had died. I had visited him before and we had become friends. I buried him."

"Ah," was all Cal could say. "But your shoulder. How could you—?"

"I didn't say it was easy," Ilesh said, with a bit of a twinkle in his eye. "It had to be done." He changed the subject. "Is it safe for you to go beyond the mountain?"

This was the question that had plagued Cal the whole time since they had started up the mountain. Even following the logging trail that met up with the track going toward Hayden would mean they'd have to go over Double O land. And Hayden itself was Double O territory. Savage's men were busy in the valley, but they would be going back to the Double O and to Hayden eventually. Would Cal have time to move on? He turned and looked to Frank, who shrugged and looked worried.

"We could chance it." Frank said. "Leave this woman and the children in Hayden and then go farther west together. Surely they wouldn't harm a woman and children in Hayden. They aren't of either the sheepherders or the farmers. We might have time, but . . ."

"But if they intercepted us and I was with you, no one in the group would fare well, would they?" Cal said.

Frank just looked at him and shrugged.

Then Ilesh spoke gently, "They might be better just with this man, Jivin. You can come up the mountain with me. You would be safe with me, at least for now. And this woman and these children would be safer from here without you."

Cal looked at Mrs. Thornton now. "It wouldn't be just me and the children, Caleb," she said. "You are one of my children too. Your safety is just as important to me. Go with your Arapaho campmate."

"You need to decide," Ilesh said quietly. "They may not be content to stay in the valley. They may come up the mountain looking for stragglers such as these."

Cal made his decision. He hoped that Ilesh wouldn't know how painful the decision was for him until later, when they were alone. "Take them, Frank. But when you get off the mountain, don't turn toward Hayden. None of you will be safe there. Head east for Steamboat and then take them all the way to Denver."

"If that's what you want," Frank said, a bit of sadness evident in his voice.

"And, Frank. When you get to Denver. Stay there. I will find you."

Frank's face opened up into a broad smile and, with one long look back at Cal, he started to get the wagon moving again south along the logging trail.

Cal turned and looked at Ilesh, whose face showed an emotion he'd never seen before but that set into its normal calm and determination to adjust to the reality of the world. Cal wouldn't have to tell Ilesh. Ilesh had figured it out for himself—and would be the first to acknowledge that Cal going to his own kind in Denver would be all for the best.

"We go to the valley beyond the mountain now. You will be safe there," Ilesh said, as he and Cal started up the narrow path toward the tree line.

"We can't go far, for a few days or more, Ilesh," Cal said. "I must go back. I have money buried at the ranch. I'll need it."

Ilesh stopped and put a hand on Cal's arm. "I know you need to go back for more than money."

"Yes," Cal said in almost a whisper. "Henry will want to rest beside Lizbeth. But I swear, Ilesh, I then will be done with the past and all of this cattlemen, sheep men, homesteader business."

"And also with the Arapaho?" Ilesh asked.

"No, never with you," Cal said, answering the question that Ilesh could not directly ask. "Even when I've gone to Denver—and, yes, to that man who was just here, to Frank—I will still come back to you, again and again. Sometimes I think that when I lived among your people was the only time I truly was in a civilized world. I don't want to lose that—or you."

"I am content," Ilesh said. And this simple statement lifted a great burden off Cal's heart.

Ridden West

Chapter One: Kansas

Sitting on a hay bale in the loft of the barn, Jeremiah ran his fingers into the blond curls of Billy's head and forced the young man's mouth down on his hard cock. Billy was on all fours between the older man's spread legs. Jeremiah moved one hand down to flare open his unbuttoned fly and gruffly demanded, "The balls too, son. They seek your love too."

Billy dutifully licked and sucked on the man's balls. The smaller, younger man was naked, except for his boots. His flannel shirt, jeans, and underdrawers had been hastily cast away to the side on a line of progress from the top of the ladder along the rough, hay-dusted wooden floorboards of the loft. Sunlight streamed in from the large opening at the end of the wall for pitching bales, but the light didn't quite reach where the two men were crouching. Jeremiah, tall, thin, gnarled, and hardbodied, was still in his britches, but his white cotton shirt was beside him on the hay bale, and his suspenders were off his shoulders and drooping at his side.

Still, he was in readiness to pop up and get himself together at the first call of his name by his wife from the adjacent house. She was ever suspicious. She was constantly checking up on where he was in relationship to where the orphans they housed were. There were things left unspoken on the farm, but very little not known. Jeremiah was careful not to touch until a boy in his care legally became a man, though. Jeremiah was a Bible reading, God fearing man, he was.

Jeremiah ran his calloused hands down the smooth, pliant skin of the back and the flanks of the young man crouched between his thighs. When he reached the nicely rounded buttocks, he slapped them, kneaded them, and spread them open. Holding one butt cheek open, he moved the other hand into the stretched crack and rubbed across the rim of Billy's butthole. Billy moaned and moved his mouth back to the thick cock, taking it half way down into his throat in one slide. Then he grunted and groaned, as Jeremiah dug a finger into the hole and gyrated it to help open the young man up. Billy would have to be open wide for him. But he had proven to do so quickly. Jeremiah extracted the finger and thumped it on the hole, being met by another moan from Billy. He thumped it again and then moved two fingers into the hole, which opened to accommodate them.

Rising from the hay bale and reversing their bodies, pushing Billy belly down on the hay, and crouching behind him and between his spread legs, Jeremiah gave more attention to the hole, fingering it, spitting on it.

"Open to me. Give yourself fully to me," he mutter. "Yes, relax, let it open."

He buried his face in the crack and began eating the hole out, encouraging it to open more, as a hand latched onto Billy's cock and balls, no more than a handful for this farmer with the large, calloused hand. Jeremiah milked the young man's cock while he ate out his ass.

It wasn't long before he was back up on his feet, between Billy's thighs, working his thick cock into the stretching—but not really fast enough—hole, while Billy clutched at the straw of the bale and buried his face in Jeremiah's white shirt, inhaling the musky sweat order of the man who had been his master for the past ten years, and his secret lover—if what was happening here could be called love—for the past four months.

Fully saddled, Jeremiah grabbed Billy's legs and pulled the young man's ankles up to hook onto his shoulders. Then he reached down and wrapped his arms under Billy's pits and pulled the young man's torso off the hay bale, arching his lithe, willowy torso up toward his chest. He moved one of his hands to where it was buried in the curly blond hair of the young man's head and pulled the head back cruelly.

Holding the young, flexible body suspended over the

hay bale in front of him, Jeremiah began to stroke inside Billy's passage, digging deep, stretching the channel walls wider as each stroke thickened and lengthened the cruel cock.

Panting hard, his hands pulled back to grip the back of Jeremiah's head in an attempt to hold himself steady in the extreme bowed, totally controlled position Jeremiah had put him in, Billy was babbling quietly to himself, saying who knows what? Jeremiah certainly didn't care. He had his eyes closed and was thrusting in ecstasy, thinking that Billy was the best one yet.

Jeremiah had done this with a succession of foster sons he had raised, subtly cultivating the boy until he had come of age and holding off on sending him out into the world until Jeremiah had initiated and had the use of him and another one of his foster sons was coming of age.

The man didn't notice when Billy jerked and spilled his seed on the dusty floorboards. He only cared that his own explosion was building—and then firing off in four strong bursts of cum up into Billy's intestines. And then Jeremiah reveled in the afterglow of the pleasure of the mellow coming back to the world as he continued to languidly stroke inside the small man's passage, until he slowly let loose of Billy's body and let it sink into a trembling pile at his feet.

Jeremiah reached down and clutched and raised Billy's head by his hair and turned Billy's face to his dripping cock, demanding in action that it be cleaned. Billy opened his mouth to the cock.

A far-off voice, a woman's voice, called, "Jeremiah, Jeremiah. Where have you gotten too? I see out in the field that the reins are slipping off the plow horse out in the field and Michael isn't being able to get them back on."

Jeremiah let loose of Billy's hair and reached over him for his cotton shirt.

"Time you got out in the potato field, Billy, and earned your keep like the other boys are doin'. Best I go sort Michael out. God help me, it's a chore keepin' all you orphan boys sorted out and contributing your keep. What do you say, boy?"

Billy looked up at the farmer who also ran the makeshift Kansas orphanage he'd been at for the past ten years. Jeremiah had stuffed the tail of the shirt into his britches waist and was buttoning up his fly. He was a tall, rugged, gaunt man, with a stern expression. Billy's image of him was always one of carrying around a Bible and thumping it as he harangued the boys on the whereabouts of the edges of the straight and narrow.

"Thank you, Brother Jeremiah," he said, by rote. "Thank you for taking us lost boys in and giving us food and shelter and work. And thank you for loving me and giving me the special attention that you do."

"And you best remember that. Now get on out into the potato field. And you know not to talk of this. This love between us is our own secret." He was looking from the hay loft out to the field, where an almost-ripe Michael was struggling at the plow. Jeremiah welcomed Michael's difficulty. Helping him with the plow would be a moment of instruction and preparation.

Billy wasn't naïve enough to think this was, indeed, love. He did receive pleasure from Jeremiah's attentions. When he'd first been taken four months earlier, it had given him release from doubts and frustration. He, in fact, would be happy receiving more of this attention from Jeremiah. If only the man weren't so stern about it all of the time. If Jeremiah took and looked like he took more enjoyment from it beyond those moments when he was past control and doing what animals naturally did, Billy would take more enjoyment from it as well. It couldn't be much of a sin if Jeremiah was doing it.

Jeremiah was still pulling his suspenders up when he came out of the barn, a gesture that wasn't lost on Mary, his wife, looking out the kitchen window. She had thought that Jeremiah was probably in the barn with Billy, the oldest of their orphans—older than she'd thought she had just yesterday discovered by going through the birth certificate records. She'd have something to say and do about that, yes she would, and soon. She then wasn't the least bit surprised seeing Billy, small bodied, which made his age deceiving, and more beautiful, with his blond curls, dark-blue eyes, ready smile, full, sensuous lips, and slim, but well muscled, body, than handsome as he came out of the barn, tucking the tail of his flannel shirt into the waist of his tight jeans.

Mary expended a puff of air and put extra elbow grease into washing out a pot. She'd do something about this—right soon.

* * * *

Billy walked out into the potato field. Four others working out there raised arms in welcome. The oldest of the orphans at the farm, actually, at nineteen, well past the time he should be here, Billy was well liked. He had a sunny disposition and was always quick to lend a hand. There was no resentment that he had not been out in the field with them earlier. A few of the boys had a strong notion why he hadn't been, and, although they felt sorry for Billy, they were just glad it was someone other than them—and that it meant that Jeremiah wasn't out here in the field ordering them around. Despite having taken them in when no one else claimed or wanted them and clothing and feeding them—and not making more work demands on them than any father would do in the hardscrabble recently minted State of Kansas in the late 1870s—Jeremiah was a hard, humorless man.

As the orphans worked, they talked.

"You must be gettin' on old enough to leave and move on to a new life," Luke said. He was taller and bigger boned than Billy was, as several of the orphans were, but he wasn't as old. His voice sounded a bit wistful. "I will be sorry to see you go, but I envy you," he continued.

"I reckon I will leave soon, yes," Billy answered.

Luke and Billy exchanged meaningful looks. They both knew that, if and when Billy left, Luke would be the next one to be worrying about special attention from Jeremiah.

"Any idea where you want to go, what you want to do?" Steven asked.

"West," Billy said. "I've always thought of going West. All the way to California."

"Panning for gold? Making your fortune?" Luke sounded hopeful.

"I think the gold has panned out in California," Billy

answered. "But the thought of California sounds like gold to me anyways."

"And it's far away from Brother Jeremiah," Clyde chimed in in a quiet voice. Clyde was a shy boy, not much larger than Billy, although near his age, and, like Billy, more beautiful than handsome.

Billy looked at Clyde. He knew that Clyde was like him in wants. They had met in the blueberry patch behind the outhouse in recent weeks, lain side by side, and given each other release with their hands. Billy wondered if, when he left, Jeremiah would be after Clyde rather than Luke as he now was after him.

"Yes it is," Billy answered, adding, "And speaking of Brother Jeremiah, we'd best be back at digging up these spuds. He's sure to count them when we're done and expect a certain number of them to be there. Although he's never likely to tell us how many he expects on the chance that we'll bring in more than that."

* * * *

Inside the house Mary was accosting her husband.

"You know, husband, that we are licensed only to keep the boys until they are eighteen."

"Of course I know that, woman. You don't have to preach my business to me." He uttered it with such finality that he probably had an inkling where Mary was going with this.

"You know your weakness, Jeremiah," Mary said, poking a finger into his chest, which looked rather amusing, as he was nearly six and a half feet tall, and she wasn't much more than five feet. "You know the laws—the law of orphans and the law of men."

"I don't know what you mean, woman."

"I mean Billy. I've been lookin' at the birth certificates, and, thank God he's nineteen, not younger, as you have allowed. But there's the orphan laws. We can't still be havin' him as an orphan."

"I don't know if I can give him up," Jeremiah said in a despairing voices. "You know my passions."

"Your passions are displaced, Jeremiah Atwell," Mary said with a good deal of force behind the statement.

"Not displaced. Just broad. I still be fancying you," Jeremiah answered, grabbing at Mary's bodice and pulling her to him, taking her mouth in a brutal kiss, as his hands ripped at the buttons of her bodice, freeing her breasts, and squeezing them, as he pushed her down on the floor, pulled up her skirting, working at the buttons of his fly, entering her strongly, and beginning to pump.

Sighing and moaning under him, Mary clutched as Jeremiah's shoulder blades. This was the Jeremiah she wanted. Not the other Jeremiah. This was the Jeremiah she'd fight for.

* * * *

Later, not long before twilight, Billy was wandering down near the stream, where the bushes were thick, when he heard them, when he heard the moaning sounds like he sometimes made himself of late. Creeping up to a clump of bushes, he spread the foliage enough to see that the cook was on her back on the ground, and Lem, one of the hired hands, was between her legs, holding her pinned to the ground with strong hands holding her upper arms to the moss. His hips were in high gear, fucking her.

Billy had barely started to watch, one of his hands unbuttoning his fly and pulling his hardening cock out, when he was jerked up from behind by a hand on the collar of his shirt, shaken hard, turned, and thrown off toward the stream bank, away from the bushes where the hired help were fucking. Jeremiah strode over and jerked Billy up again, and tossed him further down the stream bank. And then again and again, until the two of them were in a clump of bushes themselves, a stand of bushes with the trunk of a huge tree laying on the ground between the bushes.

Billy got tossed across the log, the wind forced out of his sails, the small of his back on the log, and his torso arched over it and down, so that his shoulder blades pressed into the moist moss on the other side.

Jeremiah was standing over him, breathing hard, an

201

angry look on his face, holding a short riding whip. "You are not to look at such as that," he barked. "I will provide all of that that you need to know of such as that." He leaned over and struck, three times, with the whip, twice on Billy's chest and once on his thighs. Billy winced, more in shock and surprise than pain, the flannel shirt and jeans being of heavy material, and started to roll away from where, vulnerable, he lay.

Jeremiah reached down, grabbed the front of Billy's shirt, and put him back in place. He ripped the shirt open, popping buttons left and right, and then grabbed the waistband of Billy's jeans—the young man had unbuttoned those and flared them aside himself when he was watching the hired help coupling—and jerked the jeans off Billy's legs.

He struck again and again with the whip, this time on exposed flesh, as Billy writhed under him. The whip had stung him on the belly, on the upper thighs, and on the exposed cock and balls. Billy was embarrassed that he had gone hard under the lash.

Realizing, perhaps, what he was doing—and the effect it was having on Billy—Jeremiah stood up over Billy, whip at his side, panting hard. He paused there for the longest minute, looking down at the small, more beautiful than handsome, young man. His eyes went to the manifestation of Billy's involuntary arousal, erect, twitching, and throbbing. Billy's hand went to his cock.

"My God, I've got to have you," Jeremiah muttered, as he pushed the suspenders off his shoulders and unbuttoned the fly of his trousers. He sank down on his knees in front of the log and between Billy's spread leg. His hands glided up Billy's red-welted chest, as the young man winced and groaned. Pressing his hands into the hollow of Billy's shoulders where his arms connected to his trunk, Jeremiah held the young man's torso stretched out over the tree trunk and descending to the other side.

Making little grunting sounds, Jeremiah licked and kissed up Billy's torso as if that was going to make the welts go away, while, resigned, Billy let his arms go, stretched out from his body and parallel to the tree log, putting him symbolically into a cruciform position, prepared for the sacrifice—in heat and wanting it now. He groaned and jerked as Jeremiah's cock entered him. Jeremiah's mouth found Billy's, and he went into a deep kiss. Billy lifted his ankles to Jeremiah's shoulders and the deep pumping began.

Wild with arousal himself, surprising himself that the whipping had made him hard, Billy focused his attention on the possessing cock and set his pelvis in motion, meeting Jeremiah's thrusts forward with thrusting his hips forward as well, to take Jeremiah deep as he relaxed his passage walls and set his interior muscles to undulating over the thick, plunging cock.

For the first time, it was more than Jeremiah's taking Billy for his own need—it was two lovers, both with red hot need and lust, going at each other for their own separate want of the use of the other's body. They moved their pelvises against each other in concert, thrusting and withdrawing, thrusting, thrusting, thrusting, Billy holding on for dear life, taking as much as he was giving. Fully into the fuck.

For the first time Billy could feel—could connect with—the muscles of his passage walls, which gripped and undulated over the invading shaft, caressing it as it moved inside him, causing Billy to groan as his channel muscles pulled the cock in deeper—and prompting Jeremiah to groan in pleasure as well, surely aware that, for the first time, Billy wasn't just a dormant receptacle for Jeremiah's need, but had a need for this himself. Going molten soft inside and opening as never before, Billy took the older man's cock deeper, thicker than ever before, and the two tensed together, jerked together, came together, sighed and relaxed together, tensed again together, came a second time together in a weaker afterglow, and felt their tension melt away into a soft final sigh together.

Afterward, still crouched over Billy's body and flaccid inside Billy's channel, Jeremiah pressed his lips into the hollow of Billy's throat. Pulling a bit away, he whispered. "Don't leave. I have to go for supplies for a few days, but don't let Mary let you leave while I'm gone."

Billy didn't have the foggiest notion what Jeremiah meant by that, however his thoughts soon went to the present.

He could feel the older man thickening again inside him, and he emitted a low moan, whispered, "Yes, yes, yes," under his breath despite himself, scared a bit that the lashes of the whip had only enhanced his own arousal, and clutched at Jeremiah's shoulder blades, as the man's hips went into languid motion once more.

"Yes, yes, yes, fuck me, Master," Billy murmured under his breath.

Jeremiah did so, hard, thick, and deep. The second fucking was as totally open in giving and taking as the first one had been. The two now fully lovers.

The next time they had sex, all Jeremiah had to do was show Billy the hand whip and flick it and Billy was hard, on his back, with his legs open, and panting for the cock. Billy's Achilles heel in sexual terms had been uncovered.

Chapter Two: Ridden Westward

"Is Colorado near California?"

McCoy winked at Givens and replied, "Almost spitting distance."

Billy was inside a coach traveling west from the Kansas orphan farm. They'd barely started on the journey before McCoy, the man in a black suit sitting across from Billy, started telling Billy where they were going and what the deal was.

Nothing had been said about this back at the farmhouse when the men had arrived and Mary had called Billy in to tell him that he was going with them. Jeremiah was off on his supplies buying spree. Billy had spied Jeremiah fucking Clyde in the hayloft the afternoon before Jeremiah left on his trip, so Billy didn't really care where Jeremiah was just then. He was hurt that just when he'd gotten around to wanting but Jeremiah gave, Jeremiah was giving it to someone else. And once he'd heard one of the men in the black suits tell Mary that they were headed West, Billy didn't have to hear any more to be good about going with them.

"We're going to a mining town in the Colorado Rockies called Cedar Hill," McCoy told Billy. He was leaning in toward Billy in the compartment of the couch, which meant that he almost was in Billy's lap. The distance between the two facing seats was so narrow that the man's knees were nearly in Billy's crotch. Billy's legs were spread around the man's. The other man, Givens, who was pretty silent and who was shorter, beefier, and somewhat younger than McCoy in appearance— but also wearing a black suit—was sitting beside Billy in the forward-facing seat.

A black man was up top, driving the team of horses. Billy hadn't seen many black men in Kansas, but he knew that there were some who had drifted there away from the Civil War fought some ten years earlier. If this black man had been in the Civil War, he would have had to be very young when he did it, Billy thought. He appeared to be a strapping, large-framed, very muscular young man.

"You'll be working in a saloon," McCoy continued. "They need fresh, young men coming in to work the saloons in those mining towns. You'll do quite well from the look of you."

"Thank you." Billy couldn't think of much else to say. As long as it was getting him close to California, he didn't particularly care what his job would be. It would be his first job as a man—leaving the orphanage. Even if he'd been told straight out it involved sex with men, Billy was way beyond being shocked by that.

"Mrs. Atwell says you have no relatives."

"Not that I know of—none that have shown up for the last ten years," Billy said.

"It's hard to believe you are nineteen," McCoy said. "Or even eighteen for that matter. But I have a birth certificate here that Mrs. Atwell gave me that says you are."

He looked at Billy as if he expected Billy to explain the difference between what was in print and what the man observed, but Billy had nothing to offer.

"We lose track of the passing years in the orphanage. I can't remember any life before that," was the best he could offer.

McCoy put his hands on Billy's knees and pushed the young man's legs apart a bit more. At the same time Givens put an arm around Billy's neck and palmed Billy's bicep.

"Mrs. Atwell assured me that you lay under men. Was she telling the truth?" He was giving Billy an intense look.

"Under men?" Billy answered with a questioning look.

"Yes. She said you would let a man put his pecker inside you. That's our interest—whether you'll let strangers plow you for money. I must know if she lied. If so we will take you back and recover what we paid for you. The job in Colorado requires you to let men fuck you. Will you lay under men?"

How did she know? Billy wondered, feeling panicked. He was shamed and embarrassed all at once. But why should

206

he be? He hadn't chosen that. It wasn't his fault that it seemed natural enough to him. He could never go back now. And he didn't want to go back. He wanted to go to California. He'd do anything to get there.

"I might will lay under men," he answered, hedging as far as he was concerned, but that wasn't exactly the way the two men heard it.

"Any man you're told to?" Givens asked.

"If I be paid for it, I guess it don't matter much if I know them or like them."

It was like both men had been holding their breath to that point. Smiling, McCoy moved his hands to between Billy's legs, running his fingers up and down Billy's crotch. Billy felt himself becoming aroused. Givens moved a hand to the back of Billy's neck and ran his fingers up into the blond curls on the back of Billy's head.

"We'll need to have proof of that," Givens said.

"Proof?"

"I'm such a man you'd have to lay under—so it this other man here. You'll have to lie under both of us. And of course we can't go too much further on our journey without testing out the quality of what you will do with a man."

"The quality?" Billy asked, somewhat confused.

"The quality, yes, how well you do lying under a men— how much pleasure he gets from penetrating you, moving inside you, and releasing his seed. How well you make him hard and pleasure him. Am I embarrassing you?"

"No," Billy answered not wanting to appear naïve. But scaring me more than a little, he thought.

"Have you sucked a man's pecker?"

"Yes," Billy answered. It was, after all, the truth.

"And you have had a man's pecker inside you?"

"Yes."

"Deep?"

"Yes."

"And he has moved it inside you for a while? And released his seed inside you?"

"Yes."

"Good. And we must test for endurance. I can tell that

you will be popular, in high demand. Do you think you can have one man pull out of you and another man enter you almost immediately? And even more men than two?"

"I don't know," Billy answered with a shaky voice. "There has only been one man."

"Was the man thick and long?"

"I don't know," Billy answered honestly. "How does one compare when there is only one man . . . oh."

Both men had unbuttoned themselves and had their cocks out in their hands. Billy reddened a bit.

"Yes, the man is thick and long," he answered. He didn't want to say more to make the men angry, but there was nothing special about the size of McCoy's cock, although it was growing in his hand as they spoke. Givens was quite thick, but nothing as long as Jeremiah was.

"I am going to undress and fondle you now," McCoy said. He didn't ask for permission, but he gave Billy a quizzical look.

Billy knew that it was now or never to object to this—to object to everything that these men would do to him. And, if they were laying out the job fairly, everything other men would do to him, probably many men. He set his sights on California and steeled his will. He had no skills or talents. He was coming out of an orphanage. He'd lived his entire life on a dreary farm, scratching out a dreary existence. No past or family or attachments. It was up to him to make his own way, using whatever he had to work with. He had a body that inflamed a man—Jeremiah. Maybe it would inflame other men as well. That's what he had to work with. Still, this was getting a bit too much for him. Going too fast, being too much in the open on what they wanted to do.

"I don't know about any of this. Maybe I shouldn't go with you. You could just pull over to the side here and I'd—"

The stinging slap came as a surprise. Billy's head snapped to the side, and McCoy's hand connected with another slap when he turned it back. It more than stung him. It both told him they were serious, this had gone beyond the turning back point, and it had aroused him. He felt himself harden. He lay back in the seat and gave McCoy a glazed look.

"You gonna fight us on this, boy?" McCoy growled.

"No, sir, I'm not," Billy answered meekly.

"Are you going to let me inside you—let me take my pleasure in you, in exchange for being taken to a new and better life?"

"Yes, if that is what you wish," Billy answered.

"You've done this before. This isn't taking anything from you that you haven't given before. Now, after we have our proof, you will be doing it for money—not giving it away for free. Do you understand that—accept that?"

"Yes, sir," Billy answered.

"Show me."

He moved his hand down to his crotch to cover McCoy's, looked directly into McCoy's eyes, and didn't flinch as McCoy unbuttoned his fly and pulled his cock and balls out. Billy knew that he was going hard, but, after observing what was between the legs of Jeremiah and the other orphans at the farm, he knew that he didn't measure up well. But McCoy surprised him.

"Ah, small balls and cock. There are men who will be very aroused by these."

He started tugging off Billy's jeans, while Givens palmed Billy's head, turned it to him and took Billy's mouth in a kiss. For the next several minutes, McCoy fondled and manipulated Billy's cock and balls, ending up by stroking Billy's cock and voicing pleasure at how well Billy filled out. Givens continued possessing Billy's lips while unbuttoning the young man's flannel shirt with his free hand.

As he felt himself ready to come, Billy struggled to come out of the kiss, but Givens held him close. He was pinching and thrumming Billy's nipples with his free hand. Billy gave a couple of jerks, released a muffled cry, and shot his load.

McCoy laughed. "Nothing wrong with the force of ejaculation on this one." At McCoy's command, Givens came out of the kiss.

"You said you have given a man mouth play," McCoy said. "Come down on your knees and service me."

McCoy's low moans while Billy was sucking his cock

seemed to indicate that Billy passed that test. He also left McCoy with a throbbing erection.

Givens had pulled Billy's shirt off his back as Billy was sucking off McCoy, so Billy now was naked, while the two men were fully dressed in their black suits, with just their cocks protruding from the flies of their britches.

McCoy grabbed Billy's legs under his knees and pulled him onto his thighs and then onto his throbbing cock, working hard initially, despite not being oversized, to get his bulb into Billy's entrance. But when he had, his eyes flared and he laughed, as Billy's channel pulled the cock inside. "Good, very good," he muttered.

He ran Billy's legs up his chest, grabbed hold of Billy's hips, and started pulling the young man on and off his cock. Givens went up on his knees on the seat, turned his pelvis to Billy, palmed Billy's head, and put the young man's mouth on his cock.

When McCoy had come and Billy was panting and sucking on Givens' cock, McCoy signaled Givens, who reached down and twisted around, bringing Billy's small body around to the corner of the seat, with one leg stretched along the base of the backseat rest and the ankle of the other leg being hooked on Givens' shoulder, as the stocky man grabbed, squeezed, and separated Billy's butt cheeks and brought his now-open entrance, glistening with McCoy's cum, down to sheath and draw in Givens' thick cock.

Billy moaned and sighed as Givens fucked him. Both black-suited men were impressed that Billy took them both in succession without objection or a lot of noise, other than groaning, snuffling, and an occasional encouraging, "Yes, yes, just like that." Once they started in on him, he went with the fuck, moving his pelvis in rhythm with them, pulling them in deeper when they thrust and going back up with them as they withdrew, keeping them well sheathed.

Clearly the young man enjoyed being fucked.

When Givens had finished, he reversed Billy again, setting him down in the center of the seat, while McCoy grabbed his ankles, raised and spread his legs, came down between the legs, entered him strong again, and began to pump hard.

Several minutes later, Billy was plastered to the far corner of the backseat, sitting into the corner at an angle. He was panting heavily and looking at the two men at the other end of the seat with wary eyes. Givens turned toward him, coming up on his knees and holding his thick, hard cock in his hand. He looked into Billy's eyes, and Billy returned the look.

Out of the blue Givens slapped Billy across the face. When Billy turned his face back, he was licking at a trickle of blood in the corner of his mouth and gave Givens a hooded look. "Fuck me," he murmured.

Givens slapped him again.

"Fuck me," Billy repeated, the pleading coming out in a moan.

Slowly Billy reached down, grabbed his ankles, and raised and spread his legs. He rolled his pelvis up. "Fuck me," he repeated, the invitation addressed to Givens. Givens slid across the seat on his knees, palmed and raised Billy's butt cheeks for a straight shot, and thrust inside Billy's now-gaping hole and started to pump as Billy threw his head back and cried out, "Yes! Fuck me hard!"

The young man, setting his mind to dreaming about California, obviously had passed the endurance test.

"You are a treasure," McCoy said with a tone of awe in his voice. "Men will pay well for what you just welcomed. This man at the farm. He used you roughly like this?"

"Yes. After he realized that it gave him more pleasure."

"And that it gave you more pleasure too?"

"Yes," Billy admitted.

The two men looked at each other and smiled.

A few hours later, the couch came to a stop and they all got out and moved to the side of a stream to eat the meal that Mrs. Atwell had prepared for them for their journey.

The four men separated, seemingly by class, to eat their meal. McCoy and Givens went down to beside the stream and sat on rocks. Billy, barefoot and clothed now only in his trousers, gingerly settled down, with a sigh, between the roots of an oak tree. The black driver, identified as James, stood near the driver's box of the couch.

As they neared the end of their meal, McCoy walked over and said something to James, who grinned. McCoy went back to Givens, said something to him, and then the two men walked up to rocks near the oak tree and sat down.

Billy's attention, though was on James, who started walking toward him, a big grin on his face, his short horse whip in one hand. He was pushing his suspenders over his huge biceps with the free hand and letting them drop to the side. And then he unbuttoned his fly and let the britches slide down his slim waist and hips.

Billy gasped at the sight of a cock thicker and longer than Jeremiah's. The muscles of the man's thighs bulged and, despite the slimness of his waist and hips, the man's buttocks were two plump orbs. Then his eyes went to the hand whip and he licked his lips.

Reaching Billy, James reached down and grabbed the young man by the throat, making Billy gag and clutch at the choking hold of the big, strong hand. James held him there, cruelly, off the ground, pressing his forehead to Billy's and capturing his eyes, while he stroked his cock hard with his free hand. Then he slammed Billy back down on the ground between the roots, taking the air out his lungs. Billy's eyes went big as he saw the hand go up in the air and then descend, fast. Billy gasped and groaned as the thongs of the whip caught him on his chest. He rolled over and took two more strikes on his bare back.

Then, though, Billy turned onto his back, scrabbled at the buttons of his fly, flared his trousers, and pushed them down to his knees. "Yes, fuck me," me cried out to the black bull. "I ain't gonna try to fight you off. Take it, if you want it. I want it. Put that big one inside me."

Leaning down, James pulled the trousers the rest of the way off Billy's legs, grabbed the young man's right leg and hooked the ankle on his shoulder, and grabbed the other leg and held it out to the side. The black bull sank to the ground on his knees, and Billy arched his back and cried out his passion at taking it big, black, and deep, to the leaves on the branches overhead as the black giant thrust inside a hole still gaping open from earlier penetrations and began to pump hard.

The two men in the black suits leaned forward, watching Billy's reactions carefully.

"That un likes a bit of a jolt to git goin'," Givens said.

"I can see that. There will be a lot of that where he's going, I reckon," McCoy answered. "Good thing he likes it. Great thing for our pockets that he likes it. Even better that he's a pretty boy—at least for now. A gold mine we got here, Mr. Givens."

As James set a rhythm and the shock of the assault flowed out of Billy, young man raised his torso to James' chest, unbuttoned the black man's shirt, and started sucking on the taut nipples on the man's bulging pecs. Simultaneously, he set his pelvis in motion, working with James in the deep, thick fuck.

Billy widened his stance as much as he could, dug his claws into James' shoulder blades, and used everything he'd learned in the last couple of weeks to open his channel, go soft at the core for the big, black cock, and take it in deep. He set his pelvis in countermotion to the thrusts. James opened his eyes wide, in surprise, and thrust all the harder and deeper, finding Billy's passage muscles able to clutch his cock, ripple over it, and pull it deeper. Billy's gasps and groans were a match for the black bull's own.

"Yes, take me hard! Take me deep! Work me with your big, black cock! Fill me with black buck cum!" he cried out. Billy wasn't thinking about California now. He was thinking about taking a bigger man than Jeremiah—bigger in all dimensions.

He was meant for this. He was meant to be FUCKED by a big-cocked STUD!

McCoy and Givens exchanged smiles. The young man had passed the quality test.

When the two men were spent, James walked over to the two white men.

"You gots yourselves a real sweet whore there, gentlemen," he said. "I'd pay good money to get inside that again."

"You won't be given a chance to pay for the likes of

that where that whore's going," McCoy growled. Best you get on up in the coach now. You were just a test for him— whether he can and will take a cock like you got. We see that he can. We sure can see that he will take it.

Billy still lay there, panting hard, on the ground where James had left him. He'd taken a cock the size of James' yes— and enjoyed doing so. At the same time, he sure as hell hoped they didn't get much bigger than that.

* * * *

It took the coach ten days to reach Denver. When they'd done so, Billy asked, "Could I see the Pacific Ocean from the tops of those mountains over there?"

"Not quite," McCoy said, giving Givens a wink.

Each night en route to Denver, the couch pulled up to a saloon. After a brief discussion between McCoy and the saloon manager, they were given two rooms. McCoy and Givens shared one room and James was given a pad to sleep on outside the door of the other room, which was assigned to Billy, and where he opened his legs to and otherwise entertained men sent up to the room by the saloon manager throughout the night to cover their lodging and food bill.

When Billy wasn't thinking about California and about getting almost there, he was feeling the surprise that he had discovered he walked along the clouds having a man's cock moving inside him, and that he liked variety. He had found his talent. McCoy and Givens had told him he needed some steeling and toughening in the craft before they got to their destination, so he didn't question them on whether the men plowing him in the night paid for it and, if they did, where the money was going.

Chapter Three: Colorado

They stopped at a work house in Denver and picked up Timothy. Another orphan, Timothy had aged out of an orphanage and had gone directly out on the street. A saloon owner had tried him out in his upstairs operation and had offered him a job, but Timothy wanted to work his way farther West, he'd said. So the saloon owner, for a finders' fee, had written to McCoy.

They were in Denver for three days before starting up into the Rockies. Cedar Hill was a copper mining town in a valley inside the mountain range to the northwest of Denver. It would take them another three days to get there over rough terrain. The stopover in Denver was for McCoy and Givens to put Timothy through his paces to see if he could be sold in Cedar Hill along with Billy.

Apparently he passed with flying colors. Within Billy's hearing, Givens had said, "He's a tough one. It will be a good pairing. Timothy can take the cowboys and miners and Billy the farmers and shopkeepers. That way Billy will last longer."

That didn't sound too good to Billy, although he kept thinking that he wouldn't be doing this for too long—just long enough to get a stake to go over the Rockies and down to the Pacific Ocean at the base of the range. When he'd seen the mountains from Denver and had remarked on how high they were, he'd asked if the ocean was just on the other side and had received the affirming, "Just about."

On the third day, he worked up the courage to ask Givens—not enough courage to ask McCoy—"How come this saloon in Cedar Hills has the need for two new ones? Did the old ones go over the mountains to California?"

Givens had answered, "It's a job where fresh men are always welcome, and, yes, probably, the men holding the jobs before just went on to California." Then he changed the subject. He bit his tongue from adding, "or on to glory."

When they got to Cedar Hill, mostly a scattering of shacks on a mountainside with mine shaft openings and one short street of stores, the saloon, a commercial stable, a small hotel, a doctor's office and infirmary, a jail, and a bank at the base, Billy was to find that there was to be no division of labor between him and Timothy in terms of the occupation of the clients.

As soon as the men of the town—there were few women, and no young ones, even among Billy's and Timothy's female counterparts upstairs at the saloon—heard there was fresh young male tail for sale in town upstairs over at the saloon, they were swarming in—miners, farmers, cowboys, storekeeps, and even the sheriff and his deputies. Men needed their sexual release. In circumstances where there are no or few women—on naval ships, in prisons, or in frontier mining towns like Cedar Hill, they learn to make do with what is there. What was normally in Cedar Hill other than at the saloon was mostly grizzled, rough-mannered men aging before their time. Occasionally, a young, good-looking one came thinking he was going to mine gold, but he invariably became the one mined and either moved on within days of arriving or got shot standing between two men fighting over his ass.

Billy and Timothy were handsome young men with supple skin and good muscle tone. In Cedar Hill, that otherwise was known as "fresh meat." And fresh meat didn't stay fresh here too long. That the saloon put a price on their asses took all of the guessing and running to ground work out of getting mounted and spouted.

Once in residence upstairs at the saloon, neither young man left the room assigned to him for five days. In that time, neither one closed his legs, and for that time, it was a rare occasion that one cock pulled out of either of the young men's asses more than a minute before the next one entered it for a twelve-hour period six days a week.

Billy didn't get just the storekeeps, bankers, teachers, and farmers. He got the cowboys and the miners too. The miners weren't so bad. They tended to be weaker and older and coughed a lot, taking only a few thrusts before producing weak ejaculations and being satisfied that they had managed that. The main trouble with them was the black dust under their nails and in the creases of their skin, much as the farmers had dirt there. The farmers were most diffident, hurried, and stingy with their tips—meaning they didn't tip the prostitutes.

The bankers, clerks, storekeeps, and teachers did their business quickly, entering from the back of the saloon and leaving the same way. Often a hand job or blow job was enough to give them relief and send them on their way.

The cowboys were nearly the roughest. They could ride a horse for days, so they could ride a man's ass for hours, given the money to do so. All of the men fucked with their boots on, but the cowboys, in shape, full of cum, and in town for only an hour or two, were prone to coming upstairs drunk and full of vinegar; using their boots as directional devices, toeing or kicking Billy and Timothy to the position they wanted to fuck them in; holding them down with the booted foot; and mounting and fucking them with such energy and vigor that the springs of the bed squealed and the headboards drummed against the walls of the room.

But the worst of the worst were the sheriff and his deputies. There was no one to tell them there were any limits to what they could do. They chose Billy, already exhausted, lying on his bed panting and moaning and unable to close his legs, on the fifth day.

The sheriff's idea of foreplay was fists and riding crops. The three men worked Billy over real good before they fucked him in a round-robin double penetration orgy. It only added to the liberties they took that Billy responded to the beating with arousal and begging for the fuck. After the first couple of times, he was able to handle the double fuck without passing out. Still, they did it so much that damage was unavoidable.

On the sixth day, Billy went to the doctor's infirmary, and the saloon owner put in an order for another male prostitute with McCoy and Givens, who were on their way out of town.

On the tenth day, Billy was back at work, though, and most men in town who wanted male tail and who could afford to pay for it had already spent their monthly allowance for this pleasure. Business upstairs at the Cedar Hill Saloon slowed down. Cowboys still came to town, but to hold the fort until McCoy and Givens arrived with fresh meat again, the saloon owner was directing most of these to Timothy, who indeed proved to be a tough bird. Of course he'd had two years on the streets of Denver before coming here and Billy had not.

One day there were two cowboys paying for services at the same time. The saloon owner looked them over and sent the less mean looking one to Billy's room. He had picked well.

The cowboy, giving his name as Chet, was a lover. He was young and good looking. He'd come from wealth in Virginia and was in the West for the adventure. He talked with Billy while they slowly undressed—whereas most clients were in a hurry to get Billy stripped and the only thing they needed to adjust in their clothes were the buttons on their britches' flies.

"Your body is so beautiful," he said, sitting close to Billy and stroking Billy's cock after he'd encouraged Billy to do the same for him at the same time. "How has a man as beautiful as you come to be here, in this town, in this room?"

"I was an orphan in Kansas. I'm working my way to California."

"California is my goal too," Chet said, but then, having helped Billy strip down to the skin and both of them being in erection, talking ceased and the only sounds to be heard were Chet working down Billy's lips, throat, chest, and Billy returning the favor with his tongue, teeth, and lips, as Chet laid Billy back on the bed.

"This is so nice and not what I'm used to," Billy murmured, averse to pointing out that the minutes were ticking away and wanting to be fair to this well-mannered and arousing cowboy, "And we must watch the time. Best that you put it in me now."

"I've paid for two hours of your luscious body," Chet answered. "I expect I'll put it in you and give you my seed at least twice in that time. I'm not in a hurry. I find taking it slow increases the pleasure when I've gotten inside a guy."

Before Billy could respond to that, Chet had swallowed his cock and was giving him slow, deep head. Other men sucked Billy's small cock, but few took much time with it before they were inside him and getting as much bang for their buck that they could.

Chet was taking his time, making slow love to Billy's body—worshipping Billy's body even—before gently rolling Billy onto his side, pulled into Chet's belly, bending Billy's left leg up into his stomach for a clear shot into the young man's gaping hole and at the moment of taking Billy's lips with his, slowly entering the young man's passage and languidly starting a stroking journey to the quick of him. He was right about being methodical in that Billy's passage was open to him and aching to caress the cock once it was inside him.

The one thing that Chet did that all other cowboys did, was that he kept his boots on.

Chet fucked him twice more in the two-hour session, once with both on their knees on the bed, with Billy's back pulled in close to Chet's front and his calves streaming back alongside Chet's calves. Chet was inside Billy, slow fucking him. He was cupping Billy's chin and holding Billy's head into the hollow of his shoulder. His other hand had reached around and laced Billy's balls and the root of his cock in his fingers and he was slow jacking Billy to the rhythm of the fuck of the cock.

Billy had not known that he had sighs and low, passionate moans in his quiver of responses, but he knew that now. Now he also knew what "making love" meant.

Before the two hours were up, the two were lapping each other in the bed. Chet was on his haunches on the bed, facing Billy, while Billy's thighs were straddling Chet's. Chet's cock was buried in Billy's passage. Billy was reclining back on his elbows. Chet's hands were gripping Billy's hips and pulling his passage on and off the cock. Chet had come three times, filling Billy's channel deep, and Billy had come four times, more than he had done with any other man, more than he would do in a day of many men, one after the other.

When both had ejaculated, Billy raised his chest to Chet's and they kissed passionately.

"If . . . if . . . you want, you can have me again . . . and again," Billy whispered, uncertain what to say, as he'd never had a reason to say this before. "You wouldn't have to pay. We can maybe find someplace else to meet."

"I'm only here for today," Chet said, a statement that almost caused Billy to sob. He'd finally found someone who spent time with him and fucked him right. Billy only now knew what being fucked right meant. Perhaps, he thought, it shouldn't have happened at all. It can only sour everything else now. "I'm coming back from a cattle drive, headed for Utah. It's that season. Cattlemen will be coming through here now from the cattle sales in Texas, going home to western Colorado and Utah."

"There's a western Colorado and Utah?" Billy asked. "Isn't the Pacific Ocean just across the mountains to the west?"

"No, sorry, it's still a long way from here to the coast."

Billy gave a sob. "Do the other cattlemen coming through here fuck like you do?"

"I wouldn't count on it," Chet answered, in a low voice. He was stroking Billy's blond, curly hair with his hand, as Billy shuddered in sobs. "There, there, little one, don't cry," Chet whispered. He pressed Billy's back on the bed, on his back, and stretched his own body above. Snuffling, Billy bent and spread his legs, reached down to grasp Chet's hard cock, and guided it into his passage.

Chet hadn't taken more than three strokes before there was a banging on the door and the saloon owner's call of "Time's up."

Chet quickly dressed as Billy lay on the bed and watched him with longing eyes. There wasn't much else to be said in the circumstance, so Chet just gave Billy a salute and went to the door. As he was leaving, the manager of one of the copper mines was entering, already unbuttoning his fly.

Two days later, the sheriff and his deputies arrived again. Having been told that Timothy was available, the sheriff said he preferred Billy. They nearly beat him to a pulp and double fucked him brutally. At the end of the day he was back in the doctor's infirmary.

* * * *

Bryan Barnes had come quietly into town and checked into the Cedar Hill Hotel, an establishment with all of four rooms above a dining room and with a two-seater outside behind, with the modern convenience of separate "his" and "her" compartments.

He was returning to his Utah ranch from having driven his annual selection of cattle to the Texas slaughterhouses. Cedar Hill was off the path of his return. He'd sent his son, Larry, and the rest of the crew he'd taken with him by the direct route, but Bryan had a problem. It was a problem he didn't want to share with Larry or any of the other men. Larry thought his father was coming to Cedar Hill to sample the fresh meat at the saloon that was brought in this time of year, Cedar Hill being one of the few places in the region that offered both female and male prostitutes.

It was no secret to Larry that his father went for the male tail. He did as well, and they kept their bunk room stocked with young cowboys who could please them both and who pleased each other. But they both also liked variety. Bryan especially liked something softer, less weather beaten, more experienced sport than a cowboy.

Bryan's young man, Josh, had left Bryan in Texas. Josh had been the sole property of Bryan to fuck. Even though most of the other men fucked men, Josh, trained to be a giving whore, had been kept tender and was off limits to the others, including Larry. Cowboys had congregated at the Barnes ranch because the rancher himself fucked men. So, Larry and the boys knew Bryan hadn't been getting any since they'd hit Texas. It was logical then that Bryan would go off the direct route for a couple of days to get his rocks off. That Cedar Hill had male prostitutes on tap was well known in the region. It was also known that they were brought in fresh and tender in this season.

What Bryan's ranch hands didn't know was why Josh had left Bryan and why it was that Bryan really needed to come to Cedar Hill. The reasons for both had the same root. Since sometime on the cattle trail between Utah and Texas, Bryan had stopped being able to get it up. He was in his mid-fifties, and this sometimes happened along about now, but it didn't happen to a previously virile man like Bryan. At least, that's what Bryan thought about it. And Bryan wouldn't let it happen to himself without putting up a fight.

Josh had left him because he couldn't keep the young man fucked regularly—and Bryan had let him go because he was afraid that Josh would go to Larry for satisfaction. Bryan couldn't have survived that. Larry was chomping at the bit enough to take over the ranch operations—to take over Bryan's fancy boy as well and for the fancy boy to let others know that the son satisfied him in ways the father no longer could would have emasculated the father.

Bryan came to Cedar Hill because the doctor here, Clyde Sparrow, was an old friend of his—one of the few men in the world Bryan could share his problem with and who he trusted not to gossip Bryan's problem around. Being able to get it up was a significant mark of a man's authority and power in the frontier region. Bryan couldn't afford to let his problem get out—and he couldn't go without having a tender young man in his bed and opening his thighs to Bryan and Bryan's own cock hard enough to do something about it.

As soon as he had checked into the hotel, Bryan took a walk down the wood-plank walkway to the doctor's office and went in without knocking.

Doc. Sparrow wasn't in the waiting room or his examination room. The infirmary rooms were at the back of the building. Bryan found his old friend there, and he did a double take when he got to the door of the room the doctor was in. The doctor wasn't alone. There was a young man half on a hospital bed and half off, at the foot of bed, with his back on the mattress, and his feet, his legs spread, flat on the floor. The young man had a splint on one of his arms and evidences of bandages here and there. He was wearing a nightshirt, but it was bunched up to below his pits. Doc. Sparrow was crouched below him and had the fingers of one hand up the young man's ass almost to the knuckles.

Bryan assumed it was a medical examination and would have pulled away to go wait for the doctor in the waiting room—except that the young man on the bed was the spitting image of Josh—clean, soft, pliable skin that was tanned, but not weather beaten. A body that was perfectly proportioned and lightly muscled, but not hard worked. A smooth-skinned handsome face. Just what Bryan liked to fuck. The young man moaned and Doc. Sparrow lowered his face and kissed one of the young man's nipples. Now that Bryan looked closer, he also could see that the doctor didn't just have his fingers up the young man's ass, but that the young man was moving his pelvis on this fingers—fucking himself on the doctor's hand. The young man turned his head toward the door and gave Bryan a glazed, faraway look and slight smile.

This wasn't an examination. Bryan stood there in shock and need and want—even feeling a bit of stirring in his groin, but not much. Not enough. Not by any shot. Bryan was a well-endowed man. His erection had been something to behold—when he'd managed to get it up.

He unbuttoned his jeans and handled himself now when he realized that this wasn't an examination. The doctor had his own cock out of his trousers and shortly after Bryan arrived, he stood, leaned into the pelvis of the young man, who was moaning a low moan as, hands gripping the young man's thighs, Sparrow entered his ass with his cock and started a slow pump. The young man raised his good arm, ran his fingers into the hair on the doctor's head, and turned the doctor's face toward the door. He was still looking at Bryan himself, though, while moving his pelvis in rhythm with the slow thrusts of the doctor's cock just as he had against the invasion of the man's fingers. He clearly wasn't disturbed by Bryan watching him being fucked.

Doc. Sparrow, looking over to the door, nodded his acknowledgment of Bryan's presence while his moved his hips forward and back. There was nothing shocking here for Bryan. The two men had been close friends; they'd watched each other perform with men and had shared young men and male prostitutes before. What shocked him was how much this young man reminded him of Josh.

When Bryan recovered from the shock of seeing someone so similar to his lost lover and became resigned that watching the doctor fuck the young man wasn't going to help harden his own cock no matter what he did with it with his hand, Bryan sighed, withdrew from the doorway, and went to the doctor's examination room to wait for him.

"Who is that?" Bryan asked when the doctor joined him.

"One of the new young whores for the saloon," Sparrow said. "He was working off part of his bill for me fixing him up." There was no embarrassment to be had for the doctor being caught fucking one of the saloon prostitutes.

"He looked like he's been banged up pretty good," Bryan said. His mind was already spinning. A saloon whore. One so much like Josh. If he only could get over this malady of his, there were possibilities with this young whore. If he did it for money, he'd have no expectations beyond getting the money.

"That's because he's been banged rough. Just arrived. Everyone wants to give him a ride, some a lot rougher than others. He gives a good ride. A very good ride indeed." The two men smiled at each other and the doctor continued. "The young man was pretty soft and fresh when he got here a couple of weeks ago. He's still too soft for the job in a mining town like this. I'll tell you, he's soft as a sponge deep inside. He hasn't hardened up at the core yet. He's going to have to toughen up fast, or he's going to be dead. I don't want to predict which. He's still got a sweet channel, I can say that for him. Glad I got to him before he was hardened used up. There's more of his bill to work off. So, now, Bryan, it's good to see you. What's the occasion of this visit?"

Bryan told him, all of it—what his problem was.

"Might not be too much I can do," the doctor said. "But I do have an elixir that will give you a quick hard on. If the guy you're fucking gives you good attention and you are sufficiently aroused by him, I can give you a hard with a swig of this for maybe ten, fifteen minutes. You can even bring up a little cum if you're lucky enough and your dick gets enough friction. Best I can do. What you got ain't unnatural. You're not getting any younger."

"It's something," Bryan said.

Sparrow stood to wrap the bottle and was standing at a window. "Fuck," he said.

"What is it?" Bryan asked.

"The sheriff's coming this way. He looks horny. I think there's going to be trouble if he finds this whore here. There's a window in that room. Do me—and the whore—a favor. Get the young man out of the window and back over to the saloon. If Frank over there wants to keep the boy alive, he'll hide him."

"Hide him from the sheriff?" Bryan asked, confused.

"It's the sheriff's fucking—along with his deputies'—that's got this fresh whore laid up here in the infirmary twice already. They don't know when to stop and there's no one here who can stop them. A third time, and the boy will probably be dead. The sheriff's the one man in town who can beat and fuck a whore to death if he wants to and not be charged with anything. This wouldn't be the first time. So, here's the elixir, no charge, if you help get this boy to the saloon without the sheriff getting to him first. I'd like to have another crack at him myself before the sheriff does finally find him."

* * * *

Bryan was sitting in a straight chair facing the bed in his hotel room. Billy was stretched out on the bed, facing him. Barnes had brought the young man here rather than the saloon. He figured that the sheriff would go straight from the infirmary to the saloon and that the saloon owner would give the young man over to the sheriff without a fuss. He'd really have no choice. There was no greater law in the town than the sheriff.

Barnes had his own plans for the young whore. He had an elixir to try out. He was holding one of the bottles of the liquid in his hand. As he'd hurried out of the doctor's office, Sparrow had given him three bottles and told him that, if he used them sparingly—and found someone who could get him up when he drank the elixir—the supply should last him into the new year. That is if he didn't fuck the guy more than three times a week.

"What's your name, son?" Barnes asked.

"Billy."

"I'm Bryan. Bryan Barnes. I've got a cattle spread west of here, over in Utah Territory."

Billy perked up. "West of here? Over in California?"

"Not in California, exactly, but on the way there."

"I've been trying to get to California."

Now Bryan perked up more. If the elixir worked here, that was leverage. Maybe he could convince the young man to go back to the ranch with him. He could make him think that California was near the ranch. "You work at the saloon, I understand, Billy."

"Yes, sir, I do," Billy asked.

"And you lie under men there? You let men put their dicks in you and seed you?"

"Yes, sir, I do." Billy didn't know enough to be embarrassed about that. It was reality, his whole world now.

"I want to put my dick in you, Billy. I want to loose my seed in you."

"Fine, you're a good-looking man," Billy said. "You got me out of the doctor's office with the sheriff coming. You can do what you want with me—no need for money." He started fumbling with his belt buckle with his good hand.

"But I have a little problem," Bryan said, putting a hand on Billy's to arrest the move to strip. "It's why I went to see the doctor just now. It's why he gave me this bottle of elixir. And I need a good-looking young man like you to help me get my dick hard so that I can put it in him and relieve myself of seed. Do you understand that?"

"Yes, sir, I think so. You want me to get you hard and let you fuck me." All so matter of fact.

"It will take time and effort," Bryan said. "For starters, I'll give you a dollar piece if you'll take your clothes off and let me make you come—let me put my hand and mouth on you. And I'll give you two dollars more if I can get hard enough to get inside you and give you my seed. That good with you, son?"

"Yes, sir," Billy said, already starting to work to unbutton his shirt, which wasn't easy, considering one hand was in a splint. Bryan helped him, looking on in shock at the bandage around the young man's chest and the bruises and cuts on his body. He ran his hand over Billy's chest, stopping to rub a nipple. Billy gave him a low moan.

Barnes took a swig out of one of the elixir bottles.

Billy lay there and continued moaning softly as, sitting in the straight chair pulled up to the bed, Bryan pulled Billy's jeans off his legs and gently worked the young man's body with his hands and then Billy's cock and balls with a hand, the other hand working at Billy's entrance just as the doctor had done. Barnes was good at it; he'd had a lot of experience preparing another man and having a limp dick didn't change that. Billy sighed and moved his pelvis against the penetrating fingers. Then, with Billy hard and sighing, Barnes leaned over and sucked the young man's cock to an ejaculation.

To the extent that he could, Bryan imagined that it was Josh he was working on, and he did, joyously feel a stirring in his loins. At his direction, Billy knelt between his spread thighs, with Bryan sitting on the edge of the bed, and worked Bryan's cock with his hands and mouth.

"It's got to be now," Bryan growled through clinched teeth. He wasn't his usual hard, but he was hard enough to penetrate an ass and he could feel cum building up inside him. He swiftly pulled Billy off his knees and into his lap. Quite familiar with this position, Billy reached under and held the man's cock long enough for him to sink his channel on it and then he pressed his chest to the rancher's chest. Billy was crouched on Barnes' lap with his feet flat on the mattress next to Bryan's thighs. The rancher grabbed Billy's waist and dipped him back toward his knees. Bryan's mouth went to Billy's nipples and he started thrusting his cock up into Billy's channel, while Billy vigorously rose and fell on the cock as well, being careful not to pull back so far that the cock came out of his ass. He could feel that that man wasn't rock hard. But he was long and thick.

The hard lasted for three minutes. The cum, at least some semblance of it, enough to make the rancher exclaim in victory, was spouted in just short of the three minutes. The rancher held Billy close to him, mourning his cock returning to flaccid, but cheered that it had gotten hard for a few minutes; was inside the channel of a beautiful young, soft-skinned blond man; and was slathered in his own cum. He nearly sobbed his relief, but he steeled himself. It wasn't much, but it was a start, and it was more than he'd had for the weeks of riding from Texas to Colorado.

"You earned the three dollars," he whispered to Billy. "And there will be more of that, if you'll come to Utah with me. Utah's just over the hill from California. I want you to come to Utah with me and do this with me three times a week. No more at first. But maybe later. Will you do that?"

"I could, maybe," Billy whispered.

"Will you come with me? If you stay here, the sheriff will beat you to death in fucking you. You probably won't last another week. Will you come with me?"

"Yes," Billy answered in a stronger voice.

Bryan couldn't help himself. He took another swig of the elixir and put Billy on his belly on the bed, his feet on the floor. Billy docilely lay there arms outstretched, grunting lightly, while the rancher got as many of his fingers, up to his knuckles, inside Billy's ass and worked his own cock with his hand. He sensed he was getting harder this time. Indeed, the doctor had told him that part of the problem was mental—that the fear of not being able to get it up was part of why he wasn't able to get it up. Yes, he was harder this time. This time he was able to slide in more strongly. He grabbed Billy's hips and started to pump him, Moaning, Billy pumped him back. Bryan managed to hold it longer this time, to stroke more vigorously, to fill out bigger. And Billy was doing what he could to help—pulling the cock inside him, causing his channel muscles to undulate over it, giving it a soft and spongy core to throb inside, crying out that the man was killing him with a cruel cock—if only for a few minutes before Bryan ejaculated.

But it was good—much better than before. Everything was looking much better than before. The young whore was a treasure—a miracle.

Chapter Four: Utah

The Utah ranch, although one of the richest ones in the territory, wasn't a bed of roses for Billy. Mostly it was the boredom that got him. Bryan was nice to him and kept him in the main ranch house. If he'd sent Billy to the bunkhouse, he knew Billy would be fucked silly and would be no use to him.

That meant that Billy was only fucked three times a week, and not always successfully—certainly not for long—even then. Billy had been trained to regular, rough sex, and he didn't object to it. He hadn't objected to the life of a whore other than the out-of-bounds beatings during sex and the ripe smell of some of the men. He hadn't been raised to have any contrary sense of morality and the moral authority in his life, Jeremiah, had treated him like a whore and pointed to it as Billy's natural place in life. He had conditioned himself to the impersonal, indifferent nature of being fucked in a whorehouse by a succession of men and even enjoyed the rough sex it often entailed.

Billy grew restless with the polite, fatherly, nearly sexless attention the old man gave him in the ranch house. There was no indication that he was anywhere near California or would be able to go there anytime soon. Barnes's promise of money didn't pan out. The rancher said he was paying Billy and he showed Billy that he was putting money for him in a strongbox every month, but the strongbox was going in Barnes's safe. The rancher obviously was terrified that his one chance for a regular fuck and ejaculation, such as they were, hinged on Billy being there and being willing. If Billy took his money and ran, Barnes would be left without his need being met.

After a couple of months, Billy got some relief, though. One day Larry trapped Billy in the woodshed and fucked the stuffing out of him. Larry was a rough fucker, using a bit of fist play to soften the man he was fucking before mounting him and then enjoying some choke play while he was pumping. Billy went with it—gladly—Larry was the only one within reach who could make him feel anything now when he was fucked. A bit of pain was worth someone who could ride him hard and deep for twenty minutes and seemingly hit up into his stomach with the strength of his ejaculations.

Once inside Billy that first time, Larry's knees under Billy's buttocks, the young man's bruised torso reclining back on the dirt floor of the shed, both men breathing heavily, Billy lay immobile, recovering from the blow that had dazed him and made his torso fall back. The preliminary struggle over, Larry had started to pull Billy's channel on and off his cock with strong, calloused hands grabbing the young man's hips. Billy had gone up on his elbows, given Larry a look of lust and need, and started to move his pelvis to meet Larry's thrusts with counterthrusts of his own.

Larry's anger rose. This was the saucy little piece who had captured his father's attention and who lived in comfort in the ranch house, while Larry slept with the other men in the bunkhouse.

"Fuckin' little slut," he muttered through clinched lips. He grabbed Billy by the throat, backhanded him hard in one direction and then in the other direction. He released Billy's throat, and the young man fell back onto his shoulder blades again. Larry fucked him harder and deeper, as with half-glazed eyes, Billy turned his head, smiled a little smile, and murmured, "Yes, yes, fuck me hard. Punish me." Being fucked rough brought more arousal out of Billy, and it had been so long since a man had taken him this hard. And of course he was a slut; he'd been conditioned to be a slut, a whore. The way he had survived that was to come to enjoy having a moving cock inside him, the sting of a slap on his check or buttocks.

And Larry's young, thick, vigorous cock was divine when set against three minutes of a tediously achieved erection and a weak squirt from an old man.

Fuck me hard, fuck me long with your young, vigorous cock; fuck on and on, Billy implored Larry silently. Give me a split lip, a black eye, a bruised rib as you thrust inside me thick and virile and hard. It all sends me up on the clouds. The pain heightens my arousal. It tells me I'm still alive, despite how men like you take their pleasure off and release their anger and frustration on my body.

Yes, I'm a slut, he wanted to cry out, as he set his hips in countermotion to Larry's thrusts, Larry too far gone in the fuck to notice it—or to care—this time. But I'm a slut because a parade of men like you wagging your cocks at me and sticking your dicks inside me have made me a slut. Billy pulled his chest back up to press it into Larry's heaving chest, and this time Larry's response was to embrace the younger man closely, to seek out Billy's lips, and go into a brutal kiss, including chewing on Billy's lower lip, drawing blood. Billy jerked away from the kiss, panting hard. He ran his tongue over his lip and tasted the blood. The blood told him he was alive.

This time he was the one to plaster his lips to Larry's and to open his mouth wide, giving entry—welcome—to the tongue plunging inside, gagging him. With a low rumble coming up from his belly, Larry turned Billy on his back and slapped the young man's legs apart, still possessing Billy's mouth with his. Billy dug his heels into the dirt of the floor, thrusting his pelvis up into position for the long hard slide of the cock inside him. Larry immediately started pumping hard, his head arching back in a howl to the rough wood of the shed ceiling as he blasted Billy's passage with his cum.

Billy tried to struggle up, but Larry backhanded him again so that, as Larry stood above him, buttoning his britches and looking menacing down at the blond whore, Billy fell back, near exhaustion, to the floor.

Not near enough to exhaustion after three months of frustration of the old man not being able to keep it up.

Undaunted, Billy whimpered, "Don't leave. Fuck me again." He elevated his pelvis again, pushing off on his bent legs, signaling the want for the cock again. Yes, I'm a slut, he was yelling in his mind. Men like you made me. He'd had nothing but three minutes three times a week from an old man for months.

Larry smiled cruelly. He slowly unbuttoned and pulled his cock out again, wagging it at Billy.

"So you want me again."

"Yes, yes, please," Billy murmured.

"You want me, not the old man."

"Yes."

"Just so we both know how it is. Tell my father about this and I'll cut your balls off." He laughed, stuffed his cock back in his britches, and turned and left the shed. Billy lay there, half buzzed, panting hard, and staring at the young stud who had taken him to hell—and to heaven. He was hard. Sucking on his cut lip, he reached for his cock and masturbated to a rerun in his mind of all Larry had done to him in the cruel, "fully alive" taking.

Life on the ranch wasn't great. But Larry found him and fucked him at least once a week, so Billy had something to think about when he was washing the supper dishes and sweeping out the ranch house. After that first time, Larry wasn't as rough, though. He didn't want to leave any marks his father would see and then come to him about. His father had declared Billy off limits. And his father still held the deed to the ranch.

And then Bryan suddenly, without warning, dropped dead. As his heart burst at the moment he dropped a massive load in Billy's ass channel, he died a happy man. He not only dropped dead, but he left a written will dividing the ranch between Larry and Billy.

When Larry found out, he burned the copy of the will that was in the house, but he was worried that there was another copy at the lawyer's office. The lawyer had been out to the ranch a couple of times in recent months. And the lawyer didn't like Larry that much, a dislike that Larry had too openly reciprocated.

Larry was panicked. With Bryan still laid out on the bed in his bedroom, Larry grabbed Billy, beat him down to the floor in the middle of the living area, fucked him hard and cruelly there, and then dragged the young many out into the dirt in front of the ranch house and called for a couple of horses. When they arrived, and with the ranch hands interested in what Larry proposed to do also mounting up, Larry threw Billy, his wrists bound in chains Larry had pulled out of the barn, belly down, over the back of one of the horses, and they all rode out onto the range to where a cattle birthing pen was fenced off. They tied Billy to the fence, his arms thrown over the top and his feet barely touching the ground. Larry let loose the cowboys on Billy, letting anyone who wanted to fuck the young blond have as many goes at him that it took to kill him.

They had barely started on him, though, when a gaunt stranger in a worn suit rode up and spoke in a strong voice.

"That there's my son. I'll pay you fifty dollars to let him loose and let him come with me and another ten dollars for that there horse for him to ride. If he dies here you might have a bit of explaining to do."

Larry had had time to cool down a bit and for the same worry to creep in. The lawyer just might make trouble for him if Billy just disappeared. He motioned the other cowboys off, thought a bit, and then said, "He can't stay anywhere around here if we let him go."

"I'm taking him back to Kansas. Is that far enough away for you?" Jeremiah Atwell said, taking the money out of a slit in his belt to show to Larry and the ranch hands. "Sixty dollars is a might better thing to have in your hand than the risk of a rope around your neck, I would think," Jeremiah said. "You kill the boy and you risk the rope—all of you."

Larry Barnes agreed with him. An unconscious Billy was released from the fence, thrown belly down, over the back of the horse he'd been brought here on, and his journey, once more as essentially Jeremiah's sex slave, back to Kansas began.

* * * *

They rode for no more than an hour when Billy started to come to.

"Hello world," Jeremiah said. "You can show your appreciation to me for gettin' you out of that fix in a short while. Figure we should stop by that stream over there to water and feed the horses, get you into some clothes, and put your butt rather than your belly on that horse's back. I got somethin' that will fit you, but it should be washed and dried. We can fill our bellies too."

233

Jeremiah stopped his horse in a stand of birch trees next to a stream, pulled Billy down from his horse, and pushed him down on his butt and back against a rock outcropping.

"Can you get these chains off me?" Billy asked, raising his wrists to show Jeremiah that he was bound.

"In a minute or so. You just stay put there. There are chores to do first. Remember that. The chores always come first."

He opened one of the packs on his horse's flank and came up with a pair of breeches and a flannel short, both wadded up. Wading a few steps into the stream, he washed them and then came out of the stream. The water had been only a couple of inches deep where he'd walked. His boots would be watertight enough to keep his feet dry. He beat the clothes against a rock outcropping and then stretched them out in the sun there to dry.

Then Jeremiah made a fire and put a coffee pot taken from his pack on it.

"Now for the appreciation," he said as he came over in front of Billy and started unbuttoning his fly.

Chores first and fucking second, Billy thought. Now I remember. "The chains?" he said, lifting his bound wrists for Jeremiah to see. "I can't give you proper attention chained up like this."

"Well, all right," Jeremiah said, helping to unwind the chains and tossing them to the side. "Now spread them legs for me. It's been a long time. Too long."

"Sister Mary—" Billy started to say, as he complied, reclining back, spreading his thighs, and rolling his pelvis up.

"Sister Mary ain't on God's green earth anymore," Jeremiah said. "I had a time of it findin' you again, I'll have to say. And all thanks to her too. She done got what she deserved."

Billy shivered, not wanting to think about what might have happened to Mary Atwell. Jeremiah knelt down between his thighs with a grunt, grasped his buttocks, a cheek in each hand, and raised Billy's pelvis more. He was inside and pumping with another grunt. No conversation transpired as he fucked Billy. Billy closed his eyes and took it without a sound.

There had been so many men inside him since the last time Jeremiah was there. He hardly felt a thing at first. There were few men who could make Billy feel anything in a fuck anymore. The last one had been Larry Barnes, and Billy didn't want to think of him.

But then, entering his mind, were the memories of Jeremiah from earlier, Jeremiah being his first, taking his time to seduce Billy and then holding him close, kissing his neck, throat, cheeks, and mouth tenderly that first time he was inside Billy, while Billy's sobs subsided. Jeremiah whispering of his love and gratefulness and of how he was going to take care of Billy forever as he slowly started to pump and Billy trembled under him, awash in the mix of pleasure and pain—and of the revelation, from his orphan consciousness, that here was a strong man who wanted him, wanted to be one with him so much he was inside Billy, a man who would take care of Billy. Knowing that the way to be loved by this man was to have Jeremiah's cock filling and moving his passage.

Billy started to move his hips with Jeremiah, falling into the rhythm of the fuck, and he clutched at the man's massive, moving chest. His mouth went to the flared front of Jeremiah's white shirt, and his tongue slid through the matting of the chest hair, searching and finding a taut nipple.

"We'll have none of that you little whore," Jeremiah growled, rearing back from Billy. "I see there's a lot needin' relearned on how to act proper here." He slapped Billy across the face, and, with a whimper, Billy allowed his shoulder blades to fall back on the rock, he turned his head to the side, moved into his "just another cowboy fuck" world, and lay yielding to but not involved in Jeremiah's fuck.

Jeremiah spilled his seed, pulled out of Billy with another grunt, stood up and buttoned himself up, and went looking for a slab of cured bacon to fry on the fire.

He was standing up from the fire, an iron plate in his hand with sizzling bacon on it, when he spoke next. "Here's some grub. It will give you strength and maybe more energy than you had last time. After we eat I'll fuck you again, and maybe you can show me some more appreciation when I . . ."

A funny expression came over Jeremiah's face. He

dropped the plate and pitched forward, face into the ground. The shafts of two arrows were lodged in his back.

Before Billy could cry out or anything, four Indian warriors rode into the clearing on sleek horses. They wore only loincloths and moccasins and had feathers in headbands, one more of a feathered headdress than the others. And although all were hardbodied, the apparent leader of the band was a magnificent specimen of manhood. It wasn't clear whether any of them saw Billy or suspected he was there. Coming off their horses, they gathered around the body of Jeremiah and stared down at him.

Taking the only opportunity he knew he'd ever have, Billy jumped up and ran for the nearest horse, which was one of the brave's horses. Pure adrenalin enabled him to vault on the back of the horse. He dug his heels in the side of the horse to get it to bolt and gallop away.

The leader of the braves was as fast as Billy, and filled with more adrenalin, because, before the horse could take off, he had vaulted on the back of it behind Billy, and the two of them were plastered against each other. Billy could tell that the brave was enjoying this, because he went hard in the small of Billy's back as the horse raced across a scrub plain.

Pitching Billy's body forward, the brave got his cock under the crease in Billy's bare buttocks. He grabbed the sides of Billy's chest on either side, with Billy pushed over and clutching the horse's mane in his bound hands. The brave's hard cock entered Billy's ass, and the savage let the buck of the horse as it galloped across the ground move the cock inside Billy's ass in a pumping action.

The horse made a big circle and galloped back into the clearing. The brave had shot his load inside Billy before they arrived back where the other three braves were waiting. The leader of the band pushed Billy off the horse into the arms of the three braves, who guided his descent to the ground, slapped his legs open, and beat and fucked him into unconsciousness.

When Billy came to, he was spread-eagled, still naked, on his back under the withering sun out on the edge of the scrub field and staked to the ground. The braves were gone.

He was found there by the scout from a wagon train three hours later.

"Well, lookee. What do we have here?" the man said, as he came off his horse beside where Billy was staked. "Dead or alive. Alive I see and, say, ain't you that new whore from the saloon in Cedar Hill? Wanted to have you when I last was through there, but couldn't afford it."

"Please, can you release me? Indians got the man I was traveling with—over by the stream there."

"Man take you off for a private little fuck party, did he?"

"Please, can you release me?" Billy pleaded through parched lips.

"There should be some sort of reward for that, don't you think? Don't you look pretty all staked out like that and spread apart? Makes a man's cock stand up and salute, it does—knowin' that you're a whore anyway. What say I get a bit of privilege first and then I'll help you out."

"Oh, fuck, all right," Billy muttered in exasperation.

"Yep, that's the word all right."

"What word?"

"Fuck. You say it nice and pretty. Fuck me please. Fuck me, Clem. Then I'll do it and release you."

"Fuck me. Fuck me, Clem. Please," Billy said through clinched teeth. What the hell. So many men had fucked him that this didn't mean much.

"Oh, sweet Jezuss!" Billy called out as, kneeling between his legs, Clem clasped their two cock together and stroked them until, keyed up by the attention the savages had given him, Billy released his cum, only to have it captured by Clem's hand and smeared on Billy's hole, where Clem teased the hole by swirling his cock head just within the entrance in the lube of Billy's come.

Billy was writhing to the extent the spread-eagling was permitting under the teasing of the cock.

"Please, please," Billy whimpered. "Stick it in. Give me your cock! Fuck me!"

Clem laughed. "See, you whores aren't the only ones with moves."

He grabbed his cock and slapped it around on Billy's thighs and belly, with Billy whining for it, and quite suddenly he took it in hand and thrust it inside Billy's hole up to the root. Billy cried out and strained at his bonds, as Clem pumped him hard for about twenty strokes and then stopped, holding still, until the urge for both of them to come had passed.

Clem took his time, pumping and then stopping when he came close to shooting, and then pumping again. He was just ejaculating when the first of the Conestoga wagons of the train was coming into sight. Quickly pulling out of Billy, buttoning up, and reaching over to free Billy's wrists and ankles, he muttered ominously, "Not a word of this to anyone. You do and somewhere between here and California, I'll put a blade in your ribs."

The word that thundered into Billy's brain was "California."

"This wagon train going to California?" he asked.

"Sure is," Clem answered.

Men were gathering, holding what women there were back so that they didn't see the body of Jeremiah by the stream or the naked body of Billy. They were babbling among themselves and plying Clem and Billy with questions, when a familiar voice rang out over the hubbub.

"He's hurt and needs attention. Bring him up into my wagon here. I'll take care of him."

Billy recognized the voice of the one cowboy who had been good to him in a fuck in the Cedar Hill saloon. The one man in Billy's life out of all of those men who he could say had made love to him—the cowboy Chet, from Virginia, headed for California on an adventure.

Chet took Billy up in his arms and headed for a wagon. "Make way. He's hurt," Chet was saying. "We'll take him with us. Could some of you bury that man over there? I'll take good care of this one."

And take good care of Billy, Chet certainly did. He lay between Billy's legs on flour sacks in the belly of the Conestoga wagon and fucked him slow and deep all the way to California. Two weeks to full recovery while being ridden west toward California.

238

About the Author

An artist and writer, Dirk has always been interested in history and legends, particularly those of the United States, the Mediterranean, and Asia. His works are historical, and sometimes border on fantasy. They are full of ordinary men struggling to survive and find love in difficult situations. And sometimes Dirk writes about men who are in touch with forces beyond those of mortal men, fighting for survival in more unusual ways.

Dirk's books often, but not always, contain male sex that is both forceful and rough, and at times dangerous, but is always within the context of stories of survival in more primitive and brutal times. He also writes about the power of love in turbulent times.

Dirk's America's Founding Collection is the second of a trio of historical period collections, with *Dirk's Ancient Times Collection* already in print *Dirk's America Unifies and Expands Collection* soon to be published.

He can be found at the adults only gay male site www.BarbarianSpy.com, which he shares with Sabb and habu (sr71plt). Our authors always like to receive feedback, and appreciate it when readers post reviews to Goodreads, Amazon, B&N, Smashwords and other review sites.

Books by Dirk Hessian

*Books marked with an * are available in e-book and paperback*

Xtreme Historical Erotica

Dirk's Ancient Times Collection (Print only Bundle)*

The King's Men

Shores of Tripoli*

Prophecy of Noto

Pretender's Fate

General Historical Erotic Romance

Dirk's America Unifies Collection (Print only Bundle)*

Dirk's America's Founding Collection (Print only Bundle)*

Soldier,Spy

Ridden West

Deliver a Virgin

Clouds and Rain

Confederate Gold

Puttin on the Ritz

To the Hessian Hills

Fire Down the Valley*

Constantinople*

The Beautiful Way*

Blue and Gray

Colonel's Treasure

Beginning of Time

Labyrinth